THE WHISTLEBLOWERS

THE WHISTLEBLOWERS
When land sharks baited Death

SITARAMAN

Westland Ltd

westland ltd

61 Silverline Building, 2nd Floor, Alapakkam Main Road, Maduravoyal, Chennai 600095
No. 38/10 (New No.5), Raghava Nagar, New Timber Yard Layout, Bengaluru 560026
93, 1st Floor, Sham Lal Road, Daryaganj, New Delhi 110002

First published in India by westland ltd 2014
Copyright © by Sitaraman 2014

All rights reserved
10 9 8 7 6 5 4 3 2 1

ISBN: 978-93-84030-23-0

Typeset by Ram Das Lal

CONTENTS

AYRAVATI

DEVRAJ INDRA – THE KING OF THE 36 MILLION INDIAN GODS – is the master of Ayravat, the majestic divine elephant. Legend has it that this divine elephant Ayravat, on his maiden voyage to earth some eight thousand years ago, landed first upon this city. Hence the name Ayravati for this city. There is a beautiful temple of Indra here, which contains some impressive samples of elephantine sculpture and astounding carvings depicting the story of Ayravati. The city was once ruled by the kings of the Sachidananda dynasty, who had great regard for art and sculpture. Indra's temple was originally constructed by Kandarp Sachidanand – the earliest known king of that dynasty. His successors added more sculptures and murals and the walls are now carved with many images and inscriptions in an ancient script that historians are yet to decipher fully.

Amongst the many carvings in the temple, one series portrays Ayravat in different dancing postures and a careful observer would note some thin zig-zag lines shooting off on the surface of the earth from beneath his leviathan feet. An ancient tale in the city went that when the behemoth danced, it triggered off an earthquake. Little known to the people of Ayravati, these images of the dancing Ayravat carried a more immediate significance to their lives than they could ever imagine, even in their wildest dreams.

PROLOGUE

29th July 2008

EXACTLY 5 YEARS AGO FROM THIS DATE, DEATH HAD STRUCK, suddenly and killed a vivacious soul, mutilating the body and along with it, the entrenched tenacity. Finished for good was a strong-willed effort to expose a sneaky plan that defied the law of the land and the lessons of history.

The end of a crusader. End of story.

Well, almost!

The dark memories of that day stayed alive. Seated in his study, Arun Balachander felt the tremors of an electrifying current run through him even as the skeletons came alive, destroying the graves that they had been lain under and staged their annual jig in his mental proscenium. Goosebumps numbed his arms and legs. He felt sucked into a trance. He knew that on this day in the calendar no effort on his part could protect his mind from reliving those gruelling moments from five years earlier. He shut his eyelids tight, as guilt incinerated him from within.

A loud chuckle from Shruti, his seven-year-old daughter, broke the spell. His eyes opened up and instantly, his head reeled. His eyes saw a psychedelic medley of violet, purple, orange and red circles. It took several blinks before the circles rippled away.

He tilted his face sideways and saw Shruti standing there, hands akimbo.

'What's up, dad?' She was playful and chirpy.

Struggling to appear normal, he asked, 'Aren't you going to school today?'

'Yeah. But I want a car-drop to the school. You're on leave today, aren't you?'

Arun smiled and nodded. He patted her cheeks and said, 'Sure. I'll drop you today and pick you up in the afternoon.'

Thrilled, the girl sprinted out of the room.

Shruti's fleeting intrusion had cheered him up a bit.

Arun reached for a glass of water. A parchment lying on the table caught his attention. His eyes remained glued to that piece of paper even as he sipped the water slowly from the glass. Placing the glass back on the table, he picked up the piece of paper with deep reverence for the person who'd written it – Manohar Mishra, an architect by profession and an old resident of Ayravati. Mishra had written it on the last day of his life.

Arun had read it several times earlier. He read it again.

1951 it was. 21ˢᵗ December of course! How can I ever forget that first nerve-wracking quiver that jolted me out of my deep-slumber, numbing my physical, mental and emotional sensibilities? I was thrust into the air from my king-sized bed and hurled to the floor with the force of an angry thrust. Fear gripped the bottom of my stomach, my flesh clenched together and my muscles felt frail. The walls reeled around me. The huge, invincible steel wardrobe came careening down at full pelt and smashed into the floor. It missed my head by a whisker. My brain froze and I couldn't control my bladder. I was scared beyond words!!

That was just the first quiver. Then I felt another and then one more. Each subsequent one rippled from the earlier one and grew many times stronger and impactful. I was huried deep down into the demoniac depths of a dystopian catastrophe. I didn't exist for the next 19 hours. What lay there buried under the debris and the corpses was just my physical frame.

The tremors which rocked Ayravati within a span of 10 minutes, brought upon the city, a barrage of devastation and pummelled it into submission. The tremors destroyed countless properties. Several thousands died and many more were injured.

It was nature's fury at its worst.

But life had to move on. The Office of Civic Administration (OCA), which is the present day Municipal Corporation of Ayravati (MCA), was forward-looking.

PROLOGUE

Shaken by the devastation, the OCA got seismologists and geologists to study the seismic potential of Ayravati. The cat was out of the bag: Ayravati was located in a seismic zone with a dangerously high seismic potential and there was a strong likelihood of another catastrophe of a similar nature and intensity visiting Ayravati again. Following this find, the policymakers of OCA set out some rules for civil construction in Ayravati.

The most important of all these rules was that no tall buildings should be built in Ayravati. In their futuristic wisdom they foresaw that the buildings in the city could become taller in the future. In order to put some method to the madness, they set a ceiling on the maximum number of floors in any building in Ayravati: three floors.

This rule made in 1951 gradually got diluted. It was revised to four, then to six...and so on. The OCA was rechristened the Municipal Corporation of Ayravati (MCA) sometime in the 80s. The MCA continued to increase the limit from six to seven, to eight and further on, even as I kept pleading with every successive municipal commissioner of MCA. I explained to them the background to this rule, narrated to them the calamity the city had faced in 1951 and pleaded with them to enforce the rule. But my pleas fell on deaf ears. The policymakers in MCA relaxed this rule time and again, driven by that singular swinish human trait: greed. The last revision was done by the MCA in 1997 pegging the maximum limit for any building constructed in Ayravati at 12 floors. But judging by the way things

*have gone in the past, I fear that this limit will also get
revised in the coming years.*

*My training in architecture makes me certain that
we have issued a generous invitation for disaster to strike
Ayravati again. Thousands of lives are in danger. I can
sense it lurking somewhere. The sculptures of the dancing
Ayravat are screaming their lungs out.*

*God! Take me now please. I've lived long enough. I
want to die now.*

Manohar Mishra.
Dated: 2nd October 2006

Arun sighed and put the paper back inside the desk-drawer.

He sat erect on his chair, flipped open his cell phone and
dialled the number of Ganesh Sukhtankar – his mentor and
close friend in those trying times in Ayra Housing Finance
Ltd (AHFL) where five years ago, much had happened on
account of this MCA rule and their insistence on compliance
with it.

A sonorous voice answered his call, 'How're you, buddy?'

'Ok. How about getting together for coffee?'

'Sure. Temple Coffee House. At about 10?'

'Done.'

Arun and his wife Ananya dropped Shruti at her school
and returned home. He tried conversing with Ananya, but
even to his own ears, he sounded incoherent. She soon lost
patience and got on with her chores. The clock mocked him
from the wall. He had a fair amount of time to kill before he
met Ganesh.

PROLOGUE

He went to the balcony and sat on the rocking chair, staring emptily at the vast expanse in front. As the chair rocked back and forth, he drifted back to October 2002 – to the budget meeting that had triggered off the events that had made this day so poignantly significant in his life.

Chapter – 1

THE FIRST SALVO

October 2002

THE BUDGET MEETING STARTED ON SCHEDULE AT 2.30 PM in the plush conference room on the 6th floor of the AHFL House – the corporate office of Ayra Housing Finance Limited (AHFL). AHFL was a housing finance company that offered loans to individuals to buy homes. The room witnessed a number of presentations being made through the afternoon. While several decisions for the coming business year had been made, there still remained a few unresolved issues; the meeting therefore extended beyond the scheduled hours into late evening and then into early night.

At 10.30 pm, the lights were still on in the conference

room. Five people were still in it: Cedric Calado, the Chief Executive Officer (CEO) of AHFL; Karan Agnihotri, head of Business Development (BD); Ganesh Sukhtankar, head of Risk Management and Quality (RMQ); Arun Balachander, deputy to Ganesh in RMQ and Madhukar Sinha, the Finance head of AHFL. The budget numbers, once frozen by this management team, would be presented to the Board of Directors by Cedric for their approval.

The atmosphere in the room was crackling with tension – as was usual when Karan and Ganesh came face to face.

* * *

Ayravati was now a swanky city with excellent infrastructure —great roads, bridges, super specialty hospitals and renowned educational institutions. It was located at a distance of about hundred kilometres from the commercial capital of the country. An express way and underground metro rail service had made access hassle-free. In an hour one could reach Ayravati from the metropolis.

For all of these reasons and the cheaper rates of residential and commercial property, many large corporate houses that had been operating from the metropolis gradually shifted to Ayravati. This was a boon to the real estate industry and the city had witnessed a meteoric rise in construction activity over the last fifteen years. The demand for home loans naturally increased and in a few years, the home loans industry had become cut-throat in Ayravati.

AHFL was a housing finance company that offered home

loans to individuals. The company had been formed in 1999 and it was headquartered in Ayravati. Though it had a presence in the major cities of India, it was yet to gain a strong foothold in the very competitive home loans industry in the country. Ayravati however, was its stronghold.

Ganesh Sukhtankar, head of Risk Management and Quality Unit (RMQ), had the mandate to ensure that only credit-worthy customers received loans from AHFL. Therefore his team subjected all new loan proposals sourced by AHFL's sales team to a thorough evaluation. If a loan became non-recoverable for whatever reason, as it did at times, it was Ganesh's neck on the line. However, Ganesh had a sound reputation as a finance professional in the industry and an unblemished career record of over 15 years. He had been with AHFL since the date of its inception and Cedric Calado, the CEO, held him in high regard.

Arun Balachander was Ganesh's deputy. He too had a fabulous track record in the industry, having managed home loans in different, bigger and reputed housing finance companies and banks in different parts of the country. Ganesh had hired him for his RMQ unit and Arun had gained his confidence swiftly, rising to be the second-in-command.

Karan Agnihotri headed Business Development (BD) at AHFL. Karan's unit shouldered a mandate to maximize business volumes and thereby achieve AHFL's revenue targets. The entire sales unit was under his control. Cedric had a soft corner for Karan. He felt that Karan's job was the toughest of the lot, given the severely competitive market. Cedric therefore tried to provide all possible support to Karan and at times went out of his way to bolster Karan's efforts.

As was the case in every other housing finance company in the industry, the BD and the RMQ units were hardcore professional rivals in AHFL too. Serious differences on various issues dogged their work. RMQ, through its team of underwriters, vetted the new loan applications,that had been sourced and logged in for processing by BD. The underwriters had a clear brief and thereby ensured that no file with poor or negative credentials was approved. They followed a standard evaluation process. On an average, for every two loans approved, one was rejected. Every rejected application triggered a battle of sorts. Karan would always blame RMQ for being overly rigid with file evaluations while Ganesh would counter it by saying that the customer profiles sourced by Karan's team were sub-standard in quality. This perennial saga of arguments and brawls ensured that there was never a dull moment in AHFL.

Dr.Vimal Nath Sharma, an 81 year old business tycoon, was the Chairman of AHFL. He owned several companies across varied industries and held the majority shareholding in AHFL.

* * *

As the budget meeting progressed, four of the five people in the conference room managed to reach an agreement: with some changes to the home loans product and the sales strategy of AHFL, a 30% growth in revenue was achievable next year.

Cedric however, was looking at a 40% revenue growth. The gap had to be bridged.

Karan twirled the paperweight edgily as he made a point, 'The only way I see us bridging the revenue gap of 10% in our budget is by opening up our home loans product. We're still way-off from the market benchmarks. Builders laugh at our product. Some bold opening up of the product norms is now the need of the hour. We aren't babies in the home loan market. It's been a good three years since we launched the product and it's now time for us to start running.' He paused to take a sip of water and continued, 'We need to look at new products like *high-equity loans* and *no-income-proof loans*, besides our safer vanilla products.' Then he spread his arms open dramatically and exclaimed, 'And why not builder loans? We have good relations with prominent builders and we need to leverage that. If we don't break open the shackles now, we'll keep limping along like this.'

The key point of contention in all discussions so far had been managing the builder segment in home loans. This was the most popular segment amongst home loan companies to source business from. To build a relationship with good builders, immense perseverance was needed. But once a rapport was established, builders actively partnered with lenders to facilitate growth in lending. Most of the builders' customers, i.e. the home owners, needed a loan to fund the purchase of their apartment. The builders referred the customer to the lending institution they were associated with. This arrangement worked well for everyone: the builder sold his apartment, the customer got a loan to fund his purchase and the lenders such as AHFL grew their business volumes. To initiate this association with a builder, the lender had to accord a one-time approval for the residential building project under construction. Lenders approved the project by evaluating the land title papers of the project land and the necessary statutory approvals obtained by the builder to commence the construction. The prospective homeowners then availed loans from the lender to fund their home purchase. The prospective homeowner thus became the customer of the lender and was responsible for repayment of the loan. Sometimes, lenders forged a stronger relationship with builders, by offering loans directly to builders, which were called builder loans. In the case of a builder loan, the builder becomes the direct customer of the lender and is solely responsible for the repayment of the loan. For granting a builder loan, in addition to evaluating the property papers, the lender evaluated the builder's financial papers as well. The builder mortgaged the land and building on the project site to the lender. Once the lender approved the project, the builder could advertise that fact. To a prospective buyer interested in buying an apartment, approval of the project by an institutional lender signified that the project was above-board. The lenders typically financed 75% to 85% of the cost of the apartment, with the buyer paying the rest up-front.

Reputed builders often got their projects approved by multiple lenders and flaunted all their names in their project advertisements. The lenders would then be pitched against one another, competing for their share of business from that particular project. In the face of severe competition, it was up to the sales manager of each lender, who managed the relationship with the builder, to coax the builder and get the highest referrals of home loan seekers to his company.

All the five people seated in the AHFL conference room were well aware of the market dynamics. As Karan spoke, Ganesh braced himself to respond to this tirade that was entirely directed at him. The rage was palpable in his voice when he reacted, 'Stop whining, Karan. We all know that our existing exposure to high-risk customer segments is much higher than the market average because our sales guys look for business only in the gutters and the street corners. My underwriting unit is forced to take marginal calls on a whole bunch of bad cases. Most of the cases that come to us are rejects from other lenders. We've gone bust on our product caps on these high risk segments ages ago, but we still continue to source from these segments. Mark my words: there're no free lunches. The chickens will come home to roost in the coming year and you'll see our loss curves getting steeper. I'm on a shoestring budget for bad debts and I can't afford to relax our product anymore. Our sales team does a pathetic job. This story about our relationship being strong with builders is all nonsense. The fact of the matter is, builders just don't know us at all. Your sales guys should be roughing it out in the market instead of sitting here in the air-conditioned office and cooling off. Go get some good business before you ask for any more changes to the product. And builder loans? No way!'

Assaulted by this invective, Karan turned to Cedric and said, 'We may as well kiss the 40% revenue growth goodbye.

Let the sentinels of the portfolio keep swaggering. I can't do these numbers with an RMQ unit that is so risk-averse and refuses to keep pace with the market.'

This sparring between Karan and Ganesh wasn't new to Cedric. He smiled at Karan and said, 'I did expect this stalemate somewhere. I'm sure you guys can reach 40%. Let's take a coffee break now and come back fresh.'

On that note, he signalled to his secretary Stacy, who had consented to stay back till the meeting got over, to arrange for some coffee and snacks for the group. Then he turned to the group and said, 'The next session will be the last of this meeting. We'll finalize our decisions quickly. We'll deliberate for 30 minutes post this coffee break. If nothing comes out, we'll go with a 35% growth number.'

It was a much needed break.

The men, now feeling somewhat at ease, walked out to the private terrace attached to the conference room. Ayravati glittered enticingly. The well-lit orange sulphur lights on the straight roads, the neat and clear 90 degree turns on the roads, the gentle zephyr at that time of early night were all working their magic. It was not every day that they got to stand on the office terrace at 11 pm. They savoured these few moments until they heard Stacy call out that coffee had been served in the cafeteria.

When they reassembled, Karan spoke first and once again raised the issue of builder loans, 'Why shouldn't we do builder loans? We must understand that in this booming property market, builder loans are completely safe. These loans carry high returns. Though the perceived risk is higher, the actual risk is much lower; in fact it is non-existent. This product is a must for us to strengthen relationships with builders and grow revenues.'

Builder loans being large value loans carried a significantly higher risk than individual loans to home purchasers which were much smaller in value. There were instances where builders had borrowed large sums of money from lenders and failed to pay back. Lenders then had to run from pillar to post to recover the loan. In many cases, the builders remained stubborn defaulters and refused to pay. Given this market experience, AHFL had taken a conservative stand on builder loans.

Ganesh was expecting that this would come up again. He remained defiant, 'Shot down. No builder loans. Builder loans are fraught with risks. Most builders are in any case non-compliant on legal and statutory requirements. And for the lilliputian volumes that we do, I just don't see the need to look at builder loans. We must stay away from them at least for two more years.'

Karan seethed, 'We're killing ourselves by disregarding the huge potential for business there. This product must be offered both to the top builders and the next rung . . .'

Even as Karan was labouring to put his point across, Ganesh vehemently shook his head.

Sensing that this altercation wasn't going anywhere, Cedric intervened sharply, 'Guys, I'm stepping in to resolve this. We'll not source builder loans actively. Karan, please send out a message to all to that effect.' Turning to Ganesh he said, 'But let's remain open to some one-off deals referred by known sources. No more discussions or arguments on this item.'

Ganesh had no option but to agree. Karan looked disappointed.

Cedric made his closing remarks, 'We freeze a 35% revenue growth number for the coming year. This would be the number in your performance contracts. I'm going to present this to the Board of Directors. On builder loans, just to reiterate, we won't actively source them, but would be open to the exceptional ones. Thank you all for your help in concluding the budget.'

He then glanced at Madhukar, 'Madhu, your task to consolidate all the product papers, numbers and documents begins now. I want this done meticulously and no part of the discussion should be missed out. Work with Ganesh and Karan and send the whole lot to me ASAP.'

Madhu nodded and the meeting ended. Madhu worked through the next day and collated the entire budget folder neatly for Cedric. He labelled the folder 'Final Budget Submission – Confidential', personally went across to Cedric's office and handed it to him. It was 21 October 2002.

Cedric was waiting for it. He spent an hour going through the document cover to cover. Satisfied, he asked Stacy to make multiple copies for all Board members and keep it ready for the Board meeting that was to take place two days later.

Chapter – 2

APPROVED BUILDING PLAN

October – December 2002

ON THE MORNING OF 23 OCTOBER, THE BOARD OF AHFL assembled in the sixth floor conference room to discuss and approve the budget for the coming year. Cedric made a crisp and effective presentation to the directors on the budget numbers, followed by an update on the current activities in AHFL and the new initiatives planned for the next year. He then asked the members of the board, if there were any questions. A few moments later, Dr. Sharma, the Chairman of AHFL, spoke.

'Cedric, I congratulate you and your team for putting together this wonderful strategy for the coming year. I'm fully supportive of your numbers and initiatives. I'd like to hear what the others feel.' Dr. Sharma sounded cheerful.

There were no further questions or comments from other directors. The budget was approved by the Board. Cedric thanked the Board members, 'Thank you, Dr. Sharma and members of the Board for this quick conclusion. On behalf of my team, I restate our commitment to the growth of AHFL even in the wake of cut-throat competition in the market. We have an experienced senior management team that has proved itself over the years. I'm confident of meeting the expectations of the Board and our shareholders. Thank you all once again.'

All eyes turned to Dr. Sharma for the closing remarks and he said,

'Good luck, Cedric. One of these days, I'd like the Board members here to meet up with your senior management team. I guess that'd be good for everyone.'

Cedric responded eagerly, 'That's a wonderful idea, Dr. Sharma. I'll make the necessary arrangements at the next possible opportunity.'

A few moments of silence followed. Just when they all thought that the meeting was over, Dr. Sharma said something that made everyone, particularly Cedric, a little anxious.

'Great. Now that we are through with the main agenda of this meeting, I would like to bring up a couple of issues that have bothered me over the last few months.'

Dr. Sharma glanced at the people sitting around the table and began, 'We as a lending organization, fall within the ambit of the Central Bank's regulatory authority. As we all know, the Central Bank – being the apex regulatory body for banks and financial institutions – has been constantly alerting lenders, which include finance companies and banks, about the various types of frauds that are happening in the home loans market. One of the issues on which the Central Bank recently sent an advisory to lenders, was regarding the approval of builder projects by the lenders'. He looked around the table once again and then continued, 'As per the law, the builders are supposed to obtain certain approvals from government bodies before they commence construction. These clearances, as I understand, are of two types. The first relates to clearances for land usage like urban land ceiling, non-agricultural use etc., provided by the respective government departments. The second category of approvals are provided by the civic administrative body, which is our MCA.'

He cast a quick glance again at his audience, 'MCA approves the building plan for the project. The building plan is a document that details the layout, elevation and design of the overall project and the buildings in the project. It specifies the area of apartments, types of apartments, number of floors in the building, open areas in the project etc. It's prepared by the builder's architect and taken out in ammonia prints. You must've seen those thick, large, unwieldy blue sheets of paper?' As he spoke he arced his arms on both sides to indicate the large size of those architect's drawing sheets in which the building plans are printed. 'This drawing is submitted to MCA by the builder for approval. The builder cannot commence the construction of the building until MCA approves these drawings.' He then looked at Cedric and asked, 'Have I enunciated the process correctly, Cedric?'

Cedric, who was listening attentively, responded with a jerk, 'Oh yes, Dr. Sharma. You've stated the process most succinctly.'

Dr. Sharma continued, 'If this is the process laid down in the building bye laws of MCA, I'm appalled to see that several builders, especially the influential ones, actually begin the construction of their buildings long before receiving the official approval from MCA. The construction begins soon after the drawings are submitted to MCA for approval, even if the formal approval is not yet in place.' He paused for a second to let his statement sink into the minds of the listeners around the table, who were listening attentively. He then continued, 'I'm even more surprised to see that lending organizations don't hesitate to approve such builder projects and finance the home owners there, even though the building plan is yet to be approved. They think that they'll collect the building plans later. This is wrong. The lenders are violating the law of the land. There's also a risk here. I'm aware of cases in the market where lenders have approved projects without approved plans and are now struggling to get the approved drawings from the builders. This practice must not be encouraged.' He turned his attention to Cedric and questioned, 'Cedric, I'd be particularly interested to know if we too have approved builder projects at a stage when the approved building plans aren't available? I'd like us all to be aware of the position.'

Cedric's antennae had been on red alert since the first reference to the Central Bank, which was always a sensitive topic. Cedric was aware of the advisory that Dr. Sharma was referring to. This circular from the Central Bank was not a diktat, but a cautionary note to lenders vis-a-vis builder project approvals. However, often enough the lenders didn't implement advisories in letter and spirit. The industry adopted a practical view that as long as the building plan was obtained, even if later, it wasn't a big deal. Cedric's mind raced frantically into the crevices of his memory bank to garner as much information as possible and respond to Dr. Sharma. He had not expected the aged Chairman to bring this up. Cedric was aware that at times there had been problems in collection of these building plans from builders. He did vaguely recall occasions when Ganesh had highlighted this to him and pleaded that AHFL stay away from projects that didn't have approved building plans. But in the final arguments, it was always Cedric and Karan who prevailed over Ganesh and forced him to approve builder projects without approved plans, citing the market practice.

He cleared his throat, smiled sweetly and spoke softly, 'Dr. Sharma, I'm aware of the Central Bank advisory. We have always taken regulatory notifications with utmost seriousness and you wouldn't find any instances where any has been overlooked. In AHFL, all builder project approvals are given only after appropriate due diligence on them is conducted. As regards the building plans, there have been some instances where we've faced the problem you mentioned, particularly with some top notch, category 'A' builders who enjoy an excellent market reputation and always commence construction without waiting for the final approval from MCA. In such cases we send our property appraiser, who's an external expert empanelled by AHFL, for property appraisals and valuations, to check and certify that the outer boundaries of construction in the project are as per the building bye-laws. The internal design of the building may not be certifiable since the final approved plan would not be available at that time. We get at least two independent property appraisal agencies to certify that the outer boundaries of the building are as per the bye-laws. We then approve the project. We have done this for a few select, premium builder projects. I must mention that we had no option as we were losing out on business otherwise. Of course, we have followed up and collected those plans subsequently.' Cedric uttered this last sentence with his fingers crossed under the table.

The ostensibly confident answer had the desired effect. Dr. Sharma appreciated Cedric's seemingly honest response. The Board meeting was then declared finished and the directors left the boardroom. As Dr. Sharma was leaving the room, he placed a hand on Cedric's shoulders and said, 'Be careful on this one. Let's not mess with the regulator. It's not worth it.'

Cedric promised sincerely, 'I'll personally track this down, Sir. You'll get an update from me shortly.' Dr. Sharma nodded and walked away.

Back in his cabin Cedric sank into the sofa with a sigh and stared at the ceiling thoughtfully for a few seconds until he was interrupted by a knock on the door. It was Stacy.

'Cedric, would you care for a cup of coffee?' 'Yes, Stacy. Double shot please, thanks. And please ask Ganesh, Karan and Madhu to come to my cabin soon.' He thumped the file on his table impatiently with some force.

The three men came in. Cedric shared with them the news

that the Board had approved the budget proposals. And then he recounted Dr. Sharma's concern on the building plan issue for builder projects.

'I want to know the actual position, guys.' Cedric posed this question to no one in particular.

Ganesh sniggered and said, 'Karan should be able to give you an update on this one.'

Cedric looked at Karan expectantly, who blinked a few times and then said, 'Cedric, I think there're only four or five such projects where we might not have received the building plans. I'll make sure that we get these within the next couple of days.'

At this Cedric's voice rose a few decibels, 'Karan, I've opened my big mouth and confirmed to the Board that we have *all* the building plans in our custody. My ass is on the line and yours will be too. I have to submit a factual report to Dr. Sharma on this issue soon. So please act fast.'

Ganesh made a note of it in his diary against 23 October 2002 which read, 'Building plans for projects to be collected by Karan in five cases'.

The three men returned to their respective cabins. On 24 October, Ganesh went on his scheduled annual leave for 30 days.

When Ganesh came back to work on 25 November, there was much to catch up on and the issue of pending building plans slipped his mind. It was only some time towards the third week of December, when he flipped casually through his earlier diary notes and observed the note that he had made on 23 October.

He sent for Arun and asked him, 'I believe there were five projects that we had approved without the building plans and the same were pending for collection as on 23 October. Karan had promised Cedric that he'd collect them soon. Do you have any update on this?'

'Nope. We haven't received the approved building plans for any of the builder projects approved so far.'

Ganesh hollered, 'Who's following up with Karan?'

Arun took a seat and responded calmly, 'I've been tracking these cases. Several emails were sent as reminders to the sales team asking them to arrange for the approved plans in these cases. No concrete results. And the number of projects you mentioned . . . how did you . . .?'

Ganesh interjected like a bullet from a revolver, 'Karan gave that number to Cedric.'

'But that's wrong. We have sixteen projects across the country that are at different stages of construction, for which we don't have approved building plans . . .'

Ganesh had stopped listening to Arun. He dialled Karan and let loose a volley of abuse. Arun could only hear one side of the conversation. 'Karan . . . what happened to the building plans? . . . were your boys sleeping . . . hear me out fully . . . how the hell could you commit to Cedric that there are only five projects and the plans would be received shortly . . .'

Ganesh's no holds barred approach was one of the things that the RMQ team liked about him. He could virtually say anything to anyone, say it smartly and get away with it. This gave the RMQ unit a distinct edge of aggression.

After finishing his harangue, Ganesh looked at Arun

and said, 'That idiot is on leave, but he said he will work on this over the next three days. He needed the list of the sixteen projects for which you don't have the plans. Please send the list to him immediately. And follow up with that asshole every day, until you get the approved plans.' He then added with authority, 'And stop approving any more builder projects without approved building plans, until these sixteen are obtained.'

Arun made a note in his diary and left.

Ganesh then reached Cedric's office to update him. But he was told that Cedric had left early that day to attend the felicitation ceremony for the outgoing Municipal Commissioner of Ayravati, one Mr. Hegde. The new municipal commissioner was a senior bureaucrat and was taking up this job as his last assignment before his retirement that was due in a couple of years. Ganesh was aware of the change of guard in the MCA headquarters. He decided to catch up with Cedric later and returned to his desk.

Chapter – 3

THE CRITIC

December 2002

IT WAS A SATURDAY; A HOLIDAY AT AHFL, AND ARUN WAS home. He spent the day lazing, playing with Shruti, helping Ananya cook and finally eating a hearty lunch. That evening they had an invitation. Ananya's cousin Vinay, who ran a hotel chain, had invited them for the inauguration of his new hotel in Ayravati. At 6 pm, Arun was on his way to the hotel with Shruti and Ananya.

The hotel building looked different in many ways from other hotels in the city. The name of the hotel – Hotel Airborne – flashed brilliantly in a neon signage atop the building. The hotel was designed around the theme of airplanes, which had been Vinay's fancy since childhood. The building had a distinct structure on its rooftop designed to resemble an aircraft landing on the terrace of the hotel. This structure contained the restaurants and conference rooms. The reception lounge on the upper ground floor was designed like the interiors of an airport. The hotel rooms were modelled to give visitors a business class travel experience. The hotel staff wore typical aircraft crew uniform and the duty manager wore a captain's uniform.

When Arun entered the hotel, he was given three 'boarding cards'. Arun was tickled pink to see that they looked like actual boarding cards and even had 'seat numbers' mentioned. The agenda for the evening was printed overleaf. Arun had a brief look at it:

```
Welcome speech by Vinay
Inauguration ceremony
Dancemania - a Dance presentation by The Shakers
Cocktails and Dinner
```

But he was even more surprised to see that Shruti's 'boarding card' had a different agenda printed overleaf and that read:

```
Rides at the poolside
Appointment with Santa
Grab your gifts
Child room Dinner
```

Ananya and Arun were thrilled by this customized and special attention to children. Even as they looked around, trying to figure out how to send Shruti to the poolside, a woman in crew uniform approached them and said, 'Please leave Shruti with me. I'm taking care of the child visitors here.'

Arun and Ananya smiled and let Shruti go with the woman as they proceeded further into the hotel in search of Vinay. Ananya spotted him at a distance. Vinay was a smart hotelier aged about thirty five, still single and he ran a chain of eight hotels in different cities in the country. All his hotels were either small or medium sized, but he had branded each of them with a theme to make them distinctive. On this day, Vinay was smartly attired in a black business suit, light blue shirt, a light green silk tie, gold plated tie clip, platinum coloured cufflinks and a red rose in his buttonhole. Before long, Vinay spotted them and walked upto them with a welcoming smile.

'Hey guys. Thanks a bunch for coming.' Vinay welcomed both of them with a hug. He guided them into the hotel as he enquired, 'How've you guys been? Now that I have a hotel here I'll come here often and mind you, I'm going to stay at your place and not in my hotel. I can't take this hotel food for very long. And then there's the added incentive of Shruti's company.'

Vinay chatted casually with them for some time. Then he left Ananya with his parents and other relatives who had also come down for the inauguration of the hotel and took Arun with him to show him around. He put his arm around Arun's shoulder and said, 'Great having you around, man.'

'Congratulations on your new hotel, dude. It feels good when a friend makes such enviable progress in business.'

'Thanks buddy. Let's catch Shruti at the poolside.'

The two men walked out to the poolside. It was a small sized pool, with a flat height of 5 feet all across its fifty metre length. There was a reasonably large lawn on the side, where the children were playing. Vinay located Shruti, went up to her and lifted her up. 'Hey you cutie pie, how're you? Do you know who I am?' Shruti was puzzled as she did not remember Vinay. He continued with his wide grin intact, 'I am your Vinay uncle. And here's what I have for you.' He pulled out a chocolate that looked like an airplane and handed it to Shruti. Delighted, Shruti ran back to her friends to show off her newest acquisition.

Vinay took Arun on a tour of the premises, explaining every detail, from the tariff-structure to the marketing strategies and branding. All the while, Vinay was trying to locate suitable company for Arun so that he could go back to his other guests. Suddenly, Vinay's face brightened. He hastened his pace and took long strides towards an attractive woman. She had a svelte figure, mesmerizing eyes, sharp features and was dressed in a spotless white *salwar kameez*. She stood in the middle of the reception lounge, looking around for someone. Perhaps Vinay.

Even as Arun followed him hesitantly, Vinay reached close to the woman and threw his arms around her. 'Hey Sanju! So glad you could make it.' And then he gave her a good look from top to bottom as he said, 'And baby, you're looking awesome.'

Arun hung back and started to look at the paintings on the walls. Soon, he heard Vinay call out to him. Next to him was the woman in the spotless white *salwar kameez*..Vinay introduced them to each other, 'Arun, meet my friend, Sanju. We have known each other since our college days. She's a freelance journalist and writes columns for various newspapers and magazines.' Turning to the lady he introduced Arun, 'And Sanju, this is Arun – a dear dear friend of mine, but more importantly, he's my cousin Ananya's husband. He works for Ayra Housing Finance Limited.'

Arun had a better look at the lady now. Even though her face seemed familiar, he couldn't place her. She oozed confidence and heads turned as she walked. She seemed to be about as old as Arun and Vinay. She extended her hand to Arun before he did and said, 'Good to meet you, Arun.' Her tone was warm.

Vinay rushed in, 'Sanju and Arun, you guys now please excuse me as I need to go and attend to some other matters. I'm leaving both of you in each other's company.' Then turning to Arun he asked, 'Arun, can you please walk Sanju around the hotel?'

Arun nodded.

Sanju thanked Vinay as he walked away. Left alone with Arun, she tried to make conversation. 'I'm so sorry that Vinay has dumped me on you.'

Arun laughed clumsily, 'Sanju, it's my absolute pleasure to have your company.'

Arun knew that he wasn't very good at flirting with women. However in this instance, thanks to Vinay, he looked forward to a few lively moments with Sanju. As they strolled along Arun kept narrating to Sanju whatever he remembered of Vinay's briefing. Shortly Sanju asked him, 'Arun, what do you do in AHFL?'

The way she pronounced AHFL, made Arun feel as if Sanju knew that organization.

Intrigued, he asked her, 'Are you familiar with AHFL?'

Sanju's reply rattled him. 'Yes, of course. I've personally met Dr. Sharma several times.'

This revelation stopped Arun in his tracks.

Looking at his reaction, Sanju smiled sympathetically, 'I'm not surprised at your reaction. As a freelance journalist, I've met your old man several times and interviewed him.'

His consternation ebbed, 'You've *interviewed* Dr. Sharma? About what? And have those interviews been published anywhere?

Sanju wrinkled her forehead making him feel a little dumb as she replied, 'Yes, of course! The interviews weren't published as interviews, but I quoted him in my articles.'

Arun churned his memory trying to trace the articles Sanju was referring to. He didn't remember seeing any article where Dr. Sharma had been interviewed by someone named Sanju. He queried, 'What were these articles about? I keep track of almost all his statements in press, particularly the ones relating to real estate. I couldn't have missed any.'

Sanju responded unhurriedly, 'Most of my articles deal with environmental issues. But I've written a few on illegal constructions by builders, which we see in many of our cities. I'd interviewed Dr. Sharma in that connection.'

Arun sensed that Sanju was someone who knew a lot more than he did about things that mattered to a larger spectrum of people. He was restive. 'You've written on illegal constructions? Really? When? Which magazine?' His mind attempted to recollect articles that he'd read and he tried to recall the names of journalists who had covered property related issues. The name Sanju didn't ring a bell. He kept wondering for some more time and then . . . a flash of enlightenment: With a mild apprehension, he asked, 'Are you . . . by any chance. . . Sanjeevani Desai?'

Sanju looked at him like a goddess looks at a supplicant and nodded with a smile.

Now he knew who she was. The realization dawned on Arun that the woman with whom he had been talking to in the last few minutes was an acclaimed journalist and a prominent activist on public issues. She had a reputation for being genuine and forthright. Her areas of interest included civic administration, environment, child-labour and consumer awareness. She was known to speak fearlessly in all forums; particularly on matters that the civic administration had goofed up on. The excellent research that she'd done on earthquakes and the impact management had been widely applauded. She'd been a recipient of numerous national awards and was the chairperson of the National Environment Council, which operated directly under the Ministry of Natural Resources, advising the government on various environment related issues.

Arun took a few moments to compose himself. As he was recovering, his first emotion was immense admiration for the lady, who he felt deserved all the kudos she had got for the work she'd done.

Arun extended his hand once again and in a somewhat subdued but firm tone said, 'I am thrilled to meet you . . . Ms . . . Sanjeevani. I've heard a lot about you and read your articles as well. I'm sorry, I didn't place you correctly.'

Sanju chuckled, dismissing his apology. 'Come on, you don't have to be formal. This is what happens when people get to know me for the first time. I'm not going to eat you up. And you can call me Sanju.'

The reassurance notwithstanding, Arun felt ill at ease.

'Ok. Thanks . . . er . . . Sanju.'

'Sounds better. Shall we continue the hotel tour?'

He skipped the lift and took her to the staircase, so that she could have a good look at the décor on the walls.

After a few minutes of pointless chitchat to help Arun calm down, Sanju came back to her original question, 'So, what do you do in AHFL?'

Arun now responded confidently. 'I'm in the risk management and quality unit. Since you seem to know AHFL, you must be aware of what the risk guys do.'

'I wouldn't claim perfect understanding. But I do have a fair idea. Risk management is an interesting function; but high stress, isn't it? I bet the constant pressure from the top to grow revenues keeps you all on your toes. I'd say Risk units or RMQ as you call it, are the most traumatized units in any lending organization.'

Arun cringed at this miserable portrayal of his daily grind, 'Yes. The business is under pressure to grow and by virtue of our mandate, we have to support them.'

Sanju posed a pointed question, 'So what kind of support do you guys provide to the business guys?'

Arun detested discussing work. He would've preferred polite and silly conversation to while away the time with this svelte woman. But that was not to be. With some difficulty, he controlled his urge to request for a change of topic and said, 'At RMQ, we design product norms and keep a close tab on portfolio behavior. Our underwriting unit provides the day to day support to the business for running a smooth file-decisioning process. Our fraud management and collection units work to reduce frauds and bad debts. Each activity impacts the Profit and Loss account of the organization and hits either revenues or costs or bad debts.' There, he'd given her a short overview!

Sanju picked up on his glee and acknowledged. 'Wow. That was quick.' She then rubbed it in, 'But there must be tons of conflict between you and the business guys? Can we discuss some of those? I've been waiting to meet someone down-the-line in a finance company for a long time. Lucky that I met you today. People at the top don't talk so much, you know.'

Arun wasn't exactly thrilled at being referred to as 'down-the-line.' 'I am no flunky,' he wanted to say but checked himself from blustering.

Instead he said, 'Yes, there are conflicts at various levels. We take them head on. We have open discussions and resolve the issues with the relevant people as they come up.'

She probed further, 'Who are the relevant people?'

'Could be any of the departments - sales, business, finance or operations.'

Her questions came pelting, 'Let's look at the business guys. They're the ones you have the maximum interactions with. Do you guys always manage to convince each other? What kind of compromises do you make? Can we look at some specific instances?'

Arun thought for a while and said, 'Sanju, there're several conflicts. Let me give you an idea of conflicts at different levels. At the individual loan transaction level on the ground, there're conflicts between sales guys and the underwriters on file decisions. These get thrashed out then and there, but can be really irritating if escalated to higher levels. The impact of a conflict at this level is limited only to that individual transaction. At the next level, which is the policy level, there're conflicting views on the products that are offered in the market. These are again discussed and closed between Business Development and RMQ. There's always some give and take. These conflicts have a larger impact on the company's performance. At a higher level, which is the strategic level, the impact of the conflicts is far-reaching. At this level, the roadmap for the organization is drawn up. A wrong decision here could result in an organizational collapse. At this level, the discussions are cut-throat amongst all the stakeholders and all of them sign with their blood on the roadmap for the organization. The most important pointers for any strategic decision are potential for revenue generation, cost impact and the profits.'

Arun heaved a sigh after what he thought was a reasonably elaborate oration and gleefully waited for Sanju to now switch tracks.

But she seemed least bothered about Arun's expectations and plodded on, 'So, the resolution of any conflict depends on how much revenue can be earned, how much profit can be made or if I may add, for you RMQ guys, it is about how many bad debts can be saved. And you put up with all the stress, the late nights in the office, only to do this?' There was a heavy stress on the word, 'only' and she seemed sarcastic.

Arun wondered as to what else an organization would want. He responded with aplomb, 'What else do you expect an organization to do? I'm not sure if I get your point.'

Sanju explained, 'Ok, let me restate what you just said. You categorized the different levels of conflicts as those at transaction level, policy level and strategy level and their impact on the organization. I understand that from your perspective, you're comfortable letting go at the first level. At the policy level, it's difficult for you to let go, but you can still live with it; but at the strategic level, you just don't compromise. And then there are the three drivers that provide direction to you guys on strategic issues; revenues, profits and bad debts.' She paused to let him acknowledge.

Arun agreed. He realized that she had expressed it more lucidly than him.

Sanju went on, 'Arun, if you permit, I'd like to share my serious disconnect with this approach that organizations adopt towards conflicts and their resolution drivers. I'd put it bluntly: you all epitomize mercenary behaviour. You're no better than the petty moneylender at the street-corner, if you only look at revenues, profits, costs and bad debts. I'm sure you've heard the term 'corporate citizenship'. You may have read about it in books. I'd like to ask you a direct question. What has your industry done for the society as corporate citizens? If each of you think only of making money and enhancing the bottomline, you're probably only a shade better than mercenaries.'

Arun was totally unprepared for this outburst. Resigned to a verbal battle for the next few minutes with this immensely attractive woman, Arun responded quietly, 'But what do you expect? I mentioned the three drivers because organizations exist for value enhancement for shareholders. As for corporate citizenship – we do a lot of charity. We abide by all the government rules and regulations. We pay our taxes. What more do you think should be done for us to qualify as a good corporate citizen?'

Sanju seemed to appreciate his difficulty in understanding her point.

She elucidated further, 'Ok. Let me explain. Let's talk of the Central Bank – your regulator. It keeps issuing notifications and advisories. Now you say that you abide by all the rules and regulations. Let's look at something recent. Central Bank, sometime back, sent out a guideline advising lenders such as your AHFL, not to approve any builder projects that don't have approvals for their building plans from the civic bodies like MCA. Yes or no?'

'Yes.'

'How many lenders have implemented that advisory in letter and spirit? Have you guys done it? I'll save you the embarrassment. The answer is no. Lenders like you, even now, continue to approve builder projects without collecting approved building plans. The inherent insecurity of you and your ilk makes you scamper to the nearest builder and approve his project without the proper documentation. Arun, tell me honestly, do you do this or not?'

Arun was startled at the accuracy of her information. He wondered how she could've known all about these issues which were supposedly internal trade secrets of the home loans industry.

He asked, 'Sanju, how're you so sure of all this? Let me clarify. Approved building plans are a must in all the builder projects that we approve. It's only in a few reputed builder projects that we waive this requirement in the beginning and then collect it later. We've been very particular in our follow up . . .'

She interrupted sharply, 'Load of crap! I know that approving builder projects without collecting building plans is a done thing. The builders have charmed you all so much that you don't blink even once while doing that. That's why in one of my meetings with Dr. Sharma, I'd asked him for his views on this issue and whether AHFL also indulged in similar practices. Dr.Sharma, the thorough gentleman that he is, admitted that he wasn't aware of what was happening in AHFL on this front. But he did share the view that this practice is incorrect. He promised to get back to me on AHFL practices on this. Since he hasn't got back to me in the last few months, I am forming my own conclusions. He must've posed the question to you guys and he's probably waiting for an answer. I met him subsequently as well and let me tell you that the old man was hugely embarrassed at not being able to give me an answer.'

Arun now knew what had made Dr. Sharma raise that question at the recent Board meeting. He decided to come clean with her and said, 'Sanju, I now speak to you as a friend.

You're right that due to business and competitive pressures we're driven many times to do certain things against our own wishes. At AHFL, we do have about sixteen projects that we've approved without collecting the building plans. But let me add that we do not now approve any projects, without collecting the approved plans.'

Sanju stared at him sternly, 'There you are. What do you think you guys are? Despite the Central Bank advisory you do this! Why? Revenues, profits and bad debts? Have you even considered that some of these builders, if not all, could eventually build properties that'll never comply with the rules of the civic body? Do you guys realize the risk? You'll be left holding worthless pieces of paper. You say that you abide by the law of the land. Has it ever dawned on you guys that such projects are in violation of the municipal laws? Someone wants to circumvent the laws or use the lethargy of the administrative machinery to their convenience and you mindlessly join the party. By approving such projects, you're proving that you're no different from the builder himself, when it comes to making your buck. Perhaps you'll have a million justifications for your action. I know you guys well: great at making presentations and writing documents. You'd perhaps justify it saying that such violations are minor and actually don't impact anyone. Please understand, it's not about the impact but about the law of the land. It's an MCA rule. It's what the regulator has sent you a soft advisory about. Abiding by these laws in letter and spirit is the very basic requirement for you to call yourselves good corporate citizens. And going by what you've been doing, you aren't one!'

Arun took out his handkerchief and wiped the sweat off his face. Gathering up some courage he asked, 'Sanju, what's your purpose in directing all this at me?'

Sanju shook her head from side to side vigorously, 'Arun, I'm sorry. My intent was not to attack you personally. It's just that I get very passionate when I speak on this subject and…,' she hesitated for a moment and her face grew sullen suddenly. Arun noted the hesitation and asked, 'And what?'

Sanju's voice seemed to choke for a second and she said, 'Nothing. You aren't being blamed personally. Don't worry. I know you're doing your job and so are the others. It's just that nobody is thinking of these things and I feel frustrated at times. I've tried speaking to several people in the industry, but everyone just wants more revenue. Then who will pay attention to these issues? When will we have cities fully compliant with laws?'

Arun now began to feel that there was more to the story. Her manner of speech, the passion and the frustration showed that she had run hither and thither seeking support to set this right, but no one had come forward to support her. He was curious. Gently he said, 'Sanju, I think there's something seriously bothering you on this issue. If it's ok with you, share it with me. I'm not sure if I can be of much help, but I can try.'

Sanju looked straight into Arun's eyes. 'Thanks very much, Arun. You can do a lot. One of the things that I am currently working on is influencing all the stakeholders to appreciate the importance of safety in our buildings. The stakeholders are lawmakers, builders, lenders like you and of course, the final home-owners. We should provide safe and well-equipped buildings with all necessary infrastructure to people who put in their hard-earned money to buy that one single dream home. For this, several things need to be done. For example, all builders – not just the top ones, but all – should understand the basic safety requirements for a building. The government should lay down clear rules and specify the time and costs for obtaining clearances. Most importantly, they should cut the red tape and find a way to implement the rules in letter and spirit. This needs a strong administration. Lenders such as you should cast these rules in stone and stop approving or supporting any builder project, unless all legal pre-requisites are met. If you don't get the approved building plan, don't approve the project. Don't do that business. Why can't you forego some business and some money for a larger interest?'

She paused to sip some water and continued, 'I'm working hard with several organizations and at several levels to gather support for this initiative. This can be achieved only if everyone comes forward. We all work for our families and in our busy lives, we take many things for granted. But ask someone who's lost his or her loved ones in any of the building tragedies that we've seen in India. And imagine, god forbid, if something like that should happen to *our* loved ones . . . we'll regret it for life, if we're left feeling that we didn't do something that was within our means to prevent.'

Arun absorbed every word attentively.

Sanju wasn't finished. 'Although organizations like AHFL are in the business of financing properties, I am not sure how much attention you guys give to building safety or if you guys have ever researched the building tragedies that have happened in the past?.'

Arun said in a low voice, 'You're right. We don't make an effort to ensure that the building that is financed is fully compliant with safety laws. That doesn't form a part of our mandate.'

'I know that. But can't you guys at least ensure that the building is constructed as per the approved building plan? Sure, you guys are under competitive pressure. But you should at least try to talk to your industry colleagues and convince them that as an industry, all lenders should refrain from approving any builder project without an approved plan. It must be a clear mandate for all lenders to follow.'

Arun remained silent for a while. Then he said, 'Ok Sanju. I'll give it a good try. I'll speak to people within AHFL and see if we can organize a meeting of all lenders in the industry and talk to all of them about it. We'd need to persuade a lot of people. I hope I'll be able to initiate a discussion at least.'

Sanju beamed, 'Arun, I can assure you that you wouldn't face any problems within AHFL. If you wish, I can put in a word with Dr. Sharma to support this.'

Arun retorted hastily, 'No. No. Don't take it to Dr. Sharma now. I'll manage on my own.'

'As you wish. But if you need help in moving things faster in AHFL, let me know.'

Arun then saw her face change from serious to playful as she grinned cheekily, 'So, I now rest assured that I have ground level support from the one and only Arun who is going to get the entire industry to see sense on this issue and get a consensus from all industry players that no builder projects will ever be financed by the industry minus approved project plans!'

'Yes, Ma'am!' Arun bowed gracefully.

'And you'll let me know if you need any help.'

'Yup.'

'Great.'

They loitered casually for a while. When it seemed like it was time for them to get back to the function, Sanju's phone rang. It was Vinay and he asked them to come to the lobby.

For the next couple of hours, everyone present had a blast. The dance show was energetic and the dinner, delicious. Soon it was time to leave. Arun walked up to Vinay to say good bye. Ananya and Shruti had already headed to the car. Sanju stood next to Vinay and she casually reminded Arun about the industry meet. Arun nodded. Vinay heard the exchange clearly. He walked out with Arun to see him off, leaving Sanju in the reception area. As they walked towards the car, Vinay spoke quietly, 'Sanju can sometimes be a maniac when it comes to issues close to her heart. I hope she wasn't too much of a bother.'

Arun gave him a stern glare and said, '*Saale*, you didn't tell me that she's Sanjeevani Desai. I could've got screwed if I'd acted stupid.'

'Oh yeah. I should've remembered that you act stupid often.' Vinay chuckled and said, 'Sorry boss. I thought you'd like the surprise.'

'Bloody fucking hell!'

'Point taken. I'm sorry.'

When Vinay stopped chuckling Arun said, 'I had an eventful time with her. I've taken on something about calling an industry meet to discuss some building plan issue. But I don't get this. What's driving her passion for these things?'

Vinay looked at Arun blankly for a few seconds before he said, 'She lost her parents in a building collapse in Ahmedabad. The building in which they resided just caved in. It happened a few months after the Gujarat earthquake. The repeat tremors, you remember? Keep this to yourself. She doesn't like this being discussed.'

Arun felt as if someone had smashed his jaw in. Vinay pushed him into his car and closed the door. Arun's face was colourless. Ananya saw this change of expression in Arun and became curious. She also saw Vinay when the door closed. Vinay bent down, rested his arms on the window of car, looked straight into Arun's eyes, placed a finger on his lips to gesture silence and said, 'Not one word, please.'

Vinay waved as the car sped away. Arun was in deep thought and remained silent for a long time as he drove. Ananya observed this silence and asked, 'Hellooo! Where are you? What is it that Vinay's telling you to keep quiet about? And what were you doing with that woman the entire evening? By the way, do you know who she is?'

Arun blinked and lightened up, 'Oh yes, I learnt. This bugger Vinay didn't tell me. He could've saved me some embarrassment.'

'What did you learn about her?'

'She's Sanjeevani Desai, a top rung journalist.'

'Is that all?'

'No. A lot more about her work and also that she'd interviewed my superboss, Dr. Sharma.'

'What else?'

'She knows a lot about our industry.'

'And what else?'

Arun now got desperate. 'Can you spare me the inquisition and come clean, please?'

'She and Vinay are getting engaged soon. They've known each other for quite some time. They will soon get married.'

The heaviness that had clouded his mind earlier suddenly lifted. 'Wow! I'm thrilled. That calls for a celebration! Great! Who told you this?'

'Vinay's parents.'

Chapter – 4

BREAKING THE ICE

December 2002

WALKING IN AFTER A LONG WEEKEND, ARUN NOTICED THAT half the office was empty. It was the holiday season. He grabbed his coffee and settled down at his desk to prepare a crisp summary of his discussions with Sanju. It took him about an hour to write down the points. He then walked into Ganesh's cabin placidly.

After the regular pleasantries, Arun broached the topic, 'I met someone different this weekend.'

'Oh! That's nice. Who was it?' Ganesh asked curiously.

'Sanjeevani Desai.'

Ganesh raised his brows, 'The scribe?'

'Yes.'

'How come?'

'Met her at a function. Spent a lot of time with her and got to know her a bit.'

'Uh-huh…'

Arun continued, 'She knew a lot about the home loans industry. She's met Dr. Sharma several times.'

The mention of Dr. Sharma made Ganesh sit up. 'Really?'

'Yes. In fact, she'd put our old man on the spot on a couple of occasions; especially on the builder projects that we've approved without plans.'

Arun then spent the next thirty minutes explaining to Ganesh his discussions with Sanju, her interviews with Dr. Sharma, her efforts to get the home loans industry to stop the practice of project approvals without approved building plans and his own assurance to her that he'd call for an industry meet to resolve this issue.

Ganesh listened to all of it patiently and reacted thoughtfully. 'Good grief, Arun! This explains how the old man brought it up at the Board meeting. We still haven't got back to him. I must inform Cedric about this.'

Ganesh instantly called Cedric.

'Cedric, sorry if I've caught you at a wrong time. But this is urgent.' He gave Cedric a few seconds to absorb the sudden intrusion.

'I'm all ears. Go ahead.'

'We still haven't sent a response to Dr. Sharma on his query about the building plans. And now I have information on how he got to know of this issue. I need to speak to you urgently. No update from Karan yet on the plans that haven't been collected.'

'Ah! Let me speak to Karan. You come here in an hour.'

Ganesh then told Arun, 'I'll ensure that a response goes to Dr. Sharma today. The other thing about getting all lenders to take a uniform and consistent stand in refraining from approving builder projects that don't have an approved building plan: we must do it. I'll convince Cedric to sponsor an industry meet where we could call all the Risk guys and the Business guys from other housing finance companies and discuss this issue. Prepare a list of people to call for this meet.'

Thrilled that he had got Ganesh's quick concurrence, Arun returned to his desk. Quickly he made a list of people from the industry to be invited for the industry meet and gave it to Ganesh.

An hour later, Ganesh was sitting with Cedric in his office. Cedric came straight to the point.

'I did speak to Karan and told him in clear terms that all the pending plans must be obtained before 31 December without fail. Karan will be calling me back any moment now for an update.'

Cedric was worried, 'How do I face the Board and Dr. Sharma in particular? Other members of the Board may overlook this as something minor. But the old man has specifically asked for this and he deserves a response. We've botched it up.'

Even as they deliberated on the possibilities, Cedric's phone rang. It was Karan. 'Yes, Karan! Shoot.'

As he listened he scribbled something on a piece of paper.

Ganesh got up, went around the table and positioned himself to see what Cedric was writing. The update noted by Cedric was,

Building plans already collected by the sales team - 4 projects

Building plans to be received by the sales teams within next 2 days - 2 projects

Building plans are approved. But the builders have submitted revised building plans to the authorities for approval. The revised approvals for the new designs would take some time. - 7 projects

Builder not contactable - 3 projects.

It was a miserable update by any standards. Cedric controlled his fluttering nerves. He told Karan to cancel the rest of his leave and report for work the next day.

When he hung up, Cedric had a disgusted look on his face. He was bristling with fury at the callousness with which Karan had treated the issue. As he sat there pondering over his options, Ganesh thought it was the right time to bring up another key issue that he wanted to discuss. He allowed for a few moments of silence to let Cedric calm down a bit and then put forth his thought.

'Cedric, whatever it is, we must send a report to Dr. Sharma. However, there's something that I want to share with you that would help us make this report to Dr. Sharma look constructive and progressive by nature.'

Cedric gave him a questioning look and Ganesh gave him the lie of the land. 'Over the weekend, Arun bumped into the popular journalist Sanjeevani Desai and he has gathered a lot of information.' Ganesh explained how Dr. Sharma came to place this query before Cedric at the Board meeting. Then he proposed a plan, 'Cedric, you may be aware that she's written several columns on illegal constructions. Therefore, not surprisingly, one of the things she brought up with Arun was the same issue of lenders approving builder projects without approved building plans. She requested Arun to explore the possibility of an industry meet to discuss this issue and work towards getting all in the industry to stay away from approving builder projects that don't have the approved building plans.'

Cedric heard it patiently, raised his eye-brows and asked, 'Why do you think she is bringing this up? What could be her motive?'

'I have no clue. But she's just reinforced our own thoughts. You know my views on this. So I welcome this idea. Let's try speaking to others in the industry. If the entire industry agrees to it, we shouldn't have a problem in implementing it ourselves.'

'Did she mention anything about her meeting with Dr. Sharma?'

'Just that she'd posed this question to Dr. Sharma sometime back and is still waiting for a response. She also added that when she bumped into him recently he seemed embarrassed at not being able to get back to her with the AHFL position on this issue.'

After hearing him out, Cedric said decisively, 'Let's do the industry meet. Arrange to call the relevant guys from all major competitors under one roof and thrash it out. Anyway, it's high time that the industry spoke in one voice on any particular issue. We'll bear all costs of this meeting. Make all calls from here right now.'

Ganesh was well networked in the industry and knew all the key people with the major competitors. It took him about an hour to speak to all the people he wanted to talk to and convince them to attend an industry meet. The dates were finalized and it was now left to Arun and Stacy to arrange for the logistics for everyone to travel to Ayravati for the meet.

After these calls, Ganesh and Cedric prepared a report for Dr. Sharma wherein, besides giving the factual update they also informed him of the forthcoming industry meet to nip the issue in the bud. Since the report presented a permanent solution to the problem, Cedric was confident that Dr. Sharma would appreciate it.

The report was emailed to Dr. Sharma. He received it on his blackberry almost instantly and was pleased that a step had been taken in the right direction.

* * *

Karan cancelled his leave and returned to work the next day.

Firstly, he went to Cedric's cabin. Ganesh was already sitting there. Cedric greeted Karan and said,

'I'm sorry that you had to be pulled out of your leave. But the issue was urgent.'

'I understand, Cedric.'

'You know that a response was due to Dr. Sharma for a long time on the pending building plans.' Cedric raised his eyebrows. Taking a dig at Karan he said, 'You were supposed to give me an update before the end of October, but that didn't come.'

'I'm sorry, Cedric. It somehow slipped my notice.'

Cedric remained silent to let Karan absorb the seriousness of the issue and sense a tinge of palpable embarrassment. Then, in a resigned tone he said, 'This issue has been a thorn in the flesh for Dr. Sharma. We have been informed that Sanjeevani Desai, the noted journalist, has been chasing him on this issue. We still don't know how she caught on to this, but we had to act fast. So we have sent a response to Dr. Sharma. You're copied on the message.'

'Yes. I've read it. Thanks for sending the report. I feel bad that I got you into this. I am however glad that you've called for this industry meet. This should drive some discipline in the industry.'

Ganesh added, 'Karan, you should make this pitch to the industry colleagues on behalf of AHFL. Your saying it will sound a lot more convincing than my saying it.'

Karan accepted the offer which was also perhaps a challenge.

* * *

5 January was the date of the industry meeting. All the key lenders were represented by their Business heads and their Risk function heads. Karan made a passionate speech appealing to them to reject builder projects without approved building plans. He was emphatic in stating that the extant practice of the industry was not in the spirit of the Central Bank's advisory. His speech elicited several questions. In the end, much to the relief of Ganesh and Karan, a unanimous

decision was reached whereby all the lenders from the industry agreed to Karan's appeal. It was decided to implement this norm with immediate effect.

Karan and Ganesh met Cedric that evening and briefed him about the upshot of the meeting. The thought that the entire industry would be more disciplined henceforth was gratifying. The same evening Cedric sent an email to Dr. Sharma informing him of the successful outcome of the industry meet. At that very moment, two buildings away, Shailesh Sangakartha – the Regional Sales Manager of AHFL – was cooling his heels at the office of a builder.

Chapter – **5**

THE BAIT

January 2003

45 YEARS OLD, ROOPAK CHAND WAS BORN WITH A SILVER spoon in his mouth, in a village located about 200 kilometres from Ayravati. He had an elder brother, Praveen Chand. Their pampered childhood held every luxury that they could imagine. His family commanded significant influence and clout in that part of rural India, being the wealthiest there.

Roopak's father was uneducated and he didn't care much for educating his children either. The children were sent to school at the insistence of Roopak's mother. The family owned close to 1500 hectares of fertile cultivable land spread across several villages. They also owned several ancestral properties, agricultural output processing units, hi-tech farm machinery and a large cattle farm.

Excessive luxury was a major distraction in the lives of Roopak and Praveen. Neither of them evinced any interest in studies or in any other creative activity. The brothers let loose a reign of terror in the school. Even as toddlers, they took pride in being bullies. The brothers attended school till the 8th grade, after which their father began to engage them in managing the family wealth and property.

While otherwise the going for the family was good, their father suddenly took ill and the diagnosis was blood cancer. His health deteriorated and he soon passed away. The two boys were left with the mother and a huge fortune to manage. They began to squander their wealth recklessly. Their mother tried hard to make the two boys realize the responsibilities of life. But before she could bring about any perceptible change in their attitude, she too passed away.

The boys had by then grown into young men of 22 and 24. The entire family fortune stood in their joint names as they were the only legal heirs. Praveen Chand suggested they divide the fortune between them and manage their respective portions individually. Roopak readily agreed, and he looked forward to independent control over half of his father's wealth, which was a quite a bit.

As decided, the brothers arranged for a lawyer to do the formalities required to get the wealth distributed between them. Besides the part of the wealth that was in the form of land, there were other assets such as ancestral properties, vehicles, agricultural machinery and cattle amongst others.

With the lawyer alongside, they negotiated between them over the next few days and reached a consensus on what they felt was a fair distribution between them. Once an agreement was reached, the lawyer prepared the necessary documents in their individual names and got the wealth formally registered in their respective names.

Praveen and Roopak got busy managing their wealth. Praveen had an interest in farming and he settled in the village itself.

Roopak had no interest either in farming or in staying in the village. He wanted to shift out of the village. He sold all the agricultural land in his share and invested the proceeds in different business ventures which included a transport company, a movie theatre, an illegal gambling den and a stud farm. Over time, he became a regular at Ayravati's race course. At times he lent money at exorbitant rates to builders who needed financial support to complete their real estate projects. Besides usury, he himself tried his hand at some real estate projects.

Most businesses started by Roopak failed. However, the real estate business that he had initially started on a small scale thrived and yielded excellent results. In no time, real estate became his passion and obsession. His prominence and clout in the industry grew gradually. After experimenting with small projects in the initial years, he moved to large, full scale residential projects. His projects sold well and he made good money. Enthused by his success, he headquartered himself in Ayravati and set his eyes on even bigger things.

That was twenty years ago. Over these years, Roopak had

worked hard to amass wealth that was now several times the size of what he'd initially inherited. He now owned multiple tracts of non-agricultural land across several cities in the country. His firm, Chand Builders, had acquired a reputation as one of the finest real estate companies in India, known to build the best residential projects with modern facilities. The firm enjoyed a great deal of respect and regard even in the financial world. Every lending institution vied for a relationship with the firm. Roopak was a powerful man in the real estate universe, dictating terms to customers, financiers and even to the government at times. He was a messiah for any problem within the industry. Therefore at any point in time, there were several people sitting in his office, waiting to meet him.

Roopak's office was managed by a group of gun-toting guards. It was well-known in industry circles that in the course of his rise to stardom, Roopak had crushed several people mentally, emotionally and physically, thereby making many enemies who were baying for his blood.

Notwithstanding his ruffian tendencies, he maintained a pleasantly dignified facade in front of finance companies and banks. He had borrowed money from them often enough to run his country-wide business. He was a good customer who repaid his loans on time and thus enjoyed a spectacular relationship with all his institutional lenders.

Recently, for reasons best known only to him, he asked his financial controller Dave to identify a new lending institution in Ayravati, with whom he could initiate a new business relationship. There were many lenders who would give an arm and a leg to do business with him; but his scheming mind had a definite purpose in seeking a new relationship. He wanted a lender, who would dance to his tunes. After a few days' research, Dave identified AHFL as a potential lender.

That is how it came about that Shailesh was sitting in Roopak's office that evening. Quite naturally, when Roopak crooked a finger, the likes of Shailesh came running. After an hour-long wait, Shailesh was asked to go into Roopak's cabin to meet him.

Shailesh knocked and entered the room, looked around for a few seconds, saw Roopak seated at his desk, came closer and greeted him feebly, 'Good evening . . .' But before he could finish his greeting, the phone on Roopak's desk rang. Roopak waved asking Shailesh to sit and attended to the phone by putting it on the speaker. Shailesh could hear the telephone conversation.

In his care-a-damn style Roopak said, 'Yeah.'

Shailesh had never heard such a heavy and a hoarse voice before.

The voice at the other end of the phone was respectful.

'*Bhai*, Vikas here. I'm calling from Ekdam Builder's office. Came to collect our payment, but he says he has no money. This is the fifth time I'm visiting his office for our payment. Need your permission to break his bones.'

Roopak reacted furiously, 'Tell that bastard that it'll take me no time to wipe him off the face of this earth. Before doing that, I'll squash his balls.' Simultaneously, Roopak took out a revolver from under the table and placed it on the table.

Shailesh shuddered at the sight of the revolver.

The man who had called Roopak continued, '*Bhai*, we've threatened him enough. He's not relenting. Says he'll complain to the police.'

'Tell him not to threaten me. Give him one last warning. If he doesn't cough up my money by tomorrow morning, he'll not live to see tomorrow's sunset.'

'Ok, *bhai*.'

The call ended. Roopak turned and looked at Shailesh who was sitting across and shitting bricks. Roopak gave him an abrupt smile and said, 'I don't like to do these things. But what to do? I have to run my business, no? Bastards take money when they need it, but don't give it back on time. Ok, you wait now.'

Shailesh got up to go outside and wait, but Roopak gestured for him to be seated and said, 'Wait here only.'

After a full minute of dumb silence as Roopak thoughtfully stared at the ceiling and Shailesh expectantly stared at Roopak, the builder asked quizzically, 'Ok, so why did you want to see me?'

Shailesh, scrambled for words and mumbled, 'Sir....err... ...I thought *you*'d asked me to come here to meet you.'

Roopak rolled his eyes, stared blankly for a moment and then threw his arms up and down in apparent frustration. 'So that means you don't even know why you're here? Go and find out first as to why you're here. Go, go, go! Don't waste my time.'

Shailesh had never felt so foolish. It was Roopak's office that had got in touch with Shailesh and asked him to come over. Shailesh obviously didn't check as to why this meeting had been called. He came as instructed by Roopak's office. He mustered up some courage and made a last ditch effort to get the man at the other side of the table to see some sense. 'Sir . . . Mr.Vachchani from your office asked me to come and meet you. He mentioned that you wanted to see me. I'm from AHFL.'

Hearing the name AHFL, Roopak's expression changed quickly. 'Oh. Ok. You're from AHFL! Why didn't you tell me before? I remember now. I don't forget things. You should've told me that you're from AHFL. Yes. I'd asked for a meeting with you. I'm sorry that I couldn't recognize you.'

A relieved Shailesh was overwhelmed by this sudden show of warmth from the man on the other side, who a few seconds earlier had threatened to wipe out someone from the face of this earth.

Roopak smiled, 'So what's your name?'

'I'm Shailesh. I'm the Regional Sales Manager in AHFL.'

Roopak restated his name loudly, 'Mr. Shailesh.' He looked up at the ceiling, looked back at Shailesh and asked him with a piercing look, 'Shailesh. Have we met before?'

'No, Sir. This is the first time I'm meeting you in person. But I've heard of you before. I'm glad I got this opportunity to meet you.'

Roopak nodded his head imperiously. There was no one in the industry who didn't know him or so he thought. He said, 'Shailesh, I've also heard of you and of the great work that you and your guys are doing at AHFL. I like to meet youngsters like you who are passionate about their jobs. You know, I just like to meet them. Why do we need to have a reason to meet?

I just wanted to meet you, that's all. I'm glad that I met you. Good luck.' He stopped speaking.

Shailesh didn't know whether to respond or just get up and walk away. He decided to remain seated for a few more seconds and then get up and leave if nothing happened.

Thankfully, Roopak opened his mouth again abruptly, 'So, what do you feel?' A wide grin appeared from nowhere on Roopak's face.

'Err . . . I feel good to meet you sir.'

'Yes. Exactly. I like youngsters like you. I like to be known to you people. It's important that people like you know us well and appreciate the work that we do. By the way, I'd like your views on our organization. Have you seen the buildings we've built? Do you like our work?'

Roopak was good at manipulating people. Shailesh was young and lacking in experience; he was doing exactly what Roopak wanted him to do. Soon he was all praise for Chand Builders, 'Oh yes sir. Your organization is doing great work. You are the owners of some of the best projects in the country. Besides, your reputation for timely delivery and great quality is legendary. I've seen several of your projects and I'm always impressed by them.'

'Thank you. We aim to please. Let me tell you one thing that I've learnt the hard way in life. Don't run after money. Protect your credibility. Money will follow. For me, credibility is most important and I'd go to any extent to guard it. Yes.' Roopak thumped the table and asked again. 'What do you feel? Is that the right approach?'

'Of course, sir.'

Suddenly Roopak asked, 'How's your business? How many loans do you do in a month?'

'Sir, we do about 200 loans a month from my region.'

'Is that all? But why such low figures despite good people like you?'

'Sir, we're relatively new in the industry. Our builder tie-ups are still not too many.'

'Hmmmm . . . are my boys giving enough business to AHFL?'

'No sir. We don't do much business from your projects. I'd be grateful if you can help us initiate approvals for your projects and start referring business to us. I promise the best service to your customers.'

Roopak got up from his chair and walked around the table to Shailesh.

'Don't worry, my boy. I'll help you out. I have great regard for AHFL. You guys are different. You don't cheat customers by making false promises. You stick to your commitment and I love people who honour commitments.'

The pantry boy came in, placed two cups of tea on the desk and went away. Roopak resumed his point, 'Shailesh, we want to initiate an excellent relationship with AHFL. This is only because of the great respect I have for your organization. In fact, I want an exclusive tie-up with your organization, whereby all my customers who need loans to buy apartments in any of my projects, anywhere in the country come to you and only to you. I was just wondering if that'd be acceptable to you and whether you can make it work.'

This was much more than what Shailesh was waiting to

hear. This offer could change the fortunes of his company and more importantly his own personal fortunes. If he got all the loans from Roopak's projects, he would exceed his sales targets and stand to earn a very handsome incentive. His eyes widened and he gasped audibly, 'Sir, it's absolutely possible. Are you serious? If you want that done, I'll personally take care of your cases and ensure that they're processed smoothly. Your customers will get treated as VIPs. I'll also give them a good rate.'

'Shailesh, this business will surely come to you, though over a period of time. For me, this is good because then I deal with one clean organization. What do you feel?'

Shailesh was already dreaming of sitting in front of Karan and boasting as to how he had coaxed someone as big as Roopak and convinced him to move all his referrals across the country to AHFL. His promotion as the National Sales Head of AHFL was now only a formality.

'Sir, that'd be wonderful, really. I'll coordinate all your payments centrally from here. I'll ensure that your customers get priority over everything else in AHFL.'

Roopak fuelled Shailesh's excitement, 'How much business do you do every month across the country?'

Shailesh thought for a moment and answered, 'Sir, we do about 1000 loans a month across the country.'

Roopak gave a surprised shout, 'That's puny, isn't it? What's your problem, man? Why aren't you guys able to do much more business?'

'Sir, from the next month, our targets are higher. We have to do about 1400 loans a month.'

'If you tie up with me, I can help you meet that target singlehandedly. You don't have to go anywhere else.'

While he was thrilled to hear this, Shailesh was also ashamed that the AHFL story on retail mortgage volumes was so pathetic. Roopak continued, 'My group generates close to 1500 loans a month for different lenders across the country through our projects. So you'd benefit tremendously by partnering with us. Let's make a beginning and we'll gradually build it up. I want to reach a stage where we work exclusively with you by giving all our referrals to you. Further, I want you Mr. Shailesh, to be the single point contact for us in AHFL. Are you okay with that? I don't like to go to senior people. You're the guys who do the actual work and I'm only concerned with the work.'

'It'd be my absolute pleasure, sir.'

'Young man, I wish to see you grow quickly in the organization so that you and I can do many bigger things in future.'

Shailesh was completely floored by the flattery now. He shook hands with Roopak in a daze, thanking him heartily and promising to work hard to meet his expectations.

At no cost to himself, Roopak had gained the complete loyalty of Shailesh. He had planted his first seed in AHFL.

Roopak concluded with, 'You be in touch with Vachchani. I'll tell him to start handing over our project files to you.'

'Thank you so much, Sir. I'll strive to give you the best possible service.'

Shailesh had hit a jackpot. He left Roopak's office and directly went to meet Karan in AHFL House, which was just half a furlong away.

Karan greeted Shailesh. 'Hi Shailesh, how're you, man? What brings you here?'

'I was here in Chand Builders. And I've some big news for you.'

'Chand Builders! Interesting. What's the big news?'

'I'm just walking out of a meeting with Roopak. After months of rigorous pursuit, I've got him to agree to refer loans to AHFL.'

'Wow. That's splendid, man! How many files do you think that'd get us?

'Lots. He'll refer business to us not just in Ayravati, but from across the country,'

Karan gave a low whistle, 'Wait a minute. Shailesh, are you saying that Chand Builders has agreed to refer business to us from their projects across the country? Do I hear you right?'

'Absolutely.'

'This is unbelievable. How did this happen, man? Tell me everything.'

Shailesh blew his own trumpet for the next half hour, feeding Karan a concocted story of how he and his team had spent hours, days and weeks to persuade Roopak to do business with AHFL. That Roopak would refer business to AHFL in all locations in the country was big news for Karan by any standards. This would be AHFL's first major breakthrough with any builder of repute. The existing relationships were all with smaller builders, nothing to write home about. Karan saw a king-maker in Shailesh.

'Shailesh, this is brilliant! Fantastic job! I still can't believe it.'

Shailesh tried to adopt an air of modesty, but failed miserably. Karan continued.

'Great, man. I can assure you of all the support you need. Once they start referring files, I'll personally meet up with Roopak to strengthen the relationship.'

While the two men in AHFL dreamt of a happy and rewarding association with Chand Builders, Roopak was busy plotting a devilish plan in his office.

Chapter – 6

THE BITE

February 2003 – June 2003

CHAND BUILDERS REFERRED CLOSE TO HUNDRED NEW customers to AHFL for loans in January. A hundred odd customers coming from a single source was a headline item for Karan's monthly business report. If Roopak got all his offices throughout the country to pour business into AHFL, Karan could stand tall before Cedric.

February saw the number of referrals from Chand Builders grow to 250 files. For a company that disbursed 1300 to 1400 loans in a month, this chunk of 250 loans turned the math around completely. AHFL did close to 1600 loan disbursements in February. Karan's sales team had nearly 200 more files to be logged-in for processing, but Karan told them not to log-in any more files in February, as their monthly target had been met. The files in waiting would be processed in March and help Karan reach his March targets. Roopak was well on his way to acquiring divine status in Karan's mind and was the subject of discussion in all AHFL meetings. Even Cedric now came to regard him as a critical relationship for AHFL.

March saw another 250 files from Chand Builders. Karan was now completely in Roopak's spell. The relationship with Chand Builders was turning fortunes around not just for AHFL but also for Karan at a personal level. Karan, by now, had met Roopak several times and they had become close buddies. Courtesy Roopak, Karan now flaunted memberships in some of Ayravati's toniest clubs. Their regular meetings and other favours fostered a sense of close kinship and loyalty in Karan towards Roopak. With promises from Roopak that starting June, he'd refer to AHFL a business of at least 600 files every month, Karan's world had only one name written all over it – Roopak.

The going seemed hunky-dory to all. But Arun, the dyed-in-the-wool risk guy that he was, smelt a rat. He felt it was strange that Chand Builders should refer files in such volumes to AHFL, completely out of the blue, when there were other lenders in the market who had better products on offer. Why was Roopak being so considerate to AHFL? This question troubled him. Arun did some research on the background of Chand Builders and Roopak, but could dig up nothing. He put the loan files referred by Chand Builders through a microscopic review process, but found nothing unusual with those files either.

Complaints reached Cedric through Karan that Arun was needlessly snooping into files referred by Chand Builders and delaying turnaround time. Cedric personally sent word to Arun through Ganesh asking him to get reasonable with the files from Chand Builders.

And then it happened. The day and the moment Roopak had patiently waited for arrived in early May. AHFL had closed their April business volumes at a new high – 2100 files booked in one month with Chand Builders contributing close to 600 files. The company that had done 1000 files in December 2002 had more than doubled its volumes in just four months. No ordinary feat by any standards and it was time to celebrate.

Karan arranged for a celebration and invited all his sales associates for cocktails and dinner. Roopak was invited as the guest of honour. On the day of the celebration, all key staff of AHFL gathered at the venue. Roopak walked in at the decided hour, smartly attired in a business suit. After a few pleasantries, Karan took over the microphone.

'Ladies and gentlemen, a pleasant evening to all you lovely people. As you know, we're here to celebrate our business performance in April. It's a matter of great pride for everyone here that AHFL crossed the magic 2000 number in April; the largest ever for us.' There was a spontaneous and a long round of applause. Karan waited for it to subside and continued, 'I congratulate the sales teams of AHFL who've worked hard to achieve this number. I take this opportunity to commend their contribution by giving them letters of appreciation.' At that moment someone walked up to him and whispered something in his ears. Karan then said, 'I also wish to thank our RMQ team that has supported the sales teams in achieving these numbers.' Such acknowledgement of effort for RMQ always came as an after-thought.

Karan then made the grand announcement he had planned to make. 'Today on behalf of AHFL, I'd also like to express our sincere gratitude to a very important person standing amidst us, who in spite of several options available to him, encouraged AHFL whole heartedly, thereby significantly contributing to our numbers. Please allow me to introduce a gentleman to the core and my dear friend, Mr Roopak Chand. As you all know, Roopak is the strongest pillar of the real estate industry today and it is indeed an honour that he's present here with us today.' He turned to Roopak and requested him to come forward.

Roopak was greeted with a huge round of applause from the sales team and muted applause from the RMQ team. Ganesh hadn't even come for the celebration as he knew that it would be a sales evening through and through. Arun was there however, watching everything with a deep sense of rancour. Roopak walked upto Karan and took the microphone from him. He delivered a short, patronizing speech, 'Good evening to all. I'd like to thank Karan for inviting me to this gathering. I like to work with good people. At the very first meeting with Karan, I knew that I had met someone worthy of developing a long and a strong relationship with. I've never seen anyone in my life who works with such dedication and sincerity. Karan has personally taken care to help us in getting our clients' files processed speedily in AHFL. I assure him that we'll honour our responsibility of friendship with AHFL in letter and spirit and we expect and are sure that AHFL will do the same. Thank you.'

Karan embraced him cheerfully and led him off to introduce him to the team. This overtly excessive display of friendship bothered Arun. Something was definitely amiss. The Karan-Roopak bonhomie seemed synthetic, so perfect that it could topple anytime. He left the party early and drove all the way home mulling over what he had seen.

From the party venue, everyone left after the merrymaking except for Karan, Shailesh and Roopak. They were still doing their cocktail rounds and were immersed in an animated conversation.

Karan, not having had enough of it, was expressing his adulation for his newfound friend, 'Roopak, you're fantastic, man. Your grip on the industry is strong. You dominate the market with your new projects. If you wish, you can multiply the number of projects that you do at a time and give all other builders a run for their money.' He guffawed loudly. Raising a toast to Roopak he said, 'Here's to Roopak and Chand Builders, the number one guys in the industry.' More guffaws.

Roopak had been waiting for an opportunity to broach the subject with Karan. Now was the time. He calmly waited for Karan to stop laughing and then he spoke, 'Well Karan, thanks for the compliment. But you're being optimistic. Things aren't that easy. I've got several challenges too. Do you know that we're extremely stretched on our working capital needs currently? I must continuously generate enough cash to keep all my existing projects going. Once a project commences, it cannot stop until it is completed. And each real estate project guzzles cash. Besides taking care of the project expenses, I must, without fail, pay my monthly debt commitments to other lending institutions that have trusted me with their money. Do you know that I've borrowed from other lenders in the form of builder loans? I owe a lot to those lender friends, since they helped me by giving me builder loans when I needed money the most and eased my working capital problems. But for their help, my projects would've flopped. Liquidity in the market is extremely tight, my friend. Times aren't good and Chand Builders is actually in a bit of a cash crisis. I'm sure I'll come out of it, but my purpose of telling you all this is just to let you know that it's not all hunky-dory out here. We have our own challenges too.'

This was Roopak's planned manoeuvre set to trap Karan the way he wanted. From what Roopak said, it occurred to Karan that Roopak had other relationships in the industry which were perhaps more important than AHFL. He felt a tinge of professional envy. Roopak held those relationships in high esteem with a sense of personal gratitude towards them, only because they had directly given *him* builder loans whereas AHFL, till date, had only given loans to Roopak's customers but not yet to Roopak directly in the form of builder loans.

Even as Karan mulled over what he had just heard, Roopak continued, 'Don't you worry Karan. I know how to manage these things. If I really have a cash problem, I can tap any of my existing lender relationships. They'll be only too happy to give me another builder loan; in fact, they've been asking me to take more, but I've always said no. I'd prefer to manage my work without taking on additional debt. But it's always heartening to know that there are people waiting to lend you money whenever you need it.'

The hammer hit the nail harder this time. Karan started to feel insecure about his relationship with Roopak, as he heard Roopak waxing lyrical about other lenders in the market. For the first time, Karan was worried about losing the relationship to another lender. That would mean that the immense volume of business that Roopak had been giving to AHFL would go to some other lender. Based on the informal promises Roopak had made to Karan, Karan had voluntarily committed an increase in target volumes to Cedric. But if Roopak decided to move the whole or even a part of that business away from AHFL, the committed targets would become a distant dream. Karan realized the fickleness of Roopak's allegiance towards AHFL and suddenly he could see Roopak asking, 'What's in it for me?'

Karan was thinking intently for a while when a flash of blinding light crossed his mind. Could AHFL look at a builder loan to Chand Builders? Roopak had mentioned an impending cash crunch. Karan knew that getting Cedric and Ganesh to agree to a builder loan would be difficult, but this was an extraordinary situation that demanded a favour of sorts for Chand Builders. Karan struggled with the dichotomy for some time before falling hook, line and sinker for Roopak's devious plan.

He conveyed his first inkling of willingness to Roopak

awkwardly, 'I'm sure AHFL can also look at a builder funding proposal for you, Roopak. Are you in need of funds now?'

Shrewd that he was, Roopak realized that the conversation was moving in the direction he wanted. He let Karan struggle with the dilemma, 'Oh, oh. No, Karan. You got me wrong. I don't need any money now. When we wanted the money, our lender friends approached us voluntarily and gave us the money. You guys were not in the picture at that time. And frankly, it's not my style going and asking for money. I'd do it only if I'm desperate. God has kept me comfortable. I don't need any money now. Thank you.'

Karan was showing signs of desperation now, 'I heard you mention a cash crunch earlier? If not now, would you be interested in availing a builder loan in the near future?'

Roopak spoke sardonically, 'Karan, what I meant by cash crunch was that I do not have money that I can officially disclose. But why do you ask? Don't tell me that you're really keen to give me a builder loan?' He chortled.

Karan responded, 'Well ... er, Roopak, I wouldn't want you to go to any other lender for any of your needs. Ideally, I'd want all your requirements to be met by AHFL. So if it's a builder loan, I believe AHFL can offer you one.' He signalled the bartender for a refill.

'Ok. If you insist, I'll keep that in mind. My financial requirements are managed by my financial controller, Mr. Dave. I'll convey your message to him and if he has a need for any funding, he'll contact you.' Roopak gave an abrupt smile before saying, 'He is an elderly person of 65 and has been working with me for a decade and a half now. You could also give him a call if you feel.' Roopak gave Dave's number to Karan, knowing fully well that Karan would call Dave the very next day.

That night Karan couldn't sleep. A sense of insecurity overwhelmed him. He grew anxious about the flow of business from Chand Builders.

Next day, the first thing Karan did was call Dave. He dialled Dave's number. There was no response. Karan tried after some time; no response again. Impatient, he went out to grab a cup of coffee. He came back to his desk and dialled the number again. This time it was picked up and the voice at the other end said coldly, 'Dave'.

Recognizing that it was the man himself who had come on phone, Karan spoke hastily, 'Mr. Dave, hello. My name is Karan and I'm calling from Ayra Housing Finance Limited. Is this a good time to talk to you, sir?'

'Who?' The voice sounded angry.

'Sir, my name is Karan.' Karan responded anxiously.

'Mr. Karan. I don't know you. But in any case, I'm busy now. What is it you want?'

'Mr. Dave, I wanted to speak to you about any possible funding requirement…'

Dave interjected, 'I don't think we need any funds now. Call me next month.' And Dave banged the phone down.

Karan's disappointment knew no bounds. But he made a note to call Dave again next month.

At Dave's end, within the next couple of minutes he had updated Roopak of the call from Karan and his curt response. Roopak was pleased that things were on the right track.

Karan impatiently waited for the entire month of May to pass.

On the 2nd of June, Karan called Dave and got through to him only after a couple of attempts.

'Yes.'

'Mr. Dave, I'm Karan from AHFL. We . . ..' Karan wasn't allowed to complete the sentence.

'What is it, Mr. Karan? Why have you been trying to get in touch with me for so long.?'

'Mr. Dave, I know Roopak and he asked me to speak to you.'

'But this is not a good time for me. Could you please call me next week?'

He hung up again. Karan was growing frantic and he started to believe that perhaps Chand Builders didn't need any money now and that he must grab the first opportunity when they would want funds from the market. He also noted with concern that the number of applications from Chand Builders had slowed down in May, which was disappointing after a fabulous April. AHFL only did about 1500 cases in May and this was primarily because only about 200 files came in from Chand Builders that month.

After dodging Karan a few more times, in the third week of June, Dave came on line and agreed to meet Karan to discuss with him a builder loan requirement for Chand Builders. And then Dave also voiced his expectations from Karan in a frightening tone, 'Mr. Karan, only if AHFL is serious about a relationship with Chand Builders will we discuss our builder loan requirements with you. You must ensure that the deal goes through. No bureaucratic hurdles, please. Please note that our relationship with our existing bankers is ripe and mature. I just need to make a phone call. They'd come running with the loan disbursement cheque to us. They do not ask us any questions ever. Much against my wishes, Roopak has advised me to avail this builder loan from your organisation AHFL, because you're keen to give us a builder loan. But let me make it clear: you're the one interested in doing this deal. I'm not. I have many other options. It's therefore incumbent upon you to ensure that you don't ask us funny questions during your scrutiny of our papers. If it is in your power to ensure that this deal would see a smooth sailing, let's get into it. If not, please say so right now. We'll take it in the right spirit and pursue other options. I'll look forward to a final confirmation of this in our meeting this Friday – five days from now. Hope I've made myself clear.'

Karan was not prepared for this tirade and he stuttered, 'Y…Y…Yes Mr. Dave. I hear you. I'll make sure that this goes through smoothly. You needn't worry on that count. When we meet this Friday, I'll give you a confirmation.' The call finished on that note. The next moment, a strange anxiety gripped Karan: would the deal actually sail through smoothly within AHFL? He hadn't yet discussed anything with Cedric or Ganesh. He had to do that right away! It was certainly not going to be easy, since AHFL's core strategy did not allow active sourcing of builder loans. He had to take this up with Cedric and Ganesh carefully. Karan gave himself one full day to come out with a strategy to approach the two. At the meeting on Friday, Karan had to confirm that AHFL was ready to give the loan to Chand Builders. Therefore the most critical piece was to get Cedric and Ganesh to agree in principle to this proposal. But for that, he needed a lot of information about Chand Builders.

He sent for Shailesh. Karan came straight to the point, 'Shailesh, are you aware of the discussion I had with Roopak about AHFL taking a builder loan exposure on Chand Builders?'

'Yes, Karan. I was there that night.'

'You're also aware that it's against the core thinking in AHFL to do builder loans.'

'Yes. I was actually surprised that you offered them one.'

'Never mind. At this juncture, our relationship with Roopak is precariously poised, as you can see from the drop in the loan referrals from Chand Builders in May. The writing on the wall is clear. If we don't reciprocate and show them that we too have something to offer, it's just a matter of time that they'd stop referring any cases to us.'

He waited for Shailesh to absorb the gravity of what he said.

'Yeah. I understand.'

'After much follow up, their financial controller Dave has agreed to meet me to discuss a possible funding requirement. My real intent is to ensure that AHFL gives this loan to Chand Builders. Dave has forewarned me that this deal must be a smooth affair since we seem to be more keen than them. When I meet him, I must give him the confidence that this deal will fly through AHFL. To do that, I need to get both Cedric and Ganesh on my side and that has to happen within the next couple of days. Do you get what I'm trying to say?'

'Certainly.'

Karan now came to the point, 'I need you to gather some information for me by the end of the day; it should be done discreetly from your industry network. I don't want the guys in Chand Builders to get wind of it. Do some research and identify the projects against which Chand Builders could possibly seek funding, how much they would need and how fast. Use your informal sources only and come back to me with the data ASAP.'

Shailesh liked doing this kind of work as he prided himself on his strong network within the industry. Promising to return soon with the information, he left.

In the next four hours, Shailesh made several calls. This included his sources within Chand Builders. From them, he found out the names of lenders who'd lent money to the firm earlier. From those lenders he got to know that all loans given to Chand Builders were being repaid as per schedule and that the loans had been availed several years ago. Next, he collected details of the ongoing projects of Chand Builders. There were many, not just in Ayravati, but across the country. Shailesh listed all the current projects and tabulated their information in the order of: number of flats, estimated cost of the flat, progress of construction, expected time of completion and the current sale position. Next, he dug out the names of the lenders who'd been approached by Chand Builders for a builder loan in recent months. He got three names. The three applications were for three different projects. Shailesh discovered that two of these builder loan applications were under process with two lenders, while the third application – for a project named Megacity – had already been rejected by a third lender. He enquired further about the one that had been rejected. The proposal had been rejected by Millennium Bank, which was one of the leading industry players in home loans. The reason for the rejection, he gathered, was that the bank already had a large exposure on Chand Builders and as per its internal norms, couldn't take on more. The bank did not have any issues with the project – Megacity – per se. After he was satisfied that he had all the information that he could possibly collect, Shailesh summarized it all for Karan in a report.

'Karan,

Please find below some information you may find useful for your discussions.

Location where funding would be required: Ayravati

Possible Projects where funding might be asked for,

Ocean Pearl

Whitewoods

Megacity

Current position of sale: More than 50% of flats sold in 1 and 2 above. Sale of flats yet to commence in Megacity.

Construction Progress: All projects have crossed 60% construction stage. On the Megacity project, Chand Builders had applied to Millennium Bank for a builder loan, but the same had been declined. The reason seems to be that Millennium Bank has exhausted their limit of exposure on Chand Builders.

Likely funding requirement: Rs. 400 to Rs. 600 million

Time of disbursement: Immediate

Terms: To be negotiated. Chand Builders has a tough negotiator in Dave.

Mortgage/Security: The project funded will be mortgaged to AHFL.

Regards,
Shailesh.'

Karan seemed satisfied with the information collected. He wanted to do a thorough analysis and be satisfied about the deal, in order to pitch it strongly to Cedric and Ganesh. He called his secretary and instructed her that he and Shailesh should not be disturbed. Both of them grabbed a cup of coffee each and sat down for a brain-storming session.

'Shailesh, I want us to think this through and come out with our clear views on the strengths and challenges in this deal. The challenges as I see are, first the deal size. It's too big for AHFL to finance. Second, even though we do have an ongoing relationship with Chand Builders, I'm not sure if that idiot Ganesh will buy that argument. Getting him to agree is going to be difficult. Third, Chand Builders have availed loans from many other lenders and these relationships have been on for sometime now. This raises the question of leverage; to what extent is Chand Builders financially leveraged? We don't know the answer as of now, since we don't have their financials, but it's likely that they are heavily leveraged, at least on paper. Fourth, why did Millennium Bank, that has an existing working relationship with Chand Builders, decline this proposal? What you've heard is all right. But I'd still like to be sure that this was in fact was the real reason. And let's keep this bit of information only to us. I don't want us to volunteer this information to Cedric and Ganesh. As a cardinal rule, say only as much as necessary, no more, no less.' Shailesh nodded.

Karan continued, ' Fifth, the project that's being financed should not have any legal glitches. All property documents should be in order. Chand Builders must have the approved building plan for the project. Sixth, there'll be questions about Roopak himself. To the extent we know, he's been around in the industry for a long time and has a strong reputation. His past track record with other lenders is clean. That should help.' Karan was thinking hard. He tapped his fist on his forehead a couple of times, as he was wont to do whenever he was thinking hard. He looked up at Shailesh and queried, 'What else can you think of? Of course, each of these items will get ripped to shreds. I just want to be sure that we haven't missed anything.' When nothing came forth from Shailesh, Karan said, 'Ok dude. Our work starts now. It's important that I give Cedric and Ganesh a heads up on all the issues that we have discussed today, particularly the quantum of exposure. That'll come up for severe questioning by Ganesh, who I'm sure will oppose it tooth and nail. If you ask me personally,

Rs.400 to 600 million is a tough ask. We'll see. Let me fix up a meeting with Cedric to get him on our side. Then we'll take on Ganesh.'

Karan called Stacy to check Cedric's schedule. He wanted to meet. The earliest slot available was on Wednesday morning, two days hence. Karan blocked it with Stacy and wound up his day.

Chapter – 7

GO FOR THE JUGULAR

June 2003

COME WEDNESDAY MORNING, KARAN REACHED OFFICE EARLY enough to prepare for the meeting with Cedric. Over the last two days he had thought through all the questions in his mind and concluded that giving a builder loan to Roopak was absolutely crucial, not only for AHFL, but also for his own personal growth. Karan reflected that if the relationship with Chand Builders crystallized, AHFL could leap ahead as a strong contender in the home loans market and he'd personally get credit for that. It would strengthen his position as Cedric's successor for the CEO's position; and Karan had his heart set on it. He was determined to put his best foot forward in getting the builder loan cleared. With a strong resolve, he got up and walked towards Cedric's cabin.

Outside Cedric's cabin, he met Stacy and greeted her. He enquired if Cedric was in. Stacy told him that Cedric had been in since 8.00 am as on most days and was waiting for him. Karan knocked on the door twice, entered and was the first to speak.

''Morning, Cedric.'

'Good morning, buddy. Give me a moment to send this email to the Board members. It's time for us to take stock of AHFL's performance for the current year. I'm calling for a meeting of the Board of Directors to give them an update of our business performance. We must prepare well for this meeting.'

'Tell me if some preliminary work needs to be kicked off. We do have a good story to talk about this time.'

Cedric was busy sending the mail and hence didn't respond. Once he sent the mail, he turned around and sat facing Karan.

'Mmmmmm.......Good story? Yes, of course. No questions on that. Full marks to your team for doing a great job on the new business acquisitions. The way you guys cracked Chand Builders was fantastic. So how much business are they giving us?'

'We're doing fine with Chand Builders. In April, we did about 600 individual disbursements with them. In May it came down a bit. Spoke to Roopak and he did mention about a big sales drop across the country. He has promised to make it up in the coming months. I'm not too worried on that front. I'm viewing this relationship as an important one for us to be able to deliver not just on the targets for this year, but in future years as well. Actually, the decision that we took to disallow builder projects that don't have approved building plans, impacted our business negatively. Our normal sourcing went down. Yet, with the help of Chand Builders, we neutralized the impact of that downswing. Without them, we would've been in a soup.'

Cedric concurred, 'Kudos to you and your team for managing Chand Builders well. Great going, man. Keep it up.'

Karan thought the time was appropriate for him to introduce the subject of his visit.

'Cedric, I came to discuss something important that directly concerns what we've just spoken about.'

'Go on. I'm listening.'

'I needn't emphasize the criticality of our relationship with Chand Builders. With great difficulty, Shailesh managed an entry into that organization. Roopak is an established builder with a presence not just in Ayravati, but all over the country. He has several projects that are running concurrently. Given the potential for growth in this country, this firm is only going to grow further. And if we strike a good relationship with them and fortify it now, it'll stand us in good stead in times to come. I want us to do everything we can to strengthen this relationship.'

'Undoubtedly. Agree with you a hundred percent. What do you propose? Do you want me to meet him personally? If you think that'll help . . . or do you have something else in mind?'

'Cedric, for any professional relationship to be successful, it's important that both the parties see a mutual value in the relationship. In our relationship with them, ever since we met Roopak in January, month after month they've been giving us business. Notwithstanding the fact that there are many other lending organizations who are ready to offer loans to Roopak's customers, he's favoured us. In all these months he hasn't asked for anything in return. But a time will come when he'll ask the question – what's in it for me? At that moment, if he doesn't see a value in his association with us, he'll walk away. After all, he's a businessman. To make Roopak feel that we care for him as well, I believe we should reciprocate and demonstrate to him a value in his relationship with us.'

'Come to the point, Karan. What is it that you're proposing?'

'I think we should look at taking a builder finance exposure on his firm.' Karan waited for the reaction. There was none. So he proceeded, 'Given his credentials, it'll be a worthy transaction. We'd be able to prove to Roopak that we're serious about this relationship and in the process we'd also earn some good revenue. He had taken builder loans from other lenders and his track record of repayments to them is perfectly clean. I've already checked that. His firm is currently looking for another builder loan and I feel it's an opportunity for us to show that we care. From what I know of him, it's not difficult for him to raise funds. But he'd love it if we can lend him a hand. An exposure on Chand Builders is absolutely safe and I want your support for us to do this deal.'

Karan stopped and waited for a response from Cedric.

'Hmm.' After a long pause Cedric said, 'Karan, I buy your arguments. However, organizationally we are not ready to do builder loans. Even when we did do the budget discussions, we closed it saying that we aren't actively going to source builder loan deals . . .'

'Sorry to interrupt Cedric, but please look at it from my perspective. When you all raised the issue of building plans, I agreed to discontinue doing builder projects that do not have approved building plans. We all knew very well that such a step would impact my business negatively. But I still agreed. I'm now requesting help on this one.'

Karan's tone had suddenly become aggressive. His arguments were sound and it did make a case for at least reviewing the proposition once. Cedric came around.

'Karan, a good business manager is one who spots an opportunity and converts it to actual business. Hence, despite the challenge we're likely to face in pushing this deal through, I'm inclined to give this a good consideration instead of rejecting it outright.'

Karan had won the first round.

Cedric showed an interest in knowing the specifics, 'What'll be the size of exposure?'

'I'm not sure of the details. I'm meeting his financial controller on Friday. I've understood from my network within the market that it may be between Rs. 400 and 600 million at this stage.'

Cedric was taken aback at the size of the exposure. It was impossible for AHFL to take this big an exposure in the first-ever builder loan they did. He quipped, 'Man, that's too big an amount. I don't think that we should take such a large exposure in the first instance. If at all we agree to do the deal, let's start with a smaller amount and build it up gradually.'

Karan felt compelled to give Cedric further background and spoke with his heart in his mouth, 'Cedric, Chand Builders already has several ongoing relationships with other lenders in the market and they are all willing to take additional builder loan exposures on Chand Builders. The first time I discussed builder finance with Roopak it was early May. We're now nearing end of June. This issue has been with me for a good two months now and has received in-depth deliberation, before it has come to you. I feel Chand Builders will not accept anything less than what they request. We may have to consider giving them the amount they want.'

As Karan spoke, Cedric had been thinking about the stand he should take. He agreed with Karan's view that for AHFL a sound professional association with Chand Builders would be a great strength. If that worked well, as it seemed to have in the last few months, the retail loans business of AHFL would get a significant boost. After much thought he said, 'Let's discuss this with Ganesh and get his views as well. We'll then take it forward. I presume it's not a burning urgency from a time line perspective.'

'I'm meeting Roopak's financial controller Dave on Friday. In that meeting, I should be in a position to tell him that we'd like to look at their proposal. I'm not sure if they need the money immediately, but I do feel there'd be some pressure to move fast on the disbursement of the loan as well.'

'Ok, so when should the three of us meet?"

'How about this evening?'

After checking his appointments with Stacy, Cedric said, 'Looks fine with me. Let me now check with Ganesh.' He dialed Ganesh's extension. Ganesh picked up the phone on the first ring and said, 'Hi boss.'

'Dude, short notice. But important. I'd like to meet you and Karan this evening. There's a builder finance proposal that Karan wants to discuss. How're you placed this evening?'

Even though Ganesh had always been vehemently opposed to doing builder loans, he refrained from showing any reaction to Cedric on the phone and spoke calmly.

'I'm fine with evening. What time?'

'5 pm.'

'Done.'

'Thanks.' He placed the receiver and looked at Karan. '5 pm. Now, let me tell you clearly as to what I feel about this deal.'

'I've been waiting to hear that.'

'I'm not against doing builder loans. But the justification should be adequate in terms of the exposure and the terms of the deal. We need to be thorough in our evaluation of the builder, his profile, financials, project feasibility etc. Even though Chand Builders is a big name, the amount of funding sought is too big and I can't justify this whatsoever.'

'Cedric, so I hear that you are in principle okay with the deal, but not okay with the size of the exposure. I take that feedback. Please allow me to present to you a more detailed picture after I meet up with Dave on Friday.'

'Fine. We'll also hear Ganesh's views. His view is important to me as he's the expert amongst us in evaluating a proposal of this nature.'

Green with envy at this open praise showered on his opponent, Karan reacted spontaneously, 'Cedric, I have the greatest respect for Ganesh's abilities. It's important to get his views, but we need to look at the overall interests of the organization and at times I feel Ganesh and his team aren't open to new things. They are only concerned about their bad debts and don't look at the revenue boost that comes from a new business opportunity.'

'Let's talk in the evening.'

Karan left.

Cedric could see that the evening meeting would be stormy. Karan was already showing signs of aggression. Ganesh was not one to give in easily and in the past had shown little tolerance for Karan's unconventional ideas. Ganesh's arguments were usually irrefutable. If Ganesh didn't agree to something, the only way it could pass through him was if Cedric personally told him to give up. Cedric heaved a huge sigh and asked Stacy to send in a cup of coffee.

*   *   *

Soon after Ganesh confirmed the meeting with Cedric, he called Arun to update him.

'Arun, there's something interesting. Let's go to the cafeteria and discuss this.

'Ok.'

They walked to the cafeteria and helped themselves to some grilled sandwiches and coffee.

Ganesh started, 'This bloke Karan has started showing his

true colours. He's gone and discussed some builder loan deal with Cedric. I've been called in the evening to discuss it.'

'Builder loan!'

'Wonder what it could be? Have you heard of anything from the sales team?'

'Nope. I haven't heard anything at all.'

'I just want to be well prepared for this meeting. Something is not right. What's your guess? Who could it be?'

Arun was quick to respond, 'A good guess would be Chand Builders. Karan thinks Roopak is god. The kind of loans that have been pouring in for the last few months and the way they were pushed into the system by the sales guys made it clear that Roopak was dictating terms. As you're aware, I've always wondered why Roopak is so generous to us. Our sales guys couldn't have made inroads into his camp on their own. And Millennium Bank was their favourite for financing their customers. There was no apparent reason for them to divert retail business from Millennium Bank to us. Now it all seems like a part of Roopak's gameplan: first give us the lollypop, trap us in a moral obligation and then pitch for a builder loan.'

'Hmm. What do you think of Chand Builders?'

'To be honest, I don't trust this guy Roopak. He has a good hold over the market; multiple builder loan exposures with different lenders, seamless track record on loan repayments and all that. But there's something about the guy that makes me uncomfortable. I wonder why he pulled out of Millennium Bank? Roopak has Karan under his thumb. If we don't do this builder loan, Roopak will threaten to stop referring retail business to us. And that would spell doom for Karan.'

Ganesh nodded thoughtfully and said, 'You could be right. This meeting is primarily to decide whether we'd look at this funding or not in the first place. I've done builder loans before. There're a few things about builder loans that we should consider. First, it's a question of our own philosophy on builder loans. Second, we must look at the prospective client's profile and see if it is satisfactory. Lastly, it involves our aligning fully with what I call the two 'I's. These are your own *Instinct* and your client's *Intent*. Listen to your instinct and detect the client's intent. We must get these two right. It's our job to investigate these and satisfy ourselves. With the very act of calling for a meeting and showing a willingness to discuss, Cedric has overruled the first issue. The second issue is an easy one. We just need the papers from the client to evaluate the customer's eligibility for the loan.'

Arun asked, 'What time is your meeting with Cedric?'

'5 pm.'

Arun looked at his watch. It was 2 pm. 'I'll do some spadework and get you some dope for the meeting.' He said to Ganesh.

'That'd be helpful.'

They returned to their offices. Arun browsed through his list of contacts and selected a few numbers. The first call was to his contact in the Millennium Bank. He knew a person by the name Keshav there, who was in the underwriting shop.

'Hi Keshav. How're you?'

'Arun, good to hear your voice, man. How've you been?'

'Pretty good. Just wanted to chat you up on something.'

From the silence on the other side Arun sensed that Keshav was leaving his desk and stepping out to a more private place.

'Yup. Go on.'

'Keshav, how much business does Chand Builders give you every month?'

'Chand Builders? Don't know why, but loans from them have come down in the recent months.'

'Since when has that happened? Till some months back, if my memory is right, Chand Builders gave you guys 500 to 600 loan files every month. Isn't it?'

Keshav gave a chuckle, 'Hey, you seem to be doing some real hot research on Chand Builders. But don't you worry. For old times' sake, I'll give you all the info. We've seen a drop for the last...5 or 6 months. And yes. You're right about the numbers earlier.'

Arun raised his brows and asked his next question.

'So prior to 6 months, he gave you close to 600 files every month. And that was . . .'

'About 10% of our total business volume in a month.'

'How much are you getting now?'

'Just around 50 loans. Something has definitely happened. Even these 50 odd cases seem to be coming to us directly from the individual customers themselves. I don't think there's a single case that Chand Builders has referred to us in the recent months.'

'Ok buddy. That was helpful. If I need any further info, I'll get in touch. You take care.'

Arun thanked him for the information and ended the call. His next contact was Santosh in the sales unit of

Millennium Bank; he was a deputy to the Regional Sales head in Millennium Bank. Arun had worked with Santosh in his earlier job with a public sector bank and knew him well.

He connected with Santosh on the first attempt and came straight to the point.

'Hey Santosh, need some information, *yaar.*'

'Sure. Go on.'

'How has your relationship with Chand Builders been of late?'

'We seem to be drifting apart. They started showing signs of disinterest a few months ago and the business that we used to get from them has been falling since then.'

'What could be the reason?'

'That guy's an opportunist. We turned down his builder loan proposal and he in turn stopped doing business with us. All his relationships are dependent on how people pander to his whims and fancies. Anyway, why do you ask? Has he come to you for a loan?'

'Well, I'm not too sure, but I think he has spoken to someone in AHFL for a builder loan.'

'I'm not surprised. He's been pouring business into AHFL for some time. And knowing him, I can assure you that what seems like a *request* for a builder loan, must have come to you as a command. The guy is like that. Never takes no for an answer. Very tough to deal with.'

'Have you dealt with him personally?'

'Yup. Met him several times. He's whimsical, extremely bossy and quite nutty.'

'Why did Millennium Bank reject his builder funding proposal?'

'The official reason is that we're overexposed on Chand Builders. We've certain lending limits for each builder and that has been exhausted in this case. But in the past, on some rare occasions, we've enhanced limits for special cases. In this case, we didn't and we said no to it after sleeping over the proposal for a long time. That pissed him off.'

'What was the project he wanted the funding on?'

'Megacity. The biggest residential complex in Ayravati. Flat bookings haven't yet commenced. No lender has as yet approved the project for loans to home owners. Actually Roopak himself has not approached any other lender yet. Roopak wants to build this as his dream project and is therefore extremely secretive about it. He's also looking for funding for his two other projects –Ocean Pearl and Whitewoods – quite ordinary compared to Megacity, but doing well in sales.'

'What's your take on Roopak as an individual? I mean, would you trust the guy?'

'He's never failed to repay his loans to any lender till date. It's only the past track record you can go by. I think you wouldn't have a problem on repayments if you advance him money.'

'Do you know if he is scouting elsewhere for a builder loan?'

'Could be, though I don't have the details.'

Arun thanked him and closed the call.

Arun had one more call to make. That'd give him the inside story on Chand Builders with Millennium Bank. This call was to a man named Kumaresh who was Arun's counterpart in Millennium Bank. Getting information at that level was difficult, but it worked if the informality was managed well.

Arun called Kumaresh's direct number. A recorded voice message said, 'Hi. This is Kumaresh. I'm sorry I am unable to take your call now. I'm on leave until 30th June. In an urgent situation, please contact my colleague by dialing 21 after the tone. Have a great day.' Arun hung up. He was disappointed. Now he would not get the inside story of the rejection of the Megacity project for a builder loan.

Arun then prepared a one-page summary of the discussions he had with Keshav and Santosh and gave it to Ganesh.

'Thanks for the quick effort, Arun. This whole thing about his breaking off with Millennium Bank, diverting that business to us, pretending that he's doing us a favour and then asking for a builder loan sort of gives me a strange feeling that it's not just money he wants from us. He spent a few months waiting for Millennium Bank to give their decision and then he's spent almost six months giving us individual retail files to win us over. If he was desperate for funds, he wouldn't have waited so long – a good nine months! Looks like there's something else he is after. Also, a straight player would've directly approached us for a builder loan. Why the drama? He's going out of his way to make it difficult for AHFL to reject his builder loan proposal. The intent isn't straight and we need to keep a close eye on this. There're too many loose ends.'

Arun agreed.

That evening, Ganesh reached Cedric's office early for

the meeting, thinking that Cedric may want to speak to him before the meeting commenced. This also gave him an opportunity to gauge Cedric's thoughts on the issue. Cedric smiled when he saw Ganesh and offered him a seat.

Cedric came straight to the point, 'Good you came in a little earlier. As you're aware, we have a builder loan proposal to consider. I can give you the name now. This is from,' Cedric looked straight into Ganesh's eyes and said, 'Chand Builders.' Ganesh was pleased that he and Arun had hit it bang-on.

'Ganesh, I'm aware of your views on builder loans and also the discussions that we had during budgeting. But as in the past, I trust you'll support if there is a good business opportunity and if it makes sense for us to look at it. Let us not reject it only because we didn't plan for it. I want us to give Karan an opportunity.'

'Cedric, I think we understand each other well. Our portfolio has just reached a reasonable size and is still not capable of absorbing any shocks. With incremental risks, we could end up taking incremental bad debts that were not budgeted, affecting the overall P&L position. But you're the owner of the P&L and if you believe that you can live with this additional risk, my job then is to only help you evaluate the risk properly and manage the risk later if the need arises. What irritates me at times is that Karan wants anything and everything to be done his way. Our fights stem more from the attitude and approach to the issue rather than the issue itself. If you accept this deal, I'll have no choice but to agree. But I can assure you that I'd want to know every small detail for us to be able to evaluate and satisfy ourselves fully before we cut the cheque.'

Just when Ganesh finished speaking, Karan knocked on the door and stepped in. He exchanged an uncomfortable smile with Ganesh. Cedric said, 'Karan, please take Ganesh through the discussion we have had on this deal. Once he's on the same page with us, we can put our collective minds together to decide the next steps.'

Karan explained the entire background to Ganesh in the same way he had explained it to Cedric. Ganesh listened to everything patiently and took notes. He also noted Karan's desperation.

'Karan, which is the project they're asking funds for?'

'I'm not aware right now, but I can tell you by Friday, when I'm scheduled to meet their financial controller, Mr. Dave. We've not asked for much information yet as I wanted to have an internal consensus first. But my guess is that it could be one out of their three projects in Ayravati. There's this Megacity project in the centre of this city, which is a huge project at an estimated cost of Rs. 4 billion. The other two projects are Ocean Pearl and White Woods. These two are valued at around Rs.1 billion each. I have a feeling that he'd ask us to fund either Ocean Pearl or Whitewoods. He may want a funding in the range of Rs. 400 to 600 million. I can give you exact details, as I said, after I meet Mr. Dave on Friday.'

'So the purpose of this meeting is to decide whether we want to look at this deal or not?'

'Yes.'

'I am ready to evaluate the deal in-principle. Please note: I'm just about ready to evaluate. When you speak to that guy on Friday, please be clear with him that it's perfectly possible that the deal may swing either way based on our assessment. Don't give him an impression that we're dying to do this deal as that would spell doom.' Karan had already done that and so he ignored the remark. Ganesh continued, 'Second, we'd need some information from them and I expect them to provide it all. I'll ask Arun to send you a list of documents that we need from them. I expect complete transparency from their side in sharing with us all known details of the project, including legal or technical issues if any. They should have all government approvals in place by now. We should also know from them if they've applied to any other lenders for builder loan facility and what the outcome has been. On the financials, we'd need the full set of financials for the last three years and projected cash flows for the next five years. All their financial papers must be attested by their Chartered Accountant, with his membership number written on all the papers. These and all other papers we may need to evaluate the proposal must be provided by them. ' Ganesh paused for a moment, looked at Cedric and Karan alternately and continued, 'If you guys are wondering why I'm restating all these basics again, it's because it'll only help us if we make it clear in our first meeting that these are basic hygiene processes and cannot be eliminated.'

Cedric nodded in agreement.

Ganesh had a few more things to say. 'Karan, while I'm willing to look at this deal, let me just share with both of you a few thoughts, based on my market observation. Roopak is a whimsical guy and is known to ride roughshod over people he's dealing with. I don't trust this guy. Instead of approaching us directly and asking for builder finance, he has adopted a circuitous route of first giving us tons of retail business and then putting us in an obligatory position and making it difficult for us to decline the deal . . .'

Karan interrupted here, 'Ganesh, I'd suggest that you don't shoot off your mouth here. This relationship with Chand Builders didn't walk into AHFL. It was the unstinted effort from our sales unit over several months that won this. We've slogged our butts off. If Roopak ever comes to know that we have people in AHFL who speak about his firm in such a denigrating fashion, he'd stop dealing with us right now.'

Ganesh clenched his jaw, but decided to focus on the discussion. 'Fair enough. My apologies if I made a wrong statement. But the sequence of events that have led us to this point make me uncomfortable. A direct guy would play this straight. Let's understand this and tread with adequate caution.'

Karan looked exhausted. Besides feeling that Ganesh was overbearing in his manner he also felt that Ganesh had no respect for Roopak, whom Karan held in high regard. Ganesh didn't seem to appreciate that he was talking about a VVIP client who, Karan thought, naturally deserved certain favours; after staying quiet for some time, he responded, 'I heard what you said. But Ganesh, Roopak is not just anybody and he would not like to be treated as any other customer. He isn't coming to us for money. None of his projects will stall if we don't give him money. He can very well arrange for this money and much more from many other sources. We need to be flexible in our requirements.' Karan suddenly grew hysterical now, 'Do you think we've sourced a fraud deal? Do you people even understand the difficulty that we sales guys face in the market?' He looked at Cedric and said, 'Cedric, we need to have some trust in important clients. I understand our asking for financials. But why cash flow projections? And that too for the next five years! This is utterly ridiculous. We might as well drop the deal now. I'll ring up Roopak and tell him that we don't have it in us to take a builder finance exposure and he should make his own arrangements. We can also forget about the 600 odd files that he's giving us every month. Let's keep cutting corners everywhere. We recently stopped accepting builder project files without approved building plans. Let's stop doing projects altogether, if that's what would give us peace of mind. There's no end to this. I can bet these conditions wouldn't be acceptable to Chand Builders. I cannot go into that meeting with so many conditions. We'll have to tone them down if we want a fair chance with this deal.'

Ganesh listened patiently to what he thought was pure sentimental crap. He'd seen many such flare-ups before and knew that this was Karan's most effective technique whenever he felt he needed to get something past RMQ. Ganesh responded in a controlled manner, 'Karan buddy; keep your shirt on. If you think your shouting or your emotional outburst, or better still, the blackmailing techniques, will sway me away from my purpose – which is to do my job in the best interests of the organization I work for, go take a walk. Whatever I stated as requirements will remain. If we start compromising right now, we'll keep doing that as we go on with the deal. We're evaluating a large loan proposal. Do you think they won't give the papers? On the contrary, I believe Dave will cooperate fully. He's borrowed several times in the industry and he'll be aware of the rules and regulations that most banks follow. If he's a straight guy as you say he is, he'll cooperate. If you feel awkward laying it out for him, leave that to me. I'll handle it and even say no to the deal, if required. Bottomline: the processes we need to follow will stand. I'm not going to change anything.'

Karan was seething, but reined in his temper. He just said, 'Cedric, I can't work in this uncooperative environment. I think Ganesh has now forced me to call Roopak and say sorry. You can forget about getting any further individual loan referrals from his projects.'

'Listen guys,' Cedric was unruffled, 'I get a feeling that you guys hijack the key agenda of these meetings to settle your personal scores.' He looked at Ganesh, ' I'm not talking about this deal in particular, but in general, when you specify your requirements to evaluate a case, ensure that your list contains only the necessary documents that you must have to get a good sense of the case. I don't want to rub a client the wrong way by demanding an endless list of nice-to-haves. Ensure that there's no fraud but ask only for what you definitely need.' Karan was pleased to see Ganesh in the hot seat. But soon enough Cedric looked at him and said. 'Karan, you need take care of a few things as well. Your job is to get business into the organization and manage your relationships. All the checks that we do are aimed at establishing a sense of comfort before we disburse the loan. Do not expect a cakewalk of a process where everything gets taken care of by itself. This is an extraordinary transaction and will therefore need to pass through extraordinary checks. In general, be more accommodating and appreciative of the processes and checks that we do. I see you trivializing things far too easily. We dare not take things for granted.'

The two men listening to him were slightly taken aback at Cedric's sudden aggression, even as Cedric continued talking.

'I want both of you to do all you can to get the best out of this opportunity in a manner that best suits AHFL. There are no clear answers. I'm not saying that this deal *must* be done. If we find things dodgy, say no to it. But do not say no because you in your mind think that things are not well. Go by facts, analyse things thoroughly and then come to a conclusion. For every decision, be it a yes or a no, I'll demand facts and analysis. I want very precise and clear justifications. No bullshitting. Don't tell me that you heard such and such things from the market, so and so said this or so and so said that.' He looked at Ganesh and said, 'I'm telling you now, that you'll need to back up your decision, with adequate justification.' Turning to Karan he said, 'And you, you need to bring every single tiny bit of paper that Ganesh wants for him to evaluate. No excuses. You can tell Roopak to go to hell if he refuses to give you any of the papers that Ganesh needs. I hope I am abundantly clear. In your first meeting, you must pass on this list to them and insist that you need all of this. We'll discuss the next step after your first meeting with Chand Builders. I'm closing this meeting now.' Cedric's aggression it seemed had silenced both men, for good.

On that note, the two men left Cedric's cabin.

Chapter – 8

RED HERRING

June 2003

As the meeting in the office of AHFL concluded, another meeting was underway in the office of Chand Builders. This meeting had only two men: Roopak and his most trusted colleague, Dave. They were reviewing the progress of Megacity, a high-end luxury residential apartment project. It was Roopak's dream project. His vision was to brand it as the best ever project in the history of real estate in the country. He'd taken personal interest in its design, elevation, specifications, facilities, approach, internal landscaping and every other little detail. He wanted to give the residents of Megacity the experience of a lifetime, a feeling of living in an exotic world. And to this end, he had conceptualized it brilliantly. As per the plan the project would have three blocks, with three towers in each block and three apartments on each floor. Roopak had also planned a 20 acre, eighteen-hole golf course, with free lifetime membership for the residents. As such, the project would be a dream-come-true for anyone who bought an apartment in it. It was located in the heart of Ayravati, covering a land area of about fifty acres. Even though the construction was progressing at a brisk pace, Roopak hadn't yet launched the project in the market. He had been extremely cautious about sharing information on Megacity with the general public. No advertisements, no invitations for site visits and no mention of the project in any industry forums. At the project site, a modest signboard read 'Megacity – A Trip to Dreamland'. This was all the publicity that the project had got so far. The team that worked in the project site had strict instructions not to talk about their work with anyone. The whole thing was kept under wraps and only Roopak and a few others knew the real reason for the extreme secrecy about Megacity.

Roopak and Dave had reports from the site engineer showing positive progress on every single aspect of the project. While Dave shared Roopak's excitement on the progress of the project, he was anxious.

'What's up, Dave? You look worried about something.'

'Yes. It's the cash flow. Megacity is draining a lot of cash and I'm struggling to manage the cash flow requirements for our other projects.'

'What's the position now?'

'Spends are far higher than the receipts month on month. Against cash receipts of Rs.1491 million last month, we spent Rs. 1947 million.'

'Hmmmm…'

'Roopak, it's high time we commenced the bookings for Megacity. We have now reached the 12th slab in all the wings. I need cash to keep other projects going. A lot of money is blocked in Megacity and that must be released by collections from bookings.'

'How many more months can you hang on? How are the new bookings in other projects?'

'New bookings are lukewarm. In all the seven mega projects put together that we're concurrently running, we have about 5000 flats yet to be sold. The offtake is slow. Lending rates are at an all-time high and therefore people are staying away from taking home loans. Property rates have surpassed all highs and we now seem to be hitting a threshold where it will tip. While we've held on to our rates so far, there're other big builders in the market who've reduced their rates. This has triggered a perception that property prices are dropping and that the market is going to soften. But the current problem for us is our cash position; we'll struggle to pay salaries in the coming months. I strongly feel we should open up bookings for Megacity immediately.'

Roopak was nonchalant, 'I hear you Dave, but don't worry. We've handled tougher situations before. We'll do it again.' His phone rang and he took the call. When he finished the phone call, the thread of the discussion was lost. Roopak now asked, 'What's the news on AHFL? How's that guy coming around?'

'I've kept Karan on tenterhooks. I've drilled it into his head that we're doing him a favour by asking them for a builder loan.'

'Way to go, Dave. We gave them a bit of shock in May when we reduced our referrals. We've kept it lukewarm in June as well, till now. Karan now has a taste of what we can do to his business. I guess it's time to increase the referrals, get Karan excited and help him pitch our deal better and stronger with his CEO. I'll ask Vachchani to increase the flow of files to AHFL now.'

'Sounds good.'

Roopak then asked, 'When are you scheduled to meet Karan?'

'Friday – two days from now. I have the papers ready for a discussion with him.'

'So how do you plan to present our case to Karan?'

'We need to decide on the project that we can offer as security for this builder loan. In my view, since this is the first time we are taking a loan from them, we should go in with a project that's easier for them to review and approve. I think we should offer either the Bangalore row house project, Kannada Mangala, or Ocean Pearl here.'

Roopak sniggered and said, 'Dave.'

He just kept looking at Dave for a few seconds and then continued, 'I have approached AHFL with a very specific purpose. I'll achieve that purpose eventually. The project that we offer to them as security for this builder loan has to be chosen carefully. Do you want to know what my real purpose in approaching AHFL is?'

Dave was a bit taken aback and exclaimed, 'Of course! Tell me.'

'I don't want their money.'

'Then?'

'Megacity.'

'What?'

'Yes. I want AHFL to approve Megacity.'

'I don't get you.'

'Aren't you aware of my plan for Megacity and the issue that is at the nucleus of the plan?'

'Of course I'm aware of the issue that concerns the number of floors in the project. Initially we applied for an approval to construct 12 floors in the project, which the MCA willingly approved. Later as per your desire, we submitted to MCA a revision to the original approval. In the revised submission to MCA, you've sought a special approval to construct 20 floors in Megacity and not just 12 floors as per the original approval. Now as per its bye-laws, MCA cannot accord an approval to construct anything beyond 12 floors. However you're hell-bent on constructing 20 floors in the project and in fact, you've laid the foundation of the building strong enough to take 20 floors easily. Due to this conflict with MCA, you've used your good offices in MCA and told them to put on hold our re-submitted application. They've neither approved nor rejected the revised application. You want to use this state of abeyance with MCA to your advantage. The core issue is that if we don't have the MCA approval to construct twenty floors, no lending organization would approve the project as the actual construction at site would be in direct violation of the formal approval given by MCA. And if no lender approves the project, no loans will be available to customers wanting to buy high-value apartments in Megacity. This is the issue.'

Roopak growled, 'Yes. Unfortunately yes. No lending organization would approve the project. But you just wait and see. I'll get AHFL to approve this project; and they'll do so because I won't let them get a whiff of the technical problem in the project. I'll construct twenty floors and I'll get AHFL to approve the project, despite the violation. It's a challenge. Just because the stupid MCA regulations state something, I can't stop at twelve floors, particularly when we have the privilege of owning the most prominent piece of land in Ayravati. Constructing Megacity with only twelve floors would be such a waste of that beautiful land parcel in the heart of the city. Let me see who the hell has the guts to stop me from building twenty floors there.' He then mulled over something. 'Nearly two years ago I had approached Hegde, the then municipal commissioner, for a special favour on this project. He turned out to be a stuffed shirt. It took me a long time to get him to listen to me, which happened only when I agreed to stuff him with money. He was greedy; he took money from me and before giving me the approval, retired from service. I could've got him killed, but decided against it since I didn't want to attract attention. He's staying somewhere near Bangalore now and enjoying his retirement with my money. I let him keep the money with a condition that he wouldn't open his mouth or discuss the project with anyone. So Dave, a lot has gone into this project and I have to make it happen. We need to guard this carefully. For some time, we need to maintain the perception that everything about Megacity is all right. Once the project is complete, the general public will only be surprised and awestruck. A year or so later the project will become part of the history of the city. We'll have the most influential people occupying the top floors of the project and nobody will have the balls to touch a building that's fully occupied and is so highly respected. Therefore, at this point of time, I don't want to open Megacity for bookings. The moment you open it for bookings, the first question people will ask is whether the project is approved by any lending organization. If AHFL gives us a builder loan on this project, it will automatically get approved and the home owner can then avail of loans from AHFL. We'll have a credible lender backing this project. Till then, we keep things quiet.'

Dave was astonished at this plan. He said, 'But Roopak, how do you plan to get AHFL approve Megacity, without scrutinizing the papers? They'd cotton on to the issue immediately and the cat will be out of the bag. There's no way this would escape their notice.'

Roopak replied, 'Now I shall tell you what I have in mind. When you meet up with Karan on Friday, you make a fantastic pitch to him about Chand Builders. The first 30 minutes of your meeting should be good solid sales talk. Ensure that you have a good PowerPoint presentation and make Karan feel important. You talk of our current projects, with particular emphasis on Megacity. You say that this is my dream project and it would be something never before seen in the country. You also say that the project land is not mortgaged anywhere and no financier has seen its papers yet. Emphasize that even with more than 60% of work completed the booking is still not open and that we intend to sell it at a hefty premium in the market later. Your pitch should be so sound that he should feel tempted to offer a builder loan against Megacity. Then you talk of Ocean Pearl and Whitewoods. But play them down. Keep comparing these projects with Megacity and keep mentioning that these are no comparison. Your pitch should make him yearn to finance Megacity. In the end you say that you want AHFL to finance Whitewoods. Your pitch has made him desperate to finance Megacity but you disappoint him. Do you get it?'

'Yes.'

'Having disenchanted him by asking for a builder loan for Whitewoods, you then discuss the funding amount. Our objective is to eventually replace Whitewoods with Megacity and we should smartly use the amount of loan requested as a tool to help us do that very important shuffle. Here's how we do that......'

Dave listened to the plan with rapt attention as Roopak detailed out the entire plan that he had so carefully schemed.

When the entire plan was clear, Dave's jaw hit the floor. It was an ingenious masterstroke of a plan. Dave was bowled over by the sheer artistry of Roopak's scheme. It was ultimately a mind game. Dave decided he would play it to the hilt with Karan and make sure that he won it for Roopak.

Chapter – **9**

THE QUANTUM TWIST

June 2003

FRIDAY MORNING WAS RAINY AND SLUSHY WITH DARK CLOUDS swarming in the sky. Most office-goers were huddled inside their homes, loath to step out. But Karan was raring to go. Now he even had a concurrence, in principle, from Cedric and Ganesh to evaluate the builder loan to Chand Builders and this added to his excitement. Now he only needed to get Dave to provide all the documents that Ganesh had asked for.

Karan reached office at 9.10 am. His meeting with Dave was scheduled for 9.30. Karan decided to take a stroll to the cafeteria and have a quick cup of freshly brewed coffee and return before 9.30.

When he walked into the visitors' area on his way to the cafeteria, he saw a fair and stout man with a bald pate sitting there in a formal business suit. His briefcase was on the carpeted floor. The man wore rimless eye-glasses and was reading *The Economic Times*. He checked the time and went back to the paper. Karan wasn't sure if that was Dave. AHFL did have many visitors on a daily basis, but none that early. Out of courtesy, he stopped and approached the man. 'Excuse me, sir? Are you waiting for someone?'

The man looked at his watch again, got up, straightened his coat and said, 'Oh yes. I have an appointment with Mr. Karan Agnihotri at 9.30. I reached a little early and hence chose to wait here for sometime. My name is Dave.'

Karan's eyes widened, 'Mr. Dave. Welcome. I'm Karan. Very pleased to meet you. Please join me in my office?'

'Thank you, Mr. Karan. I really don't mind waiting here for another fifteen minutes, if you have other work. The meeting was scheduled at 9.30. I didn't mean to disturb you.'

Karan persisted, 'No, no. Not at all. There's nothing else that's more important. Come this way please.'

Karan walked ahead and opened the door of his cabin, making way for Dave to get in first.

'Please be seated, Mr. Dave. Thanks so much for coming. The rains have been bad, isn't it?' Karan took a seat facing Dave.

'Oh yes. I started a little early just to be here in time as I didn't want to mess up our meeting due to the rains.'

'So nice of you to have agreed to this meeting, Mr. Dave.'

'Mr. Karan, the pleasure is absolutely mine. This business,

which I wish to discuss with you now, is part of an important agenda at Chand Builders for the current year. We want to strengthen our relationship with AHFL. Roopak has sent his personal regards to you and also specifically mentioned that in Chand Builders we have plenty of business which we wish to refer to AHFL in the months to come.' Dave kept nodding as he spoke.

Karan was pleasantly surprised by the change in Dave's conduct. In contrast to the overbearing Dave he'd been talking to all along, he was now extremely pleasant, warm and friendly. Karan couldn't quite understand what had brought about this change.

Dave then expressed his intent to move on to the subject. 'Mr. Karan, shall we get on with meeting?'

'Yes. Of course.' Karan chose his words carefully. 'You see Mr. Dave, we at AHFL welcome this opportunity to give a builder loan to Chand Builders. This, we believe, is a sound step that will be mutually beneficial. I've discussed this internally with my CEO and my colleague in our RMQ unit and they share this feeling as well. I'd now request you to let me know your specific requirement and also share some details of the project. I shall then take you through the procedure that we'd need to follow.'

'Mr. Karan, for the benefit of our meeting, I've prepared a presentation. If you don't mind, I'd like to take you through the same. Let me also assure you that we shall try to make sure that all your procedural requirements are fulfilled from our side. Please feel free to ask for whatever you want. If we have the document we shall give it to you immediately. If we don't have it ready, I'll ask for some time from you, prepare the same and give it to you. I believe in total transparency when it comes to large deals like this one.'

Karan couldn't believe he had heard Dave correctly. All his anxiety about the long list of documents required from Dave had whittled down to nothing. He also felt good that Dave had taken the trouble of making a presentation for the meeting which indicated that he was serious about it.

'Thanks very much, Mr. Dave. I'd be glad to go through the presentation.'

As per his plan, Dave's task today was to convince Karan that Roopak was relying only on him. It was a jazzy presentation with about 25 slides. Dave gave Karan a complete background of how Roopak had entered the industry almost 25 years ago and how he had expanded his operations to other cities. Dave emphasized that Roopak had acquired a lot of land in Ayravati and in many other cities 15 to 20 years ago at throwaway prices and now he was the largest single owner of non-agricultural land tracts in the country. The market value of his landholdings had now multiplied and it meant that when Roopak constructed a project now, he didn't incur any cost towards buying land. In contrast, most other builders spent 70% of their total project cost for acquiring land at current market prices. This gave Roopak a distinct advantage over every other builder. Roopak's land bank was large enough for his firm to remain the market leader for many years to come. Dave's pitch today therefore talked only of how cash rich Chand Builders was as a firm and how safe an investment it was for lenders. This message came through succinctly in his presentation. As the presentation ended, Karan felt no need to ask any further questions. He was dumbstruck. The case of Chand Builders, as presented by Dave, was unbelievably strong.

Dave then talked about the many projects that Chand Builders had completed all over the country and how quickly they had sold out. Then Dave explained to Karan the current focus of Chand Builders in the Megacity project, a project which stood on land that was purchased by Roopak almost twenty years ago at an all-time low price. It was a virtual goldmine for Roopak, once the sale of flats commenced. Dave mentioned that the apartment would have 3 blocks, with 3 towers in each block. He also added that the project would have about 60% open space. This would become a landmark in the city, because of the exotic elevation, the state-of-the-art facilities, the eighteen-hole golf course, the best security system, world-class amenities such as a fully maintained terrace-garden, a splash pool and the hi-tech car parking system and so on. Dave underscored the point that Roopak was waiting to launch Megacity in the market when the time was ripe, so that he would get the maximum premium from the buyers. He also told Karan that the project was yet to be referred to any lending organization. The day Roopak did that, the lending organizations would trip over one another to be the first in line.

Karan was speechless. He was reaching the conclusion that this builder loan to Chand Builder's was going to be a dream come true, a win-win situation for everyone concerned.

Dave ended his presentation with, 'Mr. Karan, I hope you

now appreciate the strength of Chand Builders. I'll be pleased to take any questions that you may have. We've tried to give you a fair assessment of our organization.'

Karan was taken in by the details of the Megacity project and was sure that it would be any financier's ultimate dream to finance a builder loan for that project and also provide individual housing loans to home owners there.

'Thank you for the wonderful presentation, Mr. Dave. I have no questions whatsoever. Your Megacity project looks mind blowing. It'll be a dream for anyone to buy a house in that project and surely a treat for any lender to finance the project.'

'Thank you, Mr. Karan. Yes, that project is our pride and we'll ensure that it becomes the pride of this city as well.'

'We'd love to provide a builder loan for Megacity. I'm sure when my colleagues see your presentation they'd be as captivated as I am now.'

Dave's moment had now come.

'No, Mr. Karan. We do not want any funding on Megacity. That's a huge project and we believe no lender in the market can fund us for that project.' Dave observed Karan's face carefully and continued, 'I've got a different proposal for you.'

Karan recovered from his disappointment quickly and said, 'Well, AHFL would be very keen to finance individual home owners in Megacity.'

'We'll discuss that at the appropriate time. Let me now present to you my current loan proposal. We want you to fund our Whitewoods project.' Dave continued mildly, 'The total project cost in Whitewoods is about Rs.

1 billion. Let me again add here that Roopak can do this project without any financial assistance whatsoever, but we still would like to use this opportunity to strengthen our relationship with AHFL. We only need a temporary cash arrangement and as you know now, once we open the bookings in Megacity, we'll be able to repay all our debts in full. At this stage it'll be useful if we got a small amount of Rs.500 million from AHFL.'

Despite Karan's excitement with the presentation, he grew anxious at the quantum of funding required. Dave had presented such a strong case for Chand Builders that it seemed as if any amount could be funded. However he realized that from AHFL's perspective or for that matter from any lender's perspective, Rs. 500 million was quite large. He reacted with some caution, 'Mr. Dave, with all the fine things you've told me about Chand Builders, I can only say that, you've made our task easier. I've no doubt whatsoever that we'll be able to consider your proposal positively. I now wish to take you through the requirements that we have, in order to do an initial assessment of the proposal. After the procedural perusal of the documents, I'll be able to revert to you formally with our decision.'

'I'm waiting to know your requirements. Please let me know of all the documents you need, so that I can get the work started on it.'

'I have the entire list here. Let me take you through each of these items just to confirm that you and I understand it correctly.'

He then started reading through each item and Dave took

out a notepad to write it all down. Karan said, 'Mr. Dave, don't bother writing it down, I'll mail you the list.'

'Oh don't worry about that. This is my age-old habit. I don't trust anything other than the tried and tested. Writing this down helps me remember them as well.' Karan didn't insist any further. He then read out verbatim from a printout of the mail that he had received from Arun.

'We would need (a) a detailed write up on Chand Builders and its associate entities, (b) a detailed write up on Mr. Roopak himself, his background, qualifications and experience in the industry, (c) the past three years' financials of Chand Builders, fully audited along with income tax returns or the assessment order, (d) current cash flow statement and future cash flow projections for the next five years, (e) details of bank accounts held by Chand Builders and Mr. Roopak personally, copies of bank statements of key accounts for the last 12 months, (f) details of other loans availed including amount borrowed from other lenders and repayment history certified by them, (g) copies of land papers of the project, (h) lawyers title clearance certificate and a title search certificate of the piece of land where the project is located (i) valuation of the project by two reputed valuers, (j) copies of approved building plans of your project, (k) project cost table showing each item of cost in the project and the total cost of the project, (l) current sale position of the project, (m) details of pending litigations if any and (n) a formal application to AHFL for a builder loan on Chand Builders's letter head.'

Dave wrote down each item casually and didn't seem perturbed by any of the requirements mentioned by Karan.

Finally he said, 'Just one question, Mr. Karan. Is this the complete list? As I mentioned to you, time is of essence. If there are any more documents that you'd need, please be so kind as to let me know now. Anything that can help you process this application faster will be provided by us.'

Karan now realized how right Ganesh was when he said that there was no need to be shy about stating the requirements upfront. Karan only hoped that Arun had given him the complete list. He gave a cautious response, 'I assure you Mr. Dave that this will be all in terms of documents needed. AHFL will keep any additional document requirements to the barest minimum and we'll come back to you only if it's absolutely required.'

Dave seemed satisfied with that response. Finally, he wanted to gauge Karan's comfort on the amount of funding required. As per Roopak's calculations, AHFL would find this amount of Rs.500 million difficult to fund and would come back to Chand Builders with a counter-proposal of a reduced amount. The entire plan revolved around the expectation that AHFL would struggle to meet this carefully chosen loan requirement of Rs.500 million. Once Chand Builders heard from AHFL about the reduction in the loan amount, they could then go back to AHFL with a change of project, asking for replacing Whitewoods with Megacity and demanding the full funding of Rs.500 million. That was the next stage of the plan. But first AHFL's discomfort with Rs.500 million had to be established. Dave adjusted his rimless glasses and subjected Karan to a quizzical stare, 'Mr. Karan, what's your view on the funding amount? Do you think it'll be possible for AHFL to provide it?'

Karan heard the question and as Dave had expected, he was unsure of the answer. Therefore he chose to remain non-committal. 'Mr. Dave, while our attempt would be to ensure that you get your required amount, we may in the rarest of circumstances be bound by internal restrictions. Just to give you a background, in our budgets for the current year we had not included any builder loan sanctions. Hence we'll have to reallocate funds from our other business lines and finance this loan. There may be some hiccups, but I believe that we'll be able to manage that. For us, Chand Builders is a critical relationship.'

Karan thought that he had managed to leave the question open-ended, but Dave was bent upon closing this issue. 'Mr. Karan, I understand the issues in funding arrangements. However, I would request you to try your best and provide us the entire amount. If the funding is curtailed it doesn't help us at all. My financial planning will go for a complete toss. I know you'll try your best. That's all I wanted to say. Thank you so much for your time.'

Karan realized that Dave had smartly ended the conversation by putting the ball in his court. He got up to see Dave off, 'Thank you Mr. Dave for coming to our office and sharing all the information. On receipt of all the documentation from your end, we'll work on it quickly and get back to you.'

Karan accompanied him to the basement where Dave had parked his car. After Dave left, Karan got back to his desk. He now desperately needed that cup of coffee. After the caffeine shot, he called Stacy and fixed an appointment with Cedric for the afternoon. He also asked her to include Ganesh in this meeting since he knew that Cedric would insist on it anyway. Then Karan spent the rest of his morning sprucing up his points for the discussion.

At the meeting, Karan took Cedric and Ganesh over the details of his discussion with Dave. Karan couldn't restrain a piquant smile as he spoke, which peeved Ganesh immensely. Overconfident and smug, Karan was at his crowing best talking about the case and how he and his team had been instrumental in bringing this relationship to AHFL. He detailed the Megacity project and how it was going to be a cash cow for Chand Builders. Finally he mentioned the size of the exposure, with a flutter in his stomach since in his view this was the only issue that could be shot down by Cedric or Ganesh.

Ganesh was waiting to react. The moment Karan mentioned the amount of funding required Ganesh seized the opportunity and quipped with his characteristic indifference, 'There's no way we're going to approve half-a-billion to this guy. Forget it. The amount is far too large. The retail loan business that they've been giving us can't be used as a pretext for us to dole out Rs.500 million to them. We shouldn't look at anything beyond Rs. 250 million. Even that's a tall order.'

Karan was taken aback by this tirade and was about to respond sharply when Cedric butted in, 'Ganesh, let's wait for the papers to come in and then decide the loan amount that we should approve.'

Ganesh retorted, 'Correction, Cedric. Let's look at the papers and decide if we even have to do this loan in the first place. Amount comes much later.'

Karan was frothing at the mouth. He felt that Ganesh was out to get him and feared that it would result in a situation with Roopak which could never be straightened out.

Cedric reassured Ganesh, 'Buddy, I am with you. Do a meticulous assessment and then decide.' Looking at Karan he said, 'Let us first get the documents. I too am concerned about the half billion. So let's drop this, at least for now.'

The meeting ended on a sombre note leaving Karan feeling raw and unappreciated.

Chapter – 10

THE FILE PACK

June 2003

DAVE WORKED AT FULL STEAM TO COMPILE ALL THE DOCUMENTS that Karan had asked for. He had everything ready, except for the cash flow projections. He was an expert at preparing and dressing up financials. Whenever a new project was launched by Chand Builders, Dave registered a new firm for that particular project. In this manner, Dave had registered several firms under the Chand Builders' group and used them at will to wade through convoluted taxation issues. Dave used these different establishments to split the revenues earned by Chand Builders into miniscule sums. He recorded artificially bloated costs in each firm to bring down the overall tax liability for the group to a small amount, in comparison to the actual earnings of the group. Chand Builders was the flagship firm and always remained a promoter of all other firms in the group, thereby getting a share of profits or losses from each firm. The flagship firm showed a respectable bottomline figure. Dave had the option of just showing losses even in Chand Builders, but he prudently maintained some of the entities in the group as profit-making, paying a small amount of tax: just enough to keep the tax authorities at bay and remain a non-suspect. Dave had mastered the art of managing the tax sleuths for several years now and many of the tax inspectors were now his personal friends. Showing profits in the books of Chand Builders and a few other firms in the group also made his life easier when he approached different institutional lenders for a builder loan. The lenders always expected the builder to show profits. A builder, who showed losses in his financial papers, would never be considered favourably by any lender for any type of lending. Dave used a software programme that automatically consolidated all the financials of the different firms and showed the key financials of the entire group in a single sheet. Any financial analyst looking at the one-pager would get a crisp bird's eye view of the financial position of the Chand Builders group.

On that day, Dave got out the three years' financials, tax returns and assessment orders for all the different firms and companies in the Chand Builders group and neatly placed the one-pager on top. That showed a brilliantly managed picture of the financials. It was geared to please any lending organization and bamboozle any tax officer.

He now had to get the cash flow projections prepared. He called his assistant and gave him some instructions on how that had to be done. 'Don't worry about accuracy. We just need to ensure that we show Chand Builders as capable of handling all its costs, all its debts and still have a cash surplus month on month for the next five years. The sources of cash generation would be new project bookings and payments received from flat buyers in our existing projects that are under construction. If you get any deficit anywhere, liberally introduce a new project and ensure that you show a surplus. I want this ready in the next sixty minutes.'

The next item was related to the legal papers of Whitewoods. Dave called his colleague and the Head of Projects of Chand Builders group, one Gopal Krishna.

''Morning, Gopal. Need some help. We're applying to AHFL for a builder loan against Whitewoods. Could you please send me a set of legal papers, statutory approvals and building plans of the project?'

'Sure. You'll have the file in the next ten minutes.'

'Thanks.'

Gopal was an eager beaver. All records pertaining to legal documents of all the pieces of land across the country held either by the Chand Builders group or in Roopak's personal name, were in Gopal's custody. Gopal controlled a battery of lawyers and architects, who worked full time for Chand Builders. The lawyers ensured that all the records related to title of the land in which projects were built by Chand Builders, remained clear and marketable in favour of the firm. The architects ensured that the building plans that Roopak drew mentally for any building, were converted into reality in the form of final approvals from the relevant municipal authorities in each of the cities where Chand Builders constructed its projects. However, only in the case of the Megacity project, all the plan-related issues were handled by Gopal personally, without involving any of his assistants. He took the help of a freelance liaison expert named Lokhande to liaise with MCA on plan approval issues connected to Megacity.

Gopal called for a copy of Whitewoods file, went through it to check if all the necessary documents were present. Convinced that the file was complete, he asked his assistant to send a copy to Dave.

Dave received the file from Gopal and checked it once for his own satisfaction. He then transferred all the papers provided by Gopal to the box file that he was preparing for Karan. The cash flow projections came in. Dave sifted through it and found it satisfactory. Finally, he also placed a hard copy of the PowerPoint presentation he had made to Karan in the file.

And so, in just one day the entire bulk of the file was ready for scrutiny. Dave called Karan on his direct line.

'Hello Karan, the file is ready for submission. My colleague will hand it over to you personally. Please take a look at your earliest convenience. I'd be happy to come over for another meeting to clarify any queries you may have.'

Karan was astounded at the swiftness with which Dave had completed the paperwork. That indicated that everything was above board with Chand Builders. 'Mr. Dave, I find it incredible that you have readied all the papers so quickly.'

'All our papers are kept in order and that's why I can produce it all in a jiffy. Let me take this opportunity to state that our requirement for funds is urgent and we would appreciate if you could move your office machinery fast enough so that the funds are released to us when we need them the most. If we don't get the funds now, it wouldn't serve the purpose. So thank you for your time and I am sending the file over to you right now.'

Dave closed the call and called his assistant to give instructions, 'You need to go to the office of AHFL and hand over this file to Karan. Make sure that you wear a good business suit when you go there. Keep smiling and thank him for his time. Make him feel like God.' Then he mumbled to himself, 'Such dumbasses and we must treat them like god.' The assistant chuckled. Dave's assistant just stopped short of going down on his knees before Karan. This obsequious behaviour embarrassed Karan but also gave him a secret thrill. He was used to doing the bowing and scraping. This time, he was at the other end.

Having received the file, it was now his turn to chew his nails. He was particularly worried about the stubborn character who sat two floors below, namely Ganesh. Dave's file sat like a ball of fire in Karan's hands. The urgency voiced by Dave added to his stress.

Karan looked through the papers in the file. It was such a bulky file that Karan didn't know where to start. He closed the file and thought it best to pass it on to Ganesh fast.

He sent an e-mail.

'Cedric/Ganesh,

I'm pleased to tell you that we've received the papers from Mr. Dave for us to process their builder loan for the Whitewoods project. I'm sending the file to Ganesh for his scrutiny. Please note that they've applied for a funding of Rs.500 million. Mr. Dave has emphasized that they're looking for a speedy decision. It is now incumbent on us to decide and revert to him fast. Regards, Karan.'

Karan sent across the physical file to Ganesh's cabin. At that precise moment four miles away, at the office of Millennium Bank, Kumaresh, who'd reported back to work after his vacation, was leisurely sipping a cup of coffee on his first day at the office after his vacation.

Chapter – 11

PEELING THE ONION

June 2003

GANESH REPLIED TO KARAN'S MAIL:

'Karan,

I've received the Chand Builders file. I'll review and revert soon. As I've already mentioned, being the first exposure, we must limit the quantum of funding. We cannot take an exposure of Rs.500 million at this stage. Regards, Ganesh.' The message was copied to Cedric as well.

Ganesh then gazed at the thick box file full of documents in front of him. He knew that reviewing the file was at least an hour's work. He got to work and started going through each paper in the file. Thanks to his years of experience in reviewing large and bulky files, the size of the file didn't intimidate him. The best way to study such files, as he had learnt over the years, was to look at them paper to paper, cover to cover. There were no shortcuts.

The first document he chose to read was the lawyer's report on the title ownership of the project, which ran into tens of pages. The first page of a lawyer's report usually contained what's called the *revenue address* of the land where the project was being built. This was also the address of the property as per land records with the sub-registrar's office of the government which allots a unique number, also called the survey number, for each piece of land within its jurisdiction. The postal address of the property is something that the builder subsequently provides after the building is completed. While the apartment then comes to be identified by the postal address, it's the revenue address that gives a legal identity to the land in which the building was built and it is captured in the final sale agreement with the home owner. Ganesh studied the detailed revenue address of the property. As he studied the report, he gave a vigilant but a quick glance at each page of the report. In the last page, he read the final concluding remarks of the lawyer on the property and specifically looked to see if there were any conditions attached to title certification. There were none. He seemed satisfied. Ganesh had a knack for rearranging information, as necessary, in different imaginary shapes, rows, columns, tables and pictures so that it got burnt in his memory. From the lawyer's report, he stored two critical pieces of information in his memory – the revenue address of the property and the final certification of the lawyer that the land was clear and marketable.

The next item he looked at was the set of building plans in the file that were stacked one above the other. These were large, wide ammonia prints. The location plan described the exact location of the property, mapped the project land in relation to the pieces of land to the north, south, east and west of the project land. He finished reading it and carefully folded it back. He then looked for the site plan. This contained the full layout of the project, giving a bird's eye view of the entire project. It clearly demarcated the open pieces of land in the project, water bodies, club house building, roads in and around the project and the residential blocks of buildings. For the apartment buildings, he looked for the elevation plan, scrutinized them and folded them back. Next he looked for the cross section plan, which showed him how the inside of the entire building would look, when in a fully constructed state, it was dissected from the middle. Finally Ganesh studied the floor plan for each type of flat that was proposed to be constructed. Perusal of all plans was over and he had confirmed that each was stamped and signed by the municipal authorities. He also checked to note that the revenue address of the project land was the same across all the plans and the lawyer's title report.

Then he picked up the financials and saw that Dave had provided financials of several firms. He fished out the one-pager which gave an abstract of all the key financial numbers of all the firms under Chand Builders group. He spent time only on the one pager leaving the rest of the financial scrutiny for Arun. He looked at cash flow projections given for the next five years and chuckled as he knew that they were all cooked-up numbers to show large cash surpluses. He came to bank statements that were attached in the file. They were bulky. For each month, the statement had about twenty pages and Dave had enclosed the statements for six months from three different banks. Not perturbed by the bulk of it, he spent a few seconds on each page and took a good ten minutes to go through the entire lot of bank statements given. The rest of the papers he casually flipped through and in about three quarters of an hour, he'd studied all the papers and got a fair idea of the contents of the file. He heaved a big sigh, placed the file on his desk and called Arun.

Arun entered the room, saw the bulky box file and exclaimed, 'So damn fast?'

'Yes, they've been goddamn quick and we now have it with us. I've looked through it. While I have some thoughts, I just wanted to know your views. Take your time to go through the file and come back. Let us then discuss the transaction.'

Arun took the file to his desk and studied the file almost in the same manner as Ganesh had done, but doing a much more detailed perusal of each document. He finished in two hours and returned to Ganesh's cabin.

Arun asked, 'Boss, what gives? Must we do the loan at any cost or can we say no?'

'To answer your question straight, Cedric expects us to give this a fair chance and he'd be glad if we support this loan.

Personally, if the deal is worth doing, I don't mind supporting it either. But if there are issues, we should put our foot down. Have you gone through all the file papers?'

'Yes, I have summarized my points.'

Ganesh was thoughtful for a while and then he started elaborating on his reading of the file.

'Let me first give you my feel. The papers are very well prepared and reflect a fairly strong position of Chand Builders group of entities and the Whitewoods project. The financials are brilliantly constructed. This chap Dave looks to be a near genius. He's smartly broken up their earnings across different firms to dress-up the financials beautifully and lower their overall tax liability. There is not a single firm or company that attracts any special attention because the absolute figure of turnover or profits shown in each firm is very reasonable. Chand Builders, by virtue of its position as the promoter in each of the entities, gets a share of profits or losses. Chand Builders is the flagship entity of the group and therefore is shown as the major earner. The typical life of each of the firms extends from the initiation of a project till the time it's completed. The firm is then kept on maintenance mode. During this maintenance period, the firm doesn't earn much, but is likely to have costs towards back up service for the customers of the project and would continue to show losses. Everything is within the framework of the law. It's a brilliantly managed financial structure. I've only ever seen messy builder financials. For the first time in my life, I've seen such wonderfully maintained financials of a builder. It is actually a treat reading through them.'

He paused a few moments, again leafing through the papers in the box file and then continued.

'But then, even the consolidated financial picture of this group does not justify an exposure of Rs.500 million. All the debts and their repayment amounts put together are far higher than their current cash surplus. Here's where Dave's cash flow projection comes to your rescue, though we all know that he's cooked it up only for us.' Ganesh sniggered, 'Actually it's a worthless piece of shit. But this is a document that we wanted with a purpose: to know if they'd have sufficient cash to run their different entities, service our loan and every other loan they have taken from the market. Dave understood our intent perfectly and has fed us what we wanted to eat. When your auditor questions you tomorrow as to how you approved Rs. 500 million, you'll throw the cash flow projections on his face and justify your decision. That's the only purpose the cash flow serves; to keep auditors off your back. Thus you do have a good case to lend Rs.500 million to this entity, based on the cash flows, finely maintained financials, a profitable flagship firm, excellent repayment performance on loans availed till now from the market, good track record on projects completed and so on. So, in effect it's an open and shut case.'

Arun noted the sarcasm oozing from Ganesh's words. He enjoyed these discussions with Ganesh since they were thorough and intelligent. Ganesh continued, 'But there's more to it than meets the eye. Our portfolio isn't big enough to absorb the shock, if something went wrong with this deal. We're barely crossing the Rs.7 billion mark as of today. After a couple of difficult years, our business has just begun to stabilize. That is why I was so adamant that we should not do any builder loans. But now we are in it.' He paused and heaved a huge sigh.

Arun said in a subdued voice, 'Now that we've taken it on, we have to get back to them.'

'Yup. So what are the problem areas? At this stage, we don't have too many. From your report made initially for my first meeting with Cedric and Karan we do get a few pointers.' Ganesh dug out the report from the pile of papers on his desk. He looked at it and started reading out each point, 'Roopak diverted loan files from Millennium Bank and gave them to us. Apparently Millennium Bank refused to fund Megacity.'

Ganesh looked up at Arun and said, 'We'll come to the project shortly. The first thing that strikes me from this behavior is that Roopak actually doesn't value any relationship. As long as the relationship is useful to him, he plays along, but when it doesn't help him, he kicks it away. I'd say that he's been ruthless with Millennium Bank. They'd given him enough builder loans earlier and stopped only when they reached a threshold. That's absolutely fair. And I do believe that he's wise enough to appreciate the constraints of Millennium Bank when they expressed their inability to fund Megacity. But he chose to dump them. He shifted the business referrals to AHFL. That is strange. Very strange. *What* is the real reason for him to move away from Millennium Bank?'

Arun mumbled, 'Raw arrogance, I guess.'

Arun dragged the file closer to him, flipped through a few papers and came to the copy of the presentation made by Dave to Karan. He squinted as he read something and said, 'Ganesh, this is interesting. Chand Builders is projecting their Megacity project as their most prestigious project. The project, as per the information here, is almost 60% complete. But they haven't opened up sale of flats there yet. Every single builder, right from the first day of a new project launch, opens the flat bookings and tries to gobble up earnest money from home owners as early as he can. But Chand Builders have foolishly blocked their funds in this project for more than a year now. Further, they'd applied to Millennium Bank for builder finance for this very project; which the bank refused apparently for their internal reasons..,' he paused for breath and then continued, 'What's also bizarre is, Roopak has now asked *us* to fund a different project, Whitewoods and not Megacity.'

Both racked their brains hard. Arun kept looking at the different file papers to weed out issues, if any. Suddenly Ganesh's said, 'Arun, let's note down each and every point that comes to our mind for further investigation. Make a list of all the points that you just said and the ones that I raised. Don't treat even the silliest of questions as trivial. Answers to these questions will take us to what I'd earlier referred to as the customer's *intent*. We must get to the bottom of that. Check again if your contact in Millennium Bank has resumed office? Maybe we could get some information.'

'Right away, boss.'

Arun dialed Kumaresh's number again. The phone was picked up in the first ring.

'Kumaresh here.'

'Hey there, man. How're you? This is Arun.'

'Hey man. I'm pretty good. Great to hear your voice. How've you been?'

'Couldn't be better. How was your vacation?'

'Oh, it was a great stress-buster. You know that risk guys hardly have a good time in the office. We aren't spared even on vacations. But this time, I kept my office phone switched off and didn't take any calls. Had a fabulous time. So, were you trying to reach me while I was out?'

'Yes. Actually I need some info.'

'Anything that I know is yours. Let me hear what you want and then I'll tell you how I can help.'

Arun then gave him the entire background of the newfound relationship between Chand Builders and AHFL. He also updated him of the discussions that he'd had with Keshav and Santosh, the other two people in Millennium Bank he'd spoken to earlier. 'So you get the drift. I need you to share with me all information about Chand Builders that you feel would be useful to us.'

'Got you. Let me give you the full picture. Whatever you've heard from Santosh is true. Even in our own records, the official reason for declining the builder loan proposal to Chand Builders has nothing to do with the builder profile or the project profile. We were busting the limits of financial exposure on Chand Builders. That's the reason the proposal was declined. But what also happened was, when Chand Builders approached us for funding for Megacity, as per our process we triggered the different assessments that we do to evaluate any builder loan proposal. We usually do three types of assessments – financial, project and exposure. The financial assessment was quickly done and cleared. The exposure assessment and the project assessment were underway. I was doing the project assessment. Our lawyers perused the papers of Megacity and gave a clean chit. However, our property-valuer visited the Megacity project site and commented in his report that the construction at site was being done beyond the number of floors approved as per the building plan. I called him to check. He mentioned that the plan of the building was approved for constructing only 12 floors, but the construction at the site seemed to indicate that the building was being built beyond 12 floors. This led me to investigate it further. I called the site engineer of Megacity. He just said, "Any construction we do is compliant with the approved building plans." He didn't directly answer my question about whether they're going to construct more than 12 floors or stop at the 12th floor. Then I tried to reach their sales head: a guy called Vachchani. Despite my trying several times, he didn't come on line. Thereafter I tried somebody in the MCA to know the status of this project. No breakthrough there either. Meanwhile our Board came out with a stand that they wouldn't be funding Chand Builders because our funding limit was breached. Since the deal fell through, I stopped my investigation. So if it's Megacity that you're funding, investigate this. Their other projects in Ayravati are fine. We've also cleared Ocean Pearl and Whitewoods. So if you're funding them for Whitewoods as you are saying, you have no reason to worry.'

Nobody knew that Whitewoods was a red herring.

Arun was happy with the information; he thanked Kumaresh and closed the call. He felt that the information on

Megacity wasn't of any immediate significance and just made a note of it. He thought that was no reason to worry since Chand Builders, if they wanted to build higher number of floors in Megacity, would overcome any obstacles and get the revisions to the building plans approved by MCA.

He apprised Ganesh of the discussion.

Ganesh heard Arun and agreed with his assessment on Megacity. He sauntered around the room, pondering over the various points on the proposal, eager to hit the right approach to the deal. When he couldn't make any headway, he went back to his questions. Why should Roopak break the relationship with Millennium Bank for this one deal? Why didn't he ask AHFL to fund Megacity? Could it be that these two questions were related? Despite intense deliberation, they were unable to reach a satisfactory conclusion.

Having spent sufficient time, Ganesh said, 'We've deliberated enough for a start. Let us sleep over it for now. I have a feeling that we will end up approving this case for a lower exposure. I wouldn't go beyond Rs. 250 million. You build a proposal note in the meantime, after methodically scrutinizing the file again. Then put up the proposal note to me for clearing Rs. 250 million. But take your time to mull over it. I don't want to see the proposal note at least for the next 10 days. Just because we reached a decision quickly, doesn't mean we have to tell the world. Use this time to find out more about Chand Builders and do not share any reactions with Karan.'

Arun picked up the file and left.

Chapter – 12

THE COVER UP BRIEFING

July 2003

IT HAD BEEN A WEEK SINCE DAVE HAD SUBMITTED THE builder loan file to Karan. He had received no response. Dave called Karan to check the status.

'A very good morning to you, Mr. Karan. Is it a good time to talk?'

Karan knew that Dave had called only to check about the builder loan.

'Oh yes Mr. Dave. You're welcome to call me anytime. Your proposal is under review. However, at this stage I'm not in a position to give you any concrete response. But I hope to be able to do so in the next couple of days.'

'Thank you for the update, Mr. Karan. It's been a while since we last met and I thought I'd check with you.'

After the call, Dave went across to Roopak's cabin to apprise him. Roopak was busy playing the "Angry Birds' game on his computer and was apparently not in a mood to be disturbed. But Dave had to intrude.

'Roopak, I just did a follow up with AHFL on the proposal. They don't have anything to tell us now. What should be our next step?'

Roopak was still absorbed in the game. 'We'll take our next step, when it becomes really urgent for us to get the approval of Megacity. Till then, you just relax.'

'But Roopak, it'd look silly if we don't even follow up. We must express urgency for funds and then build that urgency into approval of Megacity.'

Roopak now closed the game and looked at Dave. He got serious now.

'Well, I agree with you that we should show some urgency, but just enough to put them under stress and make them feel uncomfortable. You're not looking for an answer from them. Let them take their time to revert. It will only help us. After much delay, let them tell us that they can only give us a smaller amount. They don't have it in them to approve such a big loan. That's the time when you pounce on them and eat them up.'

'Karan tells me that they're having internal discussions. My guess is they're having differences within the organization about giving us a loan of this size. Karan is probably finding it hard to push it through his RMQ head. I've heard that their RMQ head is a hard nut to crack.'

'Dave, that's good news for us. But, keep a watch on the type of market checks they're doing on us. I don't want them to know anything about Megacity before it's time. That's all I'm worried about. Is there anyone in the market, who could be aware of our actual plans on Megacity?'

'We have tried our best to be discreet.'

'Let's also get Gopal into this. He should now be fully involved in the AHFL deliberations.'

He sent for Gopal. When Gopal came in, he said, 'Gopal, you're aware of the builder funding proposal that we've submitted to AHFL.'

'Yes sir.'

Roopak asked Dave to explain to Gopal his real plan of getting AHFL to approve and finance Megacity.

Dave explained Roopak's devious plan to Gopal and said, 'On Megacity, despite the issue of floor-violations there, you know how critical it is for us to get at least one reputed lender to approve the project. AHFL is the chosen one and we want to get this project approved by them. So, when the Megacity project file is given to AHFL for approval, replacing Whitewoods that we've currently submitted, we'll tell them that we have proposed some revisions to the building plan in Megacity and have submitted the revised proposal to MCA. That would also be the moment, when we would exhibit to AHFL an extreme urgency for disbursement of the loan. At the right time Roopak will tell Karan that he will submit to AHFL the approval of the revised plan by MCA *later*, but he needs the disbursement immediately. With his towering influence, he'll try and bulldoze AHFL through Karan to get the disbursement released for Megacity without the approved plan. If AHFL hesitates or delays in giving us the disbursement, we'll threaten complete withdrawal of the retail loan business that we give to AHFL, which currently stands at close to 750 files a month. It's expected that AHFL will come under this pressure, approve Megacity and disburse the loan immediately. It's important that we build up an emergency situation gradually, which in the end should resemble a nuclear explosion and the only way AHFL can defuse it is by releasing the disbursement. The very next day, it'll be splashed all over the papers that the Megacity project is approved by AHFL.'

Gopal appeared concerned and said, 'Roopak, you can perhaps manage AHFL. How will you manage the MCA? I don't think we can get them to approve 20 floors in Megacity. The officer whom Lokhande and I have been meeting was very firm: this approval is in total violation of the MCA bye laws. How can you then give an approved plan to AHFL; even at a later date? How are we going to manage the MCA sleuths, bypass them and construct 20 floors in Megacity?'

Roopak heard Gopal patiently and responded, 'Gopal, not to worry. If MCA is unwilling to give an approval, so be it. But I don't want them to send us a formal communication of rejection either. Let the proposal lie with them in cold storage so that we can always maintain with AHFL that the application is pending approval and we'll get it soon. Let the bureaucracy within MCA take the blame for the delay. Manage the officer in MCA who's handling our application and let the proposal gather dust in the MCA drawers. I hope the concerned officer is handling the proposal himself and hasn't passed it on to anyone else.'

Gopal replied, 'Yes. The proposal is entirely with him. We are in touch with him at least twice a week.'

'Good. Continue doing that. In the meantime, I'll seek an appointment with the Municipal Commissioner and pay him a courtesy visit. I'll get him to keep the proposal officially on hold, and prevail upon him not to stop our construction at site. I've handled several such people in the past. Leave that to me.' Then he paused for a few moments and again asked Gopal, 'How resourceful is this Lokhande guy that you have?'

'Lokhande knows the MCA like the back of his hand. Everything starting with what forms are filled in, where the files are kept and how the cupboards can be accessed, how the office boys can be used to pull out the files or do other errands, what stamps are used, who looks at the plans, who does the site inspections, where the power centres are and almost anything else that you may want from MCA. He's been doing this work for the past 15 years and moves around in MCA like an employee. In fact, he's done personal favours to many MCA employees, particularly the office boys, and therefore they're all loyal to him. But he also maintains a dignified distance in terms of using his access in there. As far as possible, he respects the procedures. All in all, immensely resourceful!'

'Sounds good. So you tell him to continue his efforts. Don't put too much pressure on the MCA officer as I don't want him to end up doing something foolhardy. As I've often repeated: please keep one thing in mind – I cannot let the Megacity project fail. I must construct 20 floors in this project, come what may.' There was heavy stress on the last three words. 'The land on which Megacity stands is prime land and I don't want to fritter it away by constructing something shitty. I want to make the best of it. This project must be built as per our plan.' He then looked at Gopal and asked, 'If it's necessary spot each and every such person, inside the MCA and outside, who may have even a whiff of the actual number of floors planned in Megacity. Work on every such individual and cover it up. Nobody should discuss Megacity in the market as an illegal project. Everyone should only believe that the building plans are pending with MCA for approval. That's our official stance. Other than the officer in MCA, who else do you think would know this? What about this guy at Millennium Bank who was trying to get information on Megacity from us. He also called the MCA, right? How did he get to know that there was an issue in Megacity?'

Gopal said, ' Millennium Bank, as per their process, had sent a property-valuer to the project site for inspection. It's possible that the valuer picked up on it during the visit to the project. The plan we'd submitted to the Millennium Bank had approval only till the 12th floor. An expert who is familiar with constructions can tell from the construction if there are any deviations from the approved plan, in the actual construction. That's what must have happened.'

Roopak was fuming now. 'That was a monumental

mistake. The first thing we must do is call our site office and inform them that nobody, I mean nobody, should be allowed entry into the project without an explicit permission from you,' he pointed at Gopal ominously, 'It's not a public park. I want us to do a few things. First, get the project site cleaned up. The construction material that's required at the site shouldn't lie out in the open. Have a temporary shed built and ensure that all building material is moved in there and put under lock and key. We will soon have a valuer from AHFL visiting us. For those few days when the valuer is likely to visit the project, restrict the construction activities at the site to the most essential. This valuer should be accompanied by our person. Identify someone who's good at handling questions. This escort should indulge the valuer in friendly, otherwise useless conversation, gift him mementos, spend time chit-chatting with him for hours in the office room, brainwash him that nothing in the project can go amiss and so on. He should do everything, except allow the valuer to do his job of proper inspection. The valuer should be subtly prevented from going near the buildings. Find such a person and train him to handle the valuer. Next time any such valuer visits the project, he should do everything at the site but the actual inspection, and he should go back fully satisfied. Also find out who are the official valuers of AHFL. After their inspection of Megacity, they should go back to AHFL and speak our language.'

Gopal said, 'We can find out from Vachchani as to who are the valuers working for AHFL. He should know this.'

Gopal called Vachchani and asked him to prepare the list of valuers of AHFL. Then he said, 'I think Vachchani is the best person to manage the valuers when they visit the project. He's good. I'll call him to my office and brief him appropriately. Leave that to me.'

The meeting was closed.

Chapter – 13

DOWNSIZING

July 2003

AT AHFL, ARUN WAS FINALISING THE PROPOSAL NOTE FOR Chand Builders for Rs. 250 million. In the last 10 days, he had done extensive research on the firm. It only reinforced that Chand Builders was a strong entity, worthy of a builder loan exposure. He printed a copy of the proposal note and kept it along with the entire file on Ganesh's table. The justification for reduction of the loan amount, as recorded in the note, read:

'The mortgage portfolio of AHFL has just started growing and it stands at about Rs.7 billion now. The portfolio is just about

two years old and AHFL has not yet seen the performance of this portfolio. Given this short portfolio experience and its small size, it's necessary to exercise abundant caution while taking single large exposures. The concentrated risk on such exposures is much higher on the portfolio, than the same risk distributed over multiple individual retail customers. In view of this, the builder loan proposal of Chand Builders is approved for their Whitewoods project for a lower exposure of Rs 250 million.'

Ganesh signed the note. This was just an in-principle approval. The project assessment, another critical part of evaluation, was still not complete. That always took more time as lawyers examined property papers in detail and valuers conducted property visits. This approval carried a condition that the final disbursement would be done subject to the lawyers' and valuers' reports on the project being satisfactory. Ganesh sent out a mail to Cedric and Karan confirming the approval and the justification for reduction of the loan amount.

Karan knew that a Rs.500 million exposure was high for AHFL. However, he doubted Dave would accept this reduction in the amount. Dave had repeatedly told him that he needed the full amount. This bothered Karan. While he wondered what to do, another mail came in from Cedric, who had responded to the message from Ganesh. To Karan's relief, Cedric stated that the three of them should discuss things first, before Karan communicated the decision to Chand Builders. For Karan, it was a reprieve of sorts. He knew that the meeting would be called soon and he needed to be ready with his arguments.

Stacy's message followed Cedric's stating that the meeting was scheduled at 9 am the next day.

Through the entire day, Karan tried to gather valid arguments to justify the Rs. 500 million loan. Finally he felt he should hinge his case on two points only. The first was that Chand Builders was a highly reputed builder and on a standalone basis qualified for this amount of exposure. Going by their past track record, they had never defaulted with other lenders. The second point was that Chand Builders would not accept any reduction in the loan amount. The whole deal would fizzle out and that would spell doom for the retail loan referrals of 700 plus cases that AHFL was currently getting from Chand Builders.

The next morning the three men met in Cedric's office. Karan initiated the discussion by stating his reasoning for doing the entire amount of Rs. 500 million. Cedric and Ganesh heard him out.

Ganesh responded with, 'Boss, I've made my position clear already. Notwithstanding Karan's points, I'm not keen to consider an exposure of Rs.500 million.'

Cedric said, 'Karan, I agree with Ganesh. We'll need to make a beginning with a small amount. This is the maximum we can do. Go ahead and confirm this to them.'

Karan tried to deliberate, but in the end Cedric prevailed. The meeting was closed leaving Karan with no choice but to convey the downsized loan amount to Dave.

Chapter – 14

FACING THE MUSIC

July 2003

IT WAS NOW OVER TWO WEEKS SINCE DAVE HAD SUBMITTED the builder loan file to Karan for evaluation. His sources had confirmed to him that AHFL had completed the checks on Whitewoods' legal papers and that the property visit by the valuer had also been done. It was time now to move to the next phase of this operation and take Karan head-on. He picked up the phone and called Karan. One thing Karan always did was to respond to phone calls immediately, however difficult the position he was in.

'Good Morning Mr. Dave.'

'Good Morning Mr. Karan. I just wanted to do my usual checking with you on the loan. It's quite sometime now and I'm sure you would've reached a conclusion on the deal. I wish to know your decision.'

Karan hesitated a little. Then he felt he would rather be done with it. So he said, 'Yes, Mr. Dave. We've done a detailed scrutiny of the proposal. After a due consideration of all the factors we have decided that we'd be able to look at a funding of Rs.250 million. However...'

Dave's moment had arrived. Without waiting to hear more, Dave started off and attacked Karan on phone like a charging bull. 'What? That is atrociously low. I wish to know why you have come to the conclusion that we, the one and only Chand Builders, aren't capable of servicing a small loan of Rs. 500 million. I am sorry, but I find it insulting to hear that our loan proposal has been shot down. You didn't even tell us in the beginning that you had a problem with the loan amount and now after taking around a month, you're telling us that you are reducing it drastically by 50%. How could you do this to us? I am thoroughly disappointed.'

When Karan managed to get a word in edgewise he stammered, 'Mr. Dave, we appreciate the strength of your organization. You are perfectly capable of servicing the loan of Rs.500 million. But....'

'Mr. Karan, I do not want reasons. I'm now going to Roopak and he'll surely blow a fuse when he hears this. You be prepared to give all your reasons to him and they better be good.'

The prospect of facing Roopak, a whimsical guy, made

Karan shudder. He was in the position of the quintessential sales guy. If there was good news, the sales guy conveys the same and walks away with all the credit and praise from the customers. But when there was bad news, he faced the customer's wrath as well. Karan held Ganesh responsible for putting him in this situation. Suddenly he realized that there was silence at the other end; Dave had already hung up.

Karan sat back and closed his eyes. He saw the entire relationship that he had created between AHFL and Chand Builders go up in smoke. He felt ill, at heart and in body. He banged his head on the table a couple of times and packed up his things. At home he took some sleeping pills and crashed out.

Next morning, Karan got up with a migraine. He anticipated Roopak's call that day. His brain began to whirr at a furious pace. Perhaps he should get Ganesh to join him in the call and let him explain why the loan amount was downsized. Karan remembered Ganesh had made the offer once.

As soon as he got into the car, his cell phone rang. It was Roopak. Karan picked it up instantly out of habit and said feebly, 'Good morning, Roopak.'

'Karan, there's nothing good about this morning. Why the fuck did you guys offer to do a builder loan with us in the first place when you don't have the balls to do this business? It was your idea and then you fucking chased Dave for a long time. We were very hesitant to give you the file, but I relented only because of your persistence and my own belief that I'd stand to gain by partnering with you. If you knew that you guys can't approve Rs. 500 million, what the hell were you thinking when you took that file?

Roopak was actually smiling and enjoying himself as he heard Karan struggling to answer him. He felt in complete control of the situation.

Karan began to speak, 'Roopak.......'

But Roopak interrupted him loudly, 'Tell me why! Why did you waste our time when it was beyond you? Do you really feel we can't service a loan of Rs. 500 million? Tell me. Answer me.'

'No Roopak, I don't think....'

'I know you don't think. That is why you have put us in this soup.'

'I didn't mean that. I do feel that you can service this and more.'

'Then why the fuck didn't you approve the entire loan amount?'

'I cannot approve it myself. The decision rests with several people within the organization and they collectively ....'

'I know that shit. I've taken several loans from other banks. I know how lenders like you operate. You have your risk departments who do a thorough appraisal and then decide. You need to bloody well realize that you have to play a key role in convincing your risk counterparts about us. In all fairness, they don't know us. It's you who knows us and you should have convinced them on our behalf. Where is your courage of conviction, man? You could've arranged a meeting between me and your risk guy. I would've gladly met him. You needed to bring them up the curve to understand our credibility and our strengths as you understand it. I view this as your complete failure to convince your risk counterpart. Did you suggest their meeting me?'

'No Roopak.'

'Why not? That would've changed things. Frankly, I thought you were capable of managing this on your own, but you've totally let us down.'

Karan was silent. It didn't occur to him that he should hit back at the conceited builder at the other end for using such derisive language against him. In his own mind he had raised Roopak to an elevated status. He forgot that there was life beyond this one single relationship with Chand Builders. For Karan, the dream of growing professionally, without Roopak's support seemed impossible to achieve and Roopak knew this. He was convinced that Karan was now dependent on him and he congratulated himself for orchestrating a fantastic plan to trap Karan.

Karan could only wear a hangdog expression and mumble, 'Sorry Roopak. I couldn't do much.'

Roopak was silent for some time. Then he said, 'OK. Since you can't do any better, I'll have to do something. I don't take no for an answer. If I leave you with a rejection, it'll have a deep impact on my market credibility. I want you to go back to your risk guys or whoever you feel is important and present the case again. Try this once more and let me know.'

Karan was desperate to get out of this ignominious conversation, 'Okay Roopak. I'll try again.'

Roopak's voice softened a bit, 'Karan. I'm sorry I used such strong language. I understand your position. It's just that I'm currently in a very tight position on money. It'll get better once I open the bookings of Megacity. But till then I need help. I can approach some other financier, but I'd be happy to do the deal with you. This just needs a bit of a push from your end. Please do that for me. If the deal doesn't go through despite your best efforts, I assure you that I'll still consider it an honour to have a good friend like you. The doors of my office are always open for you, but then it'd be only for you in your personal capacity as Karan, the handsome young dude, and not as Karan the business head of AHFL. Please, give it your best.' He then suddenly stopped talking, but didn't disconnect the phone. Karan heard him discussing something with Dave on the other end of the phone and he heard some murmurs. Roopak came back on the line. 'OK Karan, we do have some suggestions on how we can take this forward. But first, I want you to try convincing your team once more. If it doesn't work out even after your second attempt, do let me know and I'll tell you what to do.'

Roopak ended the call.

This softening of tone and particularly referring to Karan as his personal friend at the end had done the trick. Karan felt much better. Roopak had managed to curse him and yet leave him feeling better. Now that Roopak had asked him to try again, Karan decided to go hammer and tongs at Ganesh. Surprisingly, Roopak's tirade had motivated Karan significantly. He drove to work with the fires of vengeance simmering in his heart and reached the office in half the time he normally took, jogged up the stairs instead of waiting for the lift, slammed his cabin door shut as he got in, switched on his laptop and dashed off a mail to Ganesh.

'Ganesh,

This refers to the builder finance proposal of Chand Builders. I spoke to Dave and also to Roopak himself. While they thanked me for the sanctioned amount, they also reiterated that they needed the entire amount of Rs.500 million. We all know that they are a cash-rich organization and this amount is like chicken feed to Roopak. They can raise this amount from anywhere in no time. We have a greater need of their retail business and hence we must be more considerate and intelligent in our assessment of this proposal, instead of looking at the deal only from the perspective of our own little home loans portfolio which is naturally small because we've just started doing good volumes for the last one year. That still cannot be a deciding factor in approving or rejecting a loan application. I don't know what you can do. Apply logic or magic, but get the sanctioned amount revised to Rs.500 million.'

In the same mail, he wrote the following lines for Cedric,

'Cedric,

With due regard to your views on this proposal, please do note that they've threatened to withdraw the flow of individual retail loans business that they have been giving us. We're currently getting over 700 individual retail loan referrals a month from Chand Builders. That would stop, if we decline this proposal. You can do the math better than me. I rest my case.'

Though he would have preferred to make Ganesh stand in front of him, abuse him and kick him in the groin, this mail was the closest he would get to doing something like that. He believed that he had given an ultimatum to Ganesh by using the phrase 'logic or magic' and that combined with the threat of withdrawal of the business by Chand Builders should work in his favour.

Pat came Ganesh's reply to the mail.

'Karan,

I've already explained in my earlier mail the logic I'd applied to downsize the loan amount. As per your suggestion, let me now try magic.

ABRACADABRA...........ABRACADABRA

Did the loan amount increase?

No, it didn't work. Let me try again.

ABRACADABRA.....................

No. It hasn't worked.

Sorry. Magic isn't working. The approval remains at Rs. 250 million. You can tell Roopak to go fly a kite.

Ganesh.'

The message was copied to Cedric.

This reply was personally very insulting and it got Karan all fired up. He sprang up and walked upstairs to meet Cedric. He wanted to lodge a formal complaint against Ganesh for treating him with such callous disregard for his position and for being so sarcastic in his response.

He saw Stacy outside Cedric's office, wished her pleasantly and without asking her, went into Cedric's office. Such direct entry into Cedric's office was only acceptable in situations that could be categorized as emergencies As he was knocking on the cabin door, his blackberry beeped to indicate that a message has just arrived. Out of habit he stopped to check the mail. It was a mail from Cedric addressed to both him and Ganesh, asking them to exercise seriousness in office communications.

His knock got a clear and fresh response from Cedric, 'Karan, come in please.'

Karan felt encouraged and opened the door, 'Cedric. Sorry to barge into your office without prior appointment.'

Cedric motioned him to sit and immediately took charge, 'Karan, I know what you want to talk to me about. I've just sent a mail to both of you to exercise restraint in office email communications. We as senior management are supposed to be setting standards for office behaviour. I know you probably feel that at present it should apply more to Ganesh than to you, but that's not my point. Anyway, I'd like to first hear you out.'

Cedric called Stacy and asked her to inform Ganesh to meet him. He then focused on Karan and asked, 'Do you want to discuss Ganesh's mail or the exposure amount?'

Karan was feeling a little better now after Cedric's empathetic words. 'I want to talk about this mail sent by Ganesh, which is personally very insulting to me and also to my customer. We have shown complete indifference in dealing with a customer request. We are also being rude to them by saying things such as 'Roopak should go fly a kite'. What language is this? I implore you to take appropriate action.'

Cedric made an effort to reason with him.

'I agree that the message was not worded in respectable language. We'll talk to Ganesh about it. But I feel you are equally to blame. It was actually your mail that prompted him to react. You're asking him to reconsider the proposal; but on what grounds? Are you giving him any additional information that he didn't have before? No. You just mention the same thing again and again. We have discussed those points and then taken the decision. Your request for a reconsideration needs to be backed with some additional information and language that respects the earlier decision, which was taken after all due considerations.'

As he was talking to Karan, Ganesh entered. Cedric stopped and looked at Ganesh. He thought it was important to placate Karan.

'Ganesh, it's about the mail that you sent to Karan. What do you guys think the office email is for, eh? If I had received such a mail, I would have felt very offended. Please patch up with Karan immediately, with an apology. You can take it as an order from me.'

Ganesh tried to say something, 'But Cedric...'

'No buts Ganesh. First do what I tell you.'

Ganesh enjoyed watching Karan sulk in front of Cedric. So, quite unwillingly he dragged an apology out, 'I am sorry, Karan. The mail was meant to be taken in a light vein. If it has offended you, I am sorry.'

If looks could kill, Karan's would have hung, quartered and buried Ganesh right there. His voice was a whine, 'You don't even sound apologetic. There is no seriousness in what you say.'

Ganesh then came forward, sat on a chair and said, 'It's up to you to think whatever you want to.' Turning to Cedric he said, 'Cedric, I've apologized to Karan for that mail.'

Cedric said, 'Guys, take due care in future. We can't do things in jest. We're in business. I wonder sometimes if I am dealing with school children.'

Ganesh said, 'Sorry again, Cedric. I assure you that I won't start this again in future.'

'I'll hold you to this, Ganesh. Let us now discuss the matter.' Turning to Karan, 'What's Roopak saying now?'

Karan didn't want to tell Cedric and Ganesh that both Dave and Roopak had blasted him off. But he did say what both men had said about the RMQ unit.

'Both Dave and Roopak were personally very upset with our decision. They complained that the decision had been taken arbitrarily, without taking the overall proposal into consideration. They felt that the risk team should have at least met them once, before a decision was taken. They said they would withdraw their full relationship with us and stop giving us any further individual loans business if we don't consider revising the loan sanction to Rs. 500 million.'

Karan didn't realize that by revealing the threat of business withdrawal, he was diluting the bargaining strength of Roopak. He thought it would make a strong impression in the present situation. His only objective was to get the entire amount approved, by hook or by crook.

Ganesh was quick to respond, 'I reserve my reaction to the comments that Roopak or his colleague has made about the RMQ unit. But I must say that the threat of withdrawal of retail business by Chand Builders is not going to change my view on this. What's the guarantee that he'd give you tons and tons of individual loans business after we disburse the builder loan to him? What if he breaks his promise to you? Look at life beyond Chand Builders. We've made several changes to our retail home loans product to make it market friendly and customer friendly. Some of our norms are a cut above other competitive market products. After all, why do you have such a large sales team? It should be quite possible to find other sources of business in the market, besides Chand Builders. Do that instead. Let Chand Builders go to hell. '

Karan reacted with veritable outrage, 'You wouldn't say this if your ass was on the line. The market is extremely competitive and we struggle hard for every single file. Our sales managers are out on the streets begging for files from door to door.......'

'That's a complete lie. None of your sales managers are out on the streets. Whenever I've visited the branches, I've seen them sitting in the office sipping coffee. In fact, we're the only organization with cushy desks for sales managers and excellent cabins for sales heads. No other lending organization in this country offers these to its sales people, since they're supposed to be out on the field. But our sales guys never go out of the air-conditioned office. Mostly they're seen arguing with the underwriters here. '

'Well, unless the underwriter is pushed by my sales guy, the only decision that seems logical to him is rejecting a case, like you've done here. If your underwriters were to think logically and approve cases, why should my sales guys be in their office?'

'Good question. But you accept that your sales guys don't go out in the market and instead sit in the office with the underwriters. I wish to also clarify that I've not declined this proposal of Chand Builders, but only reduced the loan amount and I have given my reasoning behind that. To repeat, a Rs.500 million exposure on a single builder finance deal is one bloody hell of a risky move for a company like ours. I've checked with competitors such as Millennium Bank and others and the maximum exposure that any of them took the first time they lent to Chand Builders was only Rs. 150 million. In comparison, we've been perfectly fair in what we've approved.'

'I don't agree. So what if our portfolio is small? And why is our portfolio small? Neither will your underwriters let my sales guys do business nor will you let me do good bulk deals like this one. You guys are incorrigible. Is the entire risk community like this or what? We might as well close shop and go home.'

Ganesh, while enjoying the sight of Karan in a complaining and defeated position, decided to put his statement firmly now, 'You always make sweeping statements. That is the only trick you guys know. Cedric, I throw in the towel. It's now your call. This deal doesn't have my support.'

As the two men were sparring, Cedric – who was used to this – stopped paying attention and waited for them to calm down. After Ganesh passed the buck to him, he turned to Karan and said, 'Just go and tell Roopak that it's been discussed threadbare and there's no change in the loan amount.'

Karan was devastated. He had thought that at least this time round, Cedric would support him. Without another word, he got up and returned to his desk.

Karan didn't speak to Dave immediately. He waited for his thoughts to simmer down and allowed himself a day to mull over the whole issue. He looked at the worst-case scenario wherein, Roopak would cut-off the relationship with AHFL. Karan believed that as the business head, it was his own responsibility against all odds to protect this source of large revenues from disintegrating. He vacillated between the options available to him. The first: to push this deal within AHFL for the full amount, though he had no idea how. The second: to ask Roopak what he had in mind when he asked Karan to come back to him if his second attempt failed. Karan decided to walk that path. He also decided to inform Roopak about his own professional rivalry with Ganesh and use this opportunity to prove his loyalty to Roopak in return for Roopak's continued support to him in terms of individual retail loans business. This thought was also driven by a deep urge to avenge the personal insult hurled at him by Ganesh. He thought over this idea again and again until he reached a final conclusion.

Next morning when Karan reached office, he was supremely confident about his decision to prove his allegiance to Roopak. Before he placed his call however, he checked that the door of his cabin was properly locked. He dialled the number, 'Good morning, Roopak.'

'Hi Karan. Good morning. So what's the news for me?'

'Well Roopak, we had another round of discussions internally and both Cedric and Ganesh have declined making any changes to the loan amount. I've tried my best. It seems that the loan amount won't change.'

'Karan, I knew it was beyond you to push it. If only you'd managed this better, we could've got the disbursement by now. It is such a straightforward deal. Now I believe that we've lost our opportunity. It is so demeaning to be told that we don't deserve to get even this small loan amount. Never in my life have I faced this kind of humiliation. I don't even need that money really. I just gave you guys a chance to oblige you. But boss, you've let me down.'

He paused for Karan to react. When there was no reaction, he continued, 'But Karan, as I mentioned to you, I'm not one to take defeat lying down.' He fell silent and Karan spoke, 'Roopak, You told me that you have something else in mind. What is it? Can you share it with me? I'm prepared to do all I can to get you this approval.'

Yes! Roopak kicked the air in silent jubilation. 'Yes. I do have something in mind. I'm now giving you a package that you cannot refuse. You shouldn't refuse this, if you are looking for a good . . . no! *excellent* business opportunity. I'll put everything at stake, but never take defeat. However Karan, I need a promise from you before I make this offer to you.'

Karan thought this was the perfect opportunity to prove himself to Roopak. In his own assessment, this was a do or die situation. 'Absolutely, Roopak. If there is anything that you feel I can do, I will. It's a promise.'

'This time, you should bat for me as if it's your own deal under consideration. I'm going to give you some ammunition that you can use. But you can't let me down this time. If you think you will not be able to push it, do not forget to fix a meeting for me with your people and I'll convince them. Don't botch it up. This *must* happen.'

'All right Roopak, I understand. I will be careful. Now tell me what it is that you have.'

To Karan's utter disappointment Roopak said, 'Give me a call tomorrow. I will tell you then.'

It was a long night for Karan.

Chapter – 15

THE TRUMP CARD

July 2003

THAT NIGHT ROOPAK SAT BACK AND WENT OVER HIS PLAN again and again. He wanted to be sure that he was not making a mistake. He was on the verge of making the most important move in the whole AHFL operation. This move could make or break his ultimate plan. He was naturally a bit nervous.

Next morning Roopak reached his workplace and waited for the all-important call from Karan. He knew that Karan would call soon and he did.

Roopak picked up the phone and said, 'Hi, Karan. I knew you would call about now.'

'Roopak, you know why I have called.'

'Yes I know. Let me now share my proposal with you.' He paused for a few seconds before speaking again, 'Karan, you know the Megacity project and its background. This is my flagship project; the best project that I've ever undertaken. No other project exists in the country that can match Megacity in terms of its aesthetics, comfort and amenities. This will be one of its kind in the entire country. I have not yet opened the bookings since I want to sell it at a premium price after showcasing a significant amount of construction in the project. I've not even referred this project to any financiers till date for a project approval. The proposal to you is, my friend, you fund me Rs. 500 million against this project; the one and only Megacity, instead of Whitewoods. I promise that I'll return the money in just six months time. Also, I'm willing to offer AHFL exclusive rights to finance individual home owners in this project. Each flat costs not less than Rs. 50 million. So you can have the cake and eat it too. How do you feel about this proposal?'

It took Karan a few seconds to register the full import of what he had heard. When he understood it clearly, he couldn't believe his ears. Roopak was willing to give the humongous Megacity project as security to AHFL, only to get this amount of Rs. 500 million. It was unbelievable. He whispered in awe, 'Roopak, that's an irresistible offer. Are you serious?'

'I'm absolutely serious. I'm willing to put everything that I have to get this deal to sail through. I'll do anything to maintain and build this relationship.'

Roopak was now a superhero in Karan's mind, 'Roopak,

I'm floored by this offer. I promise that this time you can be assured that your friend will get you what you want.'

'I know Karan,that you are my friend and you'd help me out. Please do your best. However, let me be upfront: there's an issue with the project. It's not a major issue and nothing is wrong with the project. But I don't want things to get delayed at your end due to this. Till about a few months back, all lending organizations such as yours were approving builder projects even without the approved building plans along with other project papers. As per the practice then, all of you would approve the project without the building plan, start financing individual flats and later, when we had the plans approved from MCA, you collected the approved building plan from us. Sometime ago I understand there was a decision made that you would not approve any builder projects without the approved building plan being provided at the time of project approval. I fully appreciate the decision. But I am sure you still appreciate the fact that we have to deal with the bureaucracy in MCA as well. The procedures in MCA offices take a lot of time. In Megacity, we have the building plan already approved. But I'm seeking some modifications to it and the application for the modifications is pending with MCA for approval. Those modifications are critical because this is a dream project for me and I am careful about every single detail on the project. Everyone, from the commissioner himself to the junior inspector on the MCA, is known to us and has assured us that the changes will get approved. So the issue for you is that when I give you the project papers for disbursement, I'll not be able to give you my final approved building plan. But I promise that the final approved plan will be delivered to you guys within two months' time. For your own comfort, you can keep the current existing approved building plan. I need this dispensation because I just don't have any time. I now need the disbursement as of yesterday.'

Karan heard Roopak out. Given the strength of the security that was Megacity, this issue didn't seem to him a major stumbling block. He thought he had a foolproof case since the value of the project that was getting mortgaged was many times higher than the loan amount. No sensible person could refute this funding. If there was an effort on Ganesh's part to play his old tricks, he decided he'd give him a *kita* – a term he had learnt in his management school from a professor. It meant a 'kick in the ass'.

'Roopak, Don't worry about this. I'll take care of it. I've now understood this whole proposal. Let me now take it up with the guys here and get back to you.'

'Thanks Karan. I will never forget this help. And please remember, if need be arrange for a personal meeting between me and them.'

'Sure Roopak. I'll keep that in mind. Thanks for your offer and I hope that we'll soon cut your cheque for Rs.500 million. Please wait for my call.'

The phones went silent on both sides.

Karan sat grinning at his desk. He now had a golden opportunity to achieve what he had wanted. Neither Ganesh nor Cedric could say no to a loan of Rs.500 million against the Megacity project which was valued at close to Rs.4 billion. He decided not to give any more leeway to Ganesh.

He began to mull over his strategy. He asked for coffee and after a few long sips, he hit upon a plan. He decided not to take it up directly with both of them together. He thought he would deal with Cedric first, get him fully on his side and then get Cedric to deal with Ganesh. He decided he'd first go and whine to Cedric a couple of times, about how the Chand Builders' deal was unceremoniously thrown out and how it had impacted him personally. Then he would stir up a hornet's nest by constant complaints about Ganesh. Once he had gained Cedric's sympathy, he'd then produce this proposal like a rabbit out of the hat.

He acted fast and within a few minutes was sitting in front of Cedric.

'Cedric, you know that with great difficulty we managed to initiate a relationship with Chand Builders and got a number of individual loans business referred by them. Now we have messed it up and we face the imminent threat of losing a lot of business. I'll be falling back on targets. I'm still not sure if I'll ever be able to catch up. In this deal, our reason for downsizing the loan was so flimsy that I felt ashamed to convey it to Roopak. Our refusal to do this deal has already reached the market and we're being ridiculed for messing up a good relationship. It was a great opportunity missed.'

Cedric had expected complaints from Karan. He therefore took it quite calmly. As a superior, Cedric felt it was upto him to encourage him to look forward.

'I understand how bad you feel. You did your job perfectly. However, these things are a part of life and we have to be prepared to take these in our stride and move on.'

'Cedric, if it was any other deal, I wouldn't have felt so bad. It was a great opportunity for AHFL and we've lost it. Chand Builders would've given us exclusive rights on all their projects. What else do you need? That would've only meant phenomenal growth for AHFL. And you know, that the profile of customers Chand Builders refers to us for retail loans are always the best. I'm quite upset with this rejection. It would've been better, if we'd taken a dignified stance right at the start and told them that this deal was too big for us. Anyhow, I'll face the music now and keep you updated.'

He came back to his desk and phoned Roopak, explaining to him the plan and adding that he'd need a few more days to win Cedric over. Then getting Ganesh to agree would be easy. Now Roopak felt that Karan was talking sense. He lauded Karan for his clever strategy and told him that he was available for advice, whenever needed.

Over the next three days, Karan spoke to Cedric twice every day. In each of those sessions he cribbed, complained and cried about how he had to suffer due to Ganesh's stubborn stance on Chand Builders' loan proposal. This repeated hammering of the same issue had its effect on Cedric who began to feel that perhaps Ganesh and he had been a trifle rough in handling Chand Builders. Karan noted Cedric's expressions carefully and gauged that Cedric was coming around. In about a week's time Cedric started to believe that AHFL could have given the benefit of doubt to the customer. He admitted this to Karan in good faith in one of his weaker moments.

Having won the first round, Karan craftily slid the new proposal in.

'Cedric, I know that we've already taken a decision on this deal. But as I've repeatedly told you how important this was for me, I've tried to see if there were any other options for us. I've managed to salvage a modified version of the proposal, which I think makes a lot of sense. May I share it with you?'

Cedric was a little surprised to see a seemingly dead deal suddenly spring to life again. But nevertheless, he agreed to look at what Karan had in mind.

Karan then elaborated on the new and improved plan – of offering Megacity for the builder loan – that Roopak had outlined to him. He waxed so eloquent that Cedric's brow shot up at the details. Finally Cedric said, 'Let me consider this fresh proposal, think about it and revert to you, Karan.'

'Thanks Cedric. I just want to request that Ganesh not be involved before you take a stance on the issue. All I need from you is a decision on whether you're agreeable to look at an exposure of Rs. 500 million, if everything else is fine with the project. If you agree in-principle, I'll take up the rest of the issues with Ganesh directly.'

Cedric thought about it for the rest of the day. He called Karan just before work closed for the day.

'Karan, I've given it a good thought. Subject to everything else being okay with the deal, considering that we'd be funding just one-eighth of the total project cost, I am agreeable in-principle to take an exposure of Rs. 500 million. However, this is subject to everything else in the project being above board.'

Karan was over the moon. He said, 'Cedric, thank you very much for your concurrence. I'll ensure with Ganesh that everything is alright with the project. Would you please now call a meeting with Ganesh, wherein we can discuss this revised proposal?'

Cedric agreed and called for a meeting the following morning. When Ganesh heard of this meeting, he grew alert. Meetings with Karan were always loaded guns and Ganesh preferred to attend them fully prepared. Ganesh's instinct sensed that something serious was cooking on the Chand Builders deal again. Therefore he called Arun and asked him, 'These guys are raking up the Chand Builders deal again. What do you feel they will be up to this time?'

Arun thought for a while and answered, 'Ganesh, perhaps they want you to increase the exposure from Rs. 250 million to Rs. 350 million or a higher amount. Trying to reach mid-way perhaps?'

'Hey, I've made myself quite clear. I'm not going to look at anything beyond Rs. 250 million. I think both Cedric and Karan know this. So I don't think they are going to ask me to reconsider the loan amount.'

'Then . . . let me think. I'll get back to you.'

Arun went back to his desk and pondered over it. He had years of experience in the mortgage finance industry. After a while, he hit upon something that he thought he should share with Ganesh. He pulled up a chair opposite Ganesh and said, 'Something has crossed my mind.'

'What?'

'Based on my own experience with large deals like this and experienced players like Roopak, I can think of one possibility. And it's this. Probably there was some information in the Chand Builders' deal that was being kept under wraps all along and is now being brought out in the open. Roopak and company probably *wanted* us to reject their initial proposal and had planned this new thing as a backup or what we'd call Plan B. This could be stronger than the first pitch. Sometimes, Plan B is the actual trump card that's brought out later, making it extremely difficult for the lender to say no. I've seen experienced selling agencies and seasoned customers use this mode to get their cases approved. I have a feeling that they may be coming to us with their real trump card now.'

'Sounds interesting! This will surely bring some excitement into the discussion. The only trump card that could make me change my stance is a cash collateral of an equivalent amount for the additional Rs. 250 million that they want. Anything else is unacceptable. But I know that the trump card will not be a cash collateral. It has to be something else. What's your intelligent guess on this?'

Arun scratched his chin thoughtfully, 'Ganesh, I just went through all the questions that we asked ourselves initially when we evaluated the deal. One of the things that appeared strange to us was Roopak asking us to fund Whitewoods, right? He had been looking for funding against Megacity, which was earlier declined by Millennium Bank. Therefore logically Chand Builders should've approached us for funding the Megacity project. But they didn't. We questioned it among ourselves and didn't get satisfactory answers. We didn't pursue that further as Whitewoods was also a clean project to fund. Perhaps, I feel, the answer will unfold tomorrow in this meeting as the trump card. Maybe he is going to ask us to fund Megacity instead. If he does, that'll answer all our current questions,' he paused for a moment and then said, 'but also raise several more.'

There was silence in the cabin for a while. Ganesh then said, 'Would that be difficult to handle?'

'If that happens, we'd be in a tight spot. Megacity is a huge project the cost of which on paper is Rs. 4 billion. Roopak has probably told Karan to get the loan approval revised to Rs.500 million and to support his case, he is prepared to give a better security than Whitewoods, namely Megacity. And it is a security which is the special pride of Chand Builders. Never in the past has Chand Builders constructed such a massive project. It's a dream for anyone to own a home in this project. Therefore, he'll justify a higher funding by offering this prestigious project for funding. Your no to this revised proposal will be strongly contested by Karan, though I'm not sure what Cedric's reaction would be. But if you stick to your guns, it's likely that Cedric would think that you're being pointlessly stuck up.'

'Hmm . . .' Ganesh looked at Arun gravely.

'Ganesh, I'd like us to sit back and think this through carefully. If the financials and profile of the group are sound, perhaps there is a case to look at an exposure of Rs.500 million. And if it's Megacity, it's a solid mortgage security. We'll also get tremendous mileage in terms of exclusive access to offer housing loans to individual home owners there. The customers are likely to be the crème de la crème. But the question is, why us? From any other more aggressive bank, Roopak can get a higher funding on this project. Mortgaging this project worth Rs.4 billion for a funding of Rs.500 million is surely not intelligent leveraging. That's actually inefficient use of assets. How did Dave, the shrewd financial controller that he is, support this? Why are they locking up Megacity for this miserable Rs.500 million? We'll never get an honest answer from them. Maybe tommorow's meeting will shed some light on this.'

'Arun, so you are actually saying that they aren't letting us go without taking Rs. 500 million from us. You think he'd give us Megacity for that?' The frown on his face grew sharper.

'I guess so.'

Ganesh spoke very slowly, 'Arun, if Chand Builders feels that they can lay their claim on a higher loan amount of Rs. 500 million by enhancing the level of security or collateral offered to us, they have two options. The first option is, they give us something larger than Whitewoods, as you now guess they might come to us with Megacity and take Whitewoods fully out of picture. The second option is, they can just add another smaller project along with Whitewoods and give us both the projects as security for this funding and keep Megacity out of the picture. If I were them I'd do the latter because from what you say about Megacity I understand it's a real top-of-the-line luxury project and therefore I'd be surprised if they undervalue it by setting the mortgage so low.' Then after a brief thoughtful interlude he said, 'My instinct now says that something is horribly wrong here. I don't like this stubborn persistence for an amount of Rs. 500 million. And if they mortgage Megacity, it'll mean that they are desperate for that money. Given their stature, I find it hard to accept that they are desperate for funds. I feel it's not the money that's driving things. It's something else. What are we missing?'

'Well Ganesh, we're only working on one possible assumption: that they're coming back with Megacity. It's perfectly possible that there's something else.'

'Yes. In any case, whatever be the offer, I won't accept it immediately. I'll bring it back here. We'll discuss it and then get back to them.'

Chapter – 16

DIVING INTO THE DEEP BLUE SEA

July 2003

IT WAS A 9 AM MEETING AND CEDRIC, WHO WAS USUALLY IN office by 8 everyday, was unusually late that day. Ganesh arrived early and chose to wait. As Cedric walked in, Ganesh noticed that he was out of breath since he'd used the stairs to climb up to his office on the 5th floor. Cedric did this every day, as a substitute for his daily exercise. Naturally, in the process of climbing up the stairs, his heart pumped up and by the time he reached his office, he was breathing heavily. As a result, he found it difficult to talk to anyone for the first few minutes, while he recovered his breath. Usually he was at his desk before others in the office arrived. But today he was late. When he walked in to find Ganesh waiting, he felt that he could've used the lift and spared himself the embarrassment of huffing and puffing.

'Hey....huh….. Ganesh. Huh………..huh…Good morning huh…..huh…..huh…. Huh….You …..huh. huh……..reached early…huh…….huh. Hasn't.. .. .huh…… Karan come huh…….'

Cedric sank into the sofa with his arms and legs stretched. Ganesh could hear Cedric's laboured breathing, '….Huh…….. Huh…………….Huh'. Cedric reached for a glass of water and gulped it down. Ganesh said, 'Boss, please relax for a few seconds. I'll be right back.' He went out, leaving Cedric in solitude so that he could regain his composure and feel better. When Ganesh returned, Cedric was fine.

'Hey Ganesh, I do this ritual of climbing these stairs in the morning and hence this spectacle. We get very little time otherwise for any kind of physical exercise. Do you do your daily dozen?'

Before Ganesh could answer, Karan entered. Cedric said, 'Come in Karan. We were actually discussing the subject of health when you walked in. In fact, Ganesh caught me gasping for breath when I walked in. You should've actually seen me going ….huh……huh… all over.' Looking at Ganesh he said, 'If I were you, I would have laughed if I had seen someone like that.'

All of them had a chuckle. Continuing in the same vein, Cedric said, 'Guys, we need to do something about our health seriously. I'm actually worried. I don't take time out at home for any exercise. We usually go out for a walk at night, but that is not enough.' Looking at Ganesh he asked, 'But Ganesh, what do you do to maintain yourself? I don't see you even controlling your diet." Ganesh smiled. He was actually not in a mood for the banter, anxious as he was to know the purpose of this meeting.

Cedric sensed the mood and quickly came to the subject.

'Ok guys. Let's come to the point.' Looking at a piece of paper on the table, he said, 'Ganesh, we're re-opening the discussion on Chand Builders.' He looked at Ganesh, trying to gauge his reaction.

Fully prepared, Ganesh didn't show any surprise. 'I had a fair inkling that it would be so.'

'Now, our friend Roopak has come with a fresh proposal. He's keen to get the entire amount of Rs. 500 million, since he says that a lower amount doesn't serve his purpose.' As he spoke, he shifted his glance alternately between Karan and Ganesh. The latter keenly observed his body language and noted the lack of confidence in Cedric's tone. He felt this wasn't the usual Cedric. Then Cedric stopped short and asked Karan to brief Ganesh.

The shaky manner in which Cedric started the conversation and alternately looked at the two led Ganesh to conjecture that Cedric had probably taken a stance and conveyed it to Karan. This meeting apparently was only to convince Ganesh that AHFL should disburse the full Rs. 500 million to Chand Builders. His mind worked quickly. He reminded himself to hold on to his earlier decision and resist all attempts to increase the loan amount. Then Karan spoke, 'Ganesh, our approval of a Rs. 250 million has been thrown out of the window by Roopak. He's made it abundantly clear that this does not serve their purpose.'

Ganesh responded with his characteristic nonchalance, 'Tell me something new. I've heard this several times before. And frankly I don't think we should care about what Roopak feels. If he throws our offer out of the window, that's his choice. This is a free country.'

Karan was slightly taken aback by Ganesh's abrasive tone. Nevertheless, he tried to drive home his point.

'Well, let me come to the point. Now he's made a new offer to us; he wants us to fund Megacity, take that as the security for this builder loan and give him Rs. 500 million against that.'

Ganesh thought to himself, 'Ah-ha, there it is!,' and waited for Karan to finish.

Wide-eyed, Karan continued, 'The cost of the Megacity project is Rs.4 billion and this doesn't include the land cost, which was purchased by him several years ago. Megacity is a golden chance for us to cast in stone our association with Chand Builders and to comfortably lend, make tons of money, sit back and relax. We now have absolutely no justification not to approve and disburse the entire amount of Rs.500 million. It is a no-brainer now. The security offered has a value on paper that is 8 times the value of the loan. A dream situation for AHFL to make money, maintain this relationship with Chand Builders and profit by the future individual loans business that are waiting for us like ripe plums for the picking. We need to give them an immediate go-ahead on this.'

Ganesh mentally congratulated Arun for having eyes at the back of his head. He wanted to reply without overreacting. But before that he wanted to know what Cedric thought of this deal. But then he decided against it. If Cedric said that he was ready to support this deal, it would become difficult for Ganesh to take a different stance thereafter. On the contrary, if Cedric hadn't made up his mind yet, the question could embarrass him. So either way, he felt it wasn't the right thing to ask Cedric directly. He decided that he should first let both of them know his view and pre-empt Cedric. He said politely, 'Karan, I'll need some time to think through this. We may still not be able to do the full amount. Let me come back to you.'

Karan was extremely annoyed and shouted, 'What's there to think, Ganesh? Who would ever give such a large security for this small sum? We are lucky that Roopak is still with us. So far we have handled this issue ridiculously. Let me make one thing clear. I don't think there can be any answer to this deal, other than a loud and clear Yes.' Turning to Cedric he said, 'We should decide now. What's there for us to think?'

Before Cedric could speak, Ganesh replied. 'Karan, your yelling at the top of your voice won't change my decision. If you think you can bully me into making a decision, you are mistaken. I'll take my time to decide!'

This further enraged Karan and he yelled back, 'This is pure impertinence and total lack of feeling for the customer. We've already dragged our feet for several weeks. There's nothing unreasonable in asking for a quick response.' Again he appealed to Cedric, 'Boss, this needs your urgent intervention.' And again Ganesh spoke before Cedric opened his mouth, 'And neither am I saying anything unreasonable. All that I'm saying is that I'd like to think about it and get back. What is wrong with that stand?'

Cedric spoke finally, 'Okay Ganesh, when can you get back with your response?'

Sensing pressure he warned himself not to succumb to anyone and stubbornly said, 'I'll need a minimum of four days to think over this, research it and revert with a yes or a no.'

Karan was belligerent, 'I cannot take a no for an answer.'

Ganesh stood firm 'I repeat. It could be a yes or a no.'

Cedric interjected, 'Okay Ganesh. You have your four days to think over it.' Then he said, 'In my view, this looks like a good deal for us to get into. A Rs. 500-million-exposure on Megacity is worth putting our money on.'

Without asking for it, Ganesh had got his answer. He realized that Cedric was also completely sold on this proposal. He left the room quickly. Ganesh now had two clear opponents. His mind was racing. He had to get this right. Why was Karan in such a rush? What had he done to get Cedric to support him? And why Megacity? All these questions and many more, needed immediate answers and he had only four days.

He reached his desk and called Arun into his cabin. He briefed Arun on the latest and said, 'Arun, the negative vibes in my instinct have become stronger now. Karan's rush for a decision doesn't look clean. His insistence that he cannot take no for an answer also doesn't augur well. Cedric's open support for the proposal has only complicated this further. There are more questions now than we imagined. Cedric seems to be sold on this idea. Karan has worked on him independently before bringing me into the discussion. Now that he has Cedric's support, he is exerting pressure on us to give him a positive decision. We have very little time. I've managed to get four days for us to work on it. I've a feeling that Cedric didn't like my asking for this time. Cedric probably expected a decision from me immediately. But I stuck to my guns. You better get going now. Find out everything from your sources. Probe that bit about this project having some issues that your friend in Millennium Bank mentioned. Let's discuss in the next hour again.'

Arun left Ganesh's cabin to initiate his work on Megacity.

Ganesh felt an uncharacteristic and a strong nervousness grip him, particularly due to Cedric's stand on this deal. Cedric usually took a stand only after consulting Ganesh. This time he had independently taken a view, which was quite unlike him. And since he'd told Karan that he supported the deal, Ganesh now needed to have a strong reason to reject the deal. If he approved the deal and something went wrong, it would be his neck on the line. On the other hand, there never was appreciation for the good judgment calls taken by the risk unit which saved the organization from getting into troubled deals. Forever caught between the devil and the deep blue sea, that was the story of the risk guys. Ganesh felt that at least Cedric, on a personal level, had been quite open about appreciating their negative decisions as well, for the sheer saves in terms of bad debts avoided. So he held Cedric in high regard and considered it his duty to advise Cedric and protect him from any embarrassment later on. This sense of responsibility only added to the pressure.

After some time, Arun returned to Ganesh's office, 'Kumaresh's valuer stated that more than 12 floors were being constructed at Megacity although the MCA approval was only for 12 floors. Kumaresh and I discussed this and thought that Chand Builders may be in the process of getting the building plan for this project revised to accommodate more number of floors. I've asked both our valuers to visit the project and give an urgent report by 11 tomorrow.'

'Good first step. To be doubly sure, we'll still make it clear to our friends that we'll not process the loan unless we have the revised approved building plan for Megacity with us. Make a full list of documents you need due to this substitution of project and send it to Karan with a copy to me and Cedric.'

Arun did as advised.

The next day the two valuers of AHFL visited the Megacity project independently. The first one reached the project at 9 am. He was not allowed immediate entry, in keeping with Roopak's instructions. After making him wait for half an hour, when the site workers found out that he was representing AHFL, they let him in. He spent another half hour at the site. The second valuer reached at 10 am. Both men were met by Vachchani and appropriately looked after.

The valuers, who were not used to such royal treatment, were thrilled by the reception and the apparent cooperation received from the people at the site office of Megacity. Usually on any Chand Builders' project site, the valuers always found the site staff overbearing and smug. This time, as soon as they entered the project, Vachchani personally received them at the gate, took them to a special luxurious air-conditioned cabin that had excellent carpets, charming furniture and beautiful art pieces. Vachchani talked nineteen to the dozen and kept their attention diverted from their main business. He showed them the approved building plan of the project in the comfort of the cabin they were sitting in. After that, he took them on a project tour in a special site-vehicle. He showed them all the open spaces in the project, the green areas, the water bodies, the playfield, the golf course and carefully avoided taking them close to the towers under construction. The project site was already kept clean by the site manager. Hence the valuers' visit caused them no discomfort. The two valuers knew that Megacity was the most prestigious and the best project ever constructed in Ayravati. This feeling coupled with the hospitality of Vachchani, ensured that they wrote a good report about the project. The bonhomie they shared with Vachchani stopped them from noticing the obvious anomalies in the construction.

By 12 noon when Arun received the reports, he noticed that the reports had no mention of any additional floor construction in violation of the approved building plan. He even called up the valuers to double-check. The number of floors completed on the site was mentioned as twelve in the report, which also described the site in glowing terms.

Arun was quite puzzled that his valuers had failed to notice something that the Millennium Bank valuer had noticed.

That afternoon, Ganesh showed him an e-mail from Karan: *'Now that your valuers have also visited the project and given you a positive report, I'd expect a faster response from your end to clear the deal.'*

Arun was flabbergasted. Everyone knew that RMQ unit would instruct the valuers to do an inspection. Nobody outside the risk unit tracked the valuation process so closely. Only if the valuations got delayed inordinately did that issue get raised. In this case however, there was no valuation request given by Karan in the first place. Arun had done the valuation on his own, to hasten the process. So the facts Karan had mentioned in his short one-line mail, were beyond what he was supposed to know at that stage. This was intriguing. He expressed his suspicion to Ganesh. "How the hell did Karan come to know so quickly that we've sent our valuers for the inspection of the property and that they have already given us the report? And surprise surprise . . . how does he know that the reports are positive?' His voice dropped octaves as he spoke, as if he wanted to keep his words a secret. 'I have a feeling that someone in Roopak's site-office has played dirty with our valuation process by interfering with the independence of the valuers. The outcome of the valuation is therefore suspect. The valuers haven't said anything about the additional floor constructions in the project, which the valuer of Millennium Bank had mentioned in his report. And then Karan has come to know everything. This is unbelievable. These are substantive signs of the impending danger that is likely to come our way if we move ahead on this deal. Something definitely is being concealed from us. But we cannot talk about it openly since we do not know what exactly it is and who all are involved.'

Ganesh said, 'That only means that we must desist from issuing an in-principle approval.'

'Absolutely. Do not release your in-principle approval. That'll only add to our troubles. The indications aren't good.'

As they were talking in their office, Ganesh received a call from Stacy that Cedric wanted to meet him urgently. Ganesh got up from his desk and walked to Cedric's office. When Cedric urgently called somebody, it only meant a matter of burning urgency.

'Ganesh, sorry to pull you out. This time, this fellow Roopak has personally called me. This has never happened before, but he called me and expressed displeasure at our taking so much time to give him an in-principle approval on the Megacity deal. I understand from him that we've even completed the valuation of the project. Have you seen the reports? Do reports carry anything that should bother us?'

Ganesh had just heard Arun give him the story of the valuation reports. It shocked him to know that even Cedric was aware that the valuation had been done. Nevertheless, he responded in a calm and collected manner, 'Cedric, yes, we've received the reports. The reports seem all right on paper. But Arun tells me that there are a few . . . 'Cedric didn't let him complete. 'Then what're you waiting for? Why can't we give Roopak an in-principle approval now? In fact he told me that he needs money urgently and wants us to disburse fast. What's your issue?'

Realizing that Cedric was also now coming under pressure, Ganesh tried to voice his concern, 'Cedric, this Roopak guy seems to be snooping too much into what's happening in AHFL about his loan proposal. It's not a welcome situation that they are prying so much, keeping track of each and every stage of the process. They cannot dictate terms to us. We should get a free hand to complete all appraisal procedures properly. And I'm sorry to say this, but I find everyone, including you and Karan, too meddlesome. Give me the time I have asked for. Do not, for the sake of AHFL, ask me to bypass basic hygiene checks in such a large deal as this.'

'Ganesh, what I'm doing is also for the sake of AHFL. You better understand that. I'll set your comment aside for the moment and come to the issue. If you find Chand Builders too nosy, it's totally due to the fact that they are in a rush for funds and we are unduly delaying our response to them. Further, after proposing such a wonderful project as security, they have every right to know what's happening with their proposal. I'm not the least surprised by their inquisitiveness. Let us please buck up and give them a response today.'

'Today?' Ganesh screamed.

'Yes today. Before we leave the office. You're anyway going to check all the papers of the project before cutting your cheque. I don't see any sound reason for us to decline this proposal or downsize the loan amount. Your in-principle approval for half a billion should go today.'

'But Cedric, even if we want, we cannot send out the approval today because this needs the clearance of the Board of Directors. We need the Board's approval for this amount.'

'Ganesh, I know that. We'll get the Board's approval tomorrow by circulation. I've spoken to the key Board members and based on the information I've given them, they've agreed to support the decision. You can send the note to me and leave the Board approval to me. I'll take care of that.'

With these words ringing in his ears, Ganesh went back to his desk looking thoroughly disgusted. In the normal course, he would have released the in-principle approval. But the unwarranted bullying tactics and the issues in the valuation report made Ganesh want to hold it back for some time. But now after Cedric's directive, Ganesh issued the in-principle approval stating that AHFL was ready to give a loan of Rs. 500 million to Chand Builders, subject to the lawyer's report on the Megacity project being clear, the availability of the approved project plan and all project papers being submitted. The mail was sent to Karan and copied to Cedric. This was a major victory for Karan, as he'd now crossed the biggest hurdle in the deal.

As soon as the mail came in, Karan called Roopak's office. Roopak was waiting for the call. The two men congratulated each other and cheered on the phone. But Roopak knew that this in-principle approval was just a stepping stone to a final project approval that he wanted for Megacity, which he'd get only when the disbursement of the loan amount happened. Although Roopak knew that there was many a slip between this and the actual disbursement, it was a step in the right direction and he was happy.

After he sent out the mail, Ganesh forwarded it again to

Arun with a remark that no compromises should be made on the documentation. This message was also copied to Karan for his information. But Karan was on cloud nine and he paid no attention to the e-mail. He left the office early that day, to celebrate his partial victory.

Both Ganesh and Arun sensed that something was seriously amiss, but they couldn't put their finger to it. And time was brutally against them. Going by Chand Builders' past track record in submission of documents, Ganesh estimated that he'd get the property papers any moment. Between him and Arun, they had to decide on a course of action. The valuation fiasco highlighted the need to dig deep. They were unable to trust anybody. Suddenly Arun remembered Kumaresh in Millennium Bank and called him. Kumaresh picked up the phone in the first ring.

'Hey Arun. How are you, dude.?'

'Hi. Not too good. Again need some help.'

'Chand Builders again?'

'Yes. Man ... I'm in distress. We've had to give an in-principle approval to a Rs.500 million loan to them against Megacity.'

'What? I thought it was Whitewoods?'

'Yes. The project's changed. I'll tell you the story later. For now just keep this confidential. We've been forced to give an in-principle approval in a rush. Now I'm doing some heavy-lifting on project evaluation. I need information from you about that issue of number of floors. Just run it by me again?'

Kumaresh explained, 'Sure. You guys be careful. The current approved plan of Megacity that Chand Builders has permits construction of only up to 12 floors. When our valuer visited the project he saw construction happening beyond the 12th floor slab. He made a note of that in the valuation report that he submitted to us. Therefore the copy of the approved building plan that was given to us cannot be the final one. The final plan ideally should have an approval for more than 12 floors. So you guys ask for the final approved building plan. As I mentioned to you, I stopped probing the issue further, once the deal was declined by our Board.'

'Thanks. I now need a very personal favour. Get me to meet your valuer who visited the project. I want to speak to him.'

'That shouldn't be a problem. When do you want to speak to him?'

'Yesterday buddy. I am riding a mad horse. I'd like to meet him *now*.'

'Hang on. Let me speak to him right away.'

Kumaresh spoke to the valuer on another line. Within a minute he told Arun, 'I've spoken to him. He's ready to meet you now. His office is quite close to yours. Just be warned of one thing. He is an old hag. Likes to talk the hind legs off a donkey and is quite a bore.'

'The more he talks the better it is. I want him to talk.'

Arun thanked Kumaresh, took the valuer's address and hung up. He reached the valuer's office quickly. It was an old three storied building and the office was located on the 3rd floor. There was no lift and so Arun walked up the stairs. He read the name of the valuer's firm: Mishra & Co., the proprietor was Manohar Mishra.

He walked in to see an office totally disorganized with files and papers strewn all over. There were a few people in that office. In a corner he found a cabin with Manohar Mishra's name written on it. Arun knocked on the door and entered.

Mishra greeted Arun with pleasing warmth and said, 'Hello Mr. Arun. Please have a seat. I have been expecting you.'

'Mr. Mishra, Thank you for your time.' Arun took a chair and sat facing Mishra.

'It is always a pleasure to help. Tell me Mr. Arun, how can I help you?'

The meeting with Mishra lasted an hour or so. The discussion was an eye-opener. It left Arun shocked, shaken and numb. He felt ill after hearing what sounded like an apocalyptic prediction. He simply thanked Mishra and started back.

Instead of taking a cab back to the office, he walked the one kilometre or so lost in his thoughts. He had gathered critical information from Mishra and after analyzing what he had gathered, Arun reached the following conclusions:

- It was impossible for Roopak to get a formal approval from MCA to construct more than 12 floors in Megacity, notwithstanding his clout with the MCA officers.
- He and Ganesh would have to do all they could to stop this disbursement to Megacity.

Arun sat back at his desk thinking of Roopak's monumental audacity: going ahead with a construction in violation of MCA norms, something that could eventually prove to be devastating for people living there and attempting to dupe AHFL on top of that.

What Arun learnt from Manohar Mishra was that Ayravati had a high seismic potential and there was a history behind this rule that limited the maximum number of floors in a building. He learnt from Mishra that way back in 1951, after being battered badly by an earthquake, the local civic body had conducted some geological studies and fixed the limit at a maximum of three floors for any building in Ayravati. The rule had subsequently been diluted over time and the limit now stood at 12 floors. The archives in MCA, Arun visualized, would contain the history of this particular rule but he also knew that it would be impossible to dig up anything from there as it was one hell of a messed up organization. But Mishra had told him that while MCA could bend every other rule to accommodate a builder, under no circumstances would it approve a deviation from this 12 floor rule. Mishra confirmed to Arun that he had personally apprised the Municipal Commissioner of MCA of the seriousness of this issue

Arun had to share this information urgently with Ganesh. It wasn't going to be easy to get everyone else to appreciate this concern. Firstly, the information was perilously sensitive. No one would believe it unless there was some hard evidence to back it up. Karan and Cedric needed to be informed of this, but they could just brush it aside as nonsense. The moment Roopak came to know that someone was discussing this, he was going to come down heavily on such people.

He went across to Ganesh's cabin. It was empty. He chose

to wait. He got hold of a copy of the MCA building bye laws for a quick look at the rule in question. But to his utter shock, he couldn't find any such rule in the bye-laws. Nothing at all was mentioned in the bye-laws about any maximum limit to the number of floors in any building. Now Arun was worried. If there was no rule, what stopped the MCA from approving 20 floors? On what basis was this control exercised? Many questions rose in his mind.

Ganesh returned late at 8.30 pm. He called Arun and asked for an update on his meeting with Mishra. Arun narrated everything that he'd learnt from Mishra. Ganesh stared at Arun in utter shock and then shuddered in horror.

'Arun, what the hell does this mean? Are we going to finance a project without approved building plans or having illegal floors that would eventually come crumbling down killing everyone there?'

'We shouldn't. We have to do something quickly. I've just forwarded the mail of all the required documents to Karan, with particular emphasis on the approved building plan, though I now know that it's never going to come.'

'Stick to your guns on that. At my next meeting with Cedric, I'll update him on this issue. It's now clear that this man Roopak is a fraud. We should find ways to see that we reject this deal altogether. This association with Roopak is going to prove ruinous for us.'

Arun shared his concern now, 'If we tell Cedric or Karan that Roopak wouldn't get the revised approval, we need solid evidence to back our claim. I just checked the MCA bye laws to see if there are any stated rules limiting the construction to 12 floors. There's nothing written in the bye-laws to that effect. But Mishra is betting his last dollar on it.'

Ganesh mumbled, 'Oh shit, now how do we establish all this?'

While they were lost in their situation, there was a knock on the door. In walked a person bearing the file of Megacity containing the project legal papers and approved building plans.

'Sir, Mr. Karan has sent across this file to be given to you.'

Arun accepted the file and asked him, 'But I've never seen you in this office before. Who are you?'

'Sir, I work with Chand Builders. I came to give the file to Mr. Karan, who asked me to give it to you.'

Arun asked him, 'Did Karan go through this file before passing it on?'

But Ganesh chided him mildly, 'Arun, you know that idiot. He has no ability or inclination to go through a file like this.' He then looked at the man, 'Thanks. You may go now.' The man left with a smirk on his face.

There was a note attached to the file signed by Karan. 'Ganesh, this is for your immediate attention. The valuation is done and is satisfactory. The only thing left is a legal appraisal report from our lawyer. All the documents required to complete the legal appraisal are enclosed in this file. Please refer this to our lawyer. I'll ask Shailesh to sit on his head tomorrow and get the clearance. We should then be able to disburse the loan the day after, at the most.'

Ganesh was furious and called Karan immediately, 'Karan, How can we complete the project evaluation in a day? And don't you dare send Shailesh to put pressure on our lawyer! He will take not less than 7 days to do his evaluation and I do not want to pressurize him for this deal.' When Karan began to respond Ganesh interrupted him and said, 'And listen, I understand that there is some problem with the approved building plan of the project. I want Chand Builders to give us the final approved plan. Without that no disbursement will happen.'

Karan was aware of this fact, since Roopak had already mentioned this to him. 'Ganesh, the approved plan is already there in the file. Roopak has applied to MCA for approval of higher floors and will get it soon. We'll have to make an exception at the time of disbursement to say that the final approved building plan would be collected later. In any case, you already have one approved plan in the file, so you need not worry from an audit point of view. You've covered your ass.'

These business guys had no sense of discipline. 'Fuck you, Karan. The document that I have is a piece of shit. It's not about covering one's ass. It's about our own internal norms that we, only a few months ago, loudmouthed to the whole industry. I don't want to be a renegade. I won't do the disbursement without the final approved plan that has the approval for the actual number of floors that Roopak plans to construct in Megacity.'

'I'm not asking you to waive the final plan. You already have the approved plan upto the 12th floor. Let's disburse it with that. I'll ensure that you get the revised plan approved for higher floors shortly after the disbursement.'

'The answer is no. I need the final approved building plan before disbursement. Let me tell you, everything is not alright with this project. There're deviations in the project that can never be corrected. Especially the levels above the 12th floor will remain unauthorized.'

'Ganesh, please do not say baseless things that you aren't sure of. We have insulted Roopak enough. If he comes to know of this, he's going to be livid. Already people are laughing at us.'

'Karan, your arguments won't change my stance. I'll talk to you tomorrow. Let me now do my job.'

Ganesh knew that Karan's next call would be to Cedric, but he thought it was now time to call a spade a spade.

He told Arun to call the lawyer's office and ask for a special permission to accept the Megacity file that very night. He enclosed a personal note on the file addressed to the lawyer, requesting him to process the file at the earliest.

As both of them walked down to the parking lot, a thought struck Ganesh. 'Arun, can we speak to the journalist you know, Sanjeevani Desai? She was the one who prompted us to initiate the move across the housing finance industry to stop financing projects without approved building plans. Why don't you talk to her about this deal in confidence? Tell her that you're in a fix on this deal and need some information that can establish that there would be illegal floors in this building. Maybe she can help.'

'Yup. Good idea. Let me speak to her right away.'

Arun then dialed Sanju's number. No response. Arun sent a sms asking her to call back urgently.

Then they waited for Sanju's call.

* * *

Sanju was in Bangalore, sitting in a restaurant with a man named Surya Mohan or Surya, as his friends called him. Initially professional acquaintances, over time they had become good friends. Surya was tall, young and a good looking officer of the civil services cadre. Full of beans, he had been the Municipal Commissioner of Khanakpur until a few weeks ago. However, following serious differences with the political establishment, he had been transferred and was due to take over as the Municipal Commissioner of another city in Western India soon.

Sanju was prodding Surya, 'Surya, tell me about Khanakpur. What the hell did you do there that threatened the political establishment?'

'Sanju, Khanakpur was one hell of a place. Every second building there was built in violation of the building plans approved by the municipal office. There was no semblance of discipline. Wherever people saw some open space, they covered it up with concrete.'

'Gosh!'

'The first thing I did as the Municipal Commissioner was investigate and identify the municipal officers who had allowed such unauthorized buildings to proliferate. I identified about 20 such people and suspended all of them.'

'Must've been mayhem?'

'I didn't have a choice, neither did I give them a choice.

I formed a team of energetic people to run what I called "Project Reconstruction." We sent notices to all those people who owned properties that were built in violation of municipal bye-laws. The notice advised that the owners should pull down the deviated portions of their properties themselves, failing which our demolition team would arrive, tear down the property and recover demolition charges from the owners. People thought I was joking. They took the notice as a joke. But you know me. My team and I actually did the deed.'

Sanju chuckled, 'Project Reconstruction, is it? You should have named it "Project Demolition" instead.'

Surya grinned, 'This irked the power centres as they saw their vote bank eroding. The Chief Minister called me and told me to stop all demolition activity. He tried to bully me. I told him to go take a hike. I told him in clear terms that this wouldn't stop until the city was cleaned up.'

Sanju was astounded, 'I admire you, Surya. Only the rarest of people can do it. No wonder the media calls you *The Bulldozer Man.*'

Surya rolled his eyes, 'You should've seen that place. Any person with good sense couldn't have turned a blind-eye to it. I just did what I thought was right. This CM – when he realized that he couldn't stop me, called an official meeting of all his legislators and these guys passed a resolution stating that if the owners of deviated properties paid a one time regularization fee, the violations in their properties would get regularized.'

'Shucks.'

'That was the end of it. Most property owners came forward and paid the regularization fee, which was a pittance. The municipal office was unfortunately bound by this amendment and we couldn't proceed with our project. I was frustrated and threw in the towel.'

'I'm proud of you, Surya. What you did is now known to everyone at the national level.'

'Whatever. But look the new city I'm posted to: Channe – again swarming with illegal constructions.'

'So you now know what to do.'

'Absolutely. Something that bugs me no end is this utter disregard for safety rules. I guess I'll have a busy time there right from day one.'

'I wish there were thousands of officers like you.'

'Sanju, I could say the same for you. The truth is we're all guided by our conscience. I don't want any undue credit.'

They finished dinner and Sanju returned to her hotel room.

It was only then that Sanju noticed a missed call on her cell phone and saw Arun's sms. It was quite late. But it seemed urgent and so she called back.

Arun and Ganesh were in Temple Coffee House when Sanju's call came.

'Hi, Arun. Just saw your message. How've you been?'

'Sanju, thanks for calling back despite the late hour. I've got something urgent to discuss with you.'

'Sure. Just that I'm currently in Bangalore. So if you want to meet up, it won't be possible for another week. But talk, we surely can.'

'Oh, ok. Didn't know that you were out of station. Never mind. We can discuss it over phone. It's about a builder loan proposal. Chand Builders has applied to us for a builder funding proposal of Rs. 500 million.'

The moment she heard the name, she reacted even before Arun spoke further.

'Arun, that place is hell. Try to avoid if possible. I can vouch for the fact that Roopak, despite the good name he's earned in the market, is a monster and can be extremely mean and cunning. Wrong person for you to do business with. What have you gotten into with him?'

'Our business guys have developed a close relationship with Roopak and over the last few months Chand Builders has been giving AHFL a lot of individual loans referrals. Our guys want to further this relationship with Roopak. My colleague Ganesh and I are under tremendous pressure to disburse a builder loan to Roopak for his project Megacity. We're trying our best to find something that can help us decline the deal. We've caught on to something, but need solid evidence to back up our claim.'

'What have you known and about what?'

'Do you know anything about the Megacity project?'

'Frankly I don't. I only know that there's a project by this name coming up in Ayravati.'

'Roopak's planning to construct a high rise structure there that will have more than 12 floors.'

'More than 12 floors?' she yelped. 'How can he do that? The MCA doesn't permit more than 12 floors. In fact I've been fighting with the MCA to bring it down to 8. Twelve is the maximum number of floors that you can have in any building currently in Ayravati.'

'Do you know Mishra? He also mentioned this to me.'

'Yes. I know Mishra very well.'

'But Sanju, why is this not mentioned anywhere in the MCA bye-laws?'

'I am not surprised that the MCA bye-laws have no mention of this. That document is some forty years old.'

'No, I am talking of the latest version.'

'The latest version is just a reprint, which happens year on year. Every year, MCA passes a resolution that the building bye-laws have been reviewed. But the review is just a formality. The same document gets reprinted as the latest version. The only thing that's changed over the last several decades is the limit on the maximum number of floors that can be constructed in a building in Ayravati. This explicit rule of not allowing more than 12 floors would've been formalized through a separate circular, a copy of which would be available somewhere in one of those dusty files in the broken MCA cupboards. Mishra has also been trying to prevail upon the MCA to bring this limit down as he knows the real background on the origins of this rule. Did he share that with you?'

'Yes. He did.'

'So that's it. Megacity can't have more than 12 floors.'

'But Roopak is saying that he has applied for a special approval and he is sure of getting it. Can he really get MCA to approve this?'

'I doubt it. Now tell me what you want me to do?'

'We don't want to do this deal. We desperately need

something to prove that what Roopak is planning in Megacity is illegal. There is no municipal rule documented that can prove this. No one in MCA would speak about it and neither will MCA formally approve the revision. How can we get some evidence to prove that this is illegal and thereby decline this deal?'

'I'm sure everyone in MCA is covered by Roopak. They would just keep mum and watch him do what he wants to do; no use going there. The best thing you can do is to continue insisting for the final building plan approved by MCA. In the meantime, let me try to get some more information. How urgent is this whole thing?'

'We have to disburse the amount soon; maybe in the next couple of days. We have very little time.'

Sanju went silent for a few moments and then said, 'What immediately strikes me is that Mr. Hegde, who was the earlier municipal commissioner of MCA, has retired and lives somewhere close to Bangalore. There's a remote chance that he can give us some information that can help us. It's worth a try. But I'll need at least two days to do this.'

Arun shrugged: beggars couldn't be choosers.

'Ok, Sanju. We'll try to hold them at bay until you get back to us. Thanks for your help.'

After the call, Arun briefed Ganesh on his discussions with Sanju and Ganesh said, 'Thanks dude. There is a silver lining to every dark cloud. Don't worry. Tomorrow will be a better day.'

They drove home, marking an end to what was largely a day of frustrations.

Chapter – 17

THE 'STING' WAY

July 2003

THAT MORNING IN BANGALORE SANJU WOKE UP EARLY AND had a quick breakfast. She had come there to attend a series of workshops on environmental awareness, which were likely to continue for another seven days. But she felt that Arun's issue was an important one and hence decided to put her best foot forward. She had the personal number of the former Municipal Commissioner of MCA, Mr. Hegde, who had retired last December. She knew him well and she was confident that he could throw some light on this issue of MCA's restrictions on the number of floors allowed in a building. She hesitated a moment and then dialled his number. Someone came on the line and said, 'Hegde here.'

'Mr. Hegde, I'm Sanjeevani here.'

'Who?'

'Mr. Hegde, I'm Sanjeevani, the journalist.'

'Uh-huh...What do you want?'

'I want to meet you for about 30 minutes sometime, within the next two days if possible. I'll be grateful if you can spare that time.'

'What is it regarding?'

'I need some information regarding an old residential builder project scrutinized by MCA that you may be aware of.'

'Of what use would any of that information be now? I'm now retired.'

'Sir. Please. It's important. I...'

He agreed. 'Ok. Tomorrow at 12 noon. I don't have more than 30 minutes.'

'Thank you very much, sir.' She took down the address where she needed to meet him and closed the call.

Now that the appointment with Hegde was fixed, Sanju thought through and listed the questions that she wanted to pose to him. She also wondered as to how to convert the conversation with Hegde into some form of presentable evidence which could be used by Arun or Ganesh. As she kept pondering over it, she hit upon a plan. She realized that the only way Hegde's words could be converted into any form of evidence was by recording the conversation. The old man would certainly not agree to it willingly. So she'd have to do a sting operation. She decided to go out on a limb. With a mini recording device that could record for three quarters of an hour, she felt she could convert this conversation with Hegde into some form of useful evidence. As she thought more about it, she was convinced about the idea and was in fact thrilled at the prospect of a sting operation.

Later that day she went to an electronics shop and bought, not one but two, units of small digital voice-recorders which could be easily hidden in her handbag. She ensured that the instruments had a good enough capability to pick up conversation from a few metres away. She tested them in the shop itself and was satisfied. She kept both of them in her handbag in an effort to get used to carrying them around comfortably.

Chapter – 18

THE FINAL RACE

27th July 2003

AFTER TALKING TO SANJU, ARUN AND GANESH WERE thinking of ways to put-off the disbursement till she got back to them. But the next morning started off on a stressful note for Ganesh.

He received a mail from Cedric asking for a meeting to discuss the next steps in the Megacity deal. He realized that this was his last chance to bring home to Cedric the risks on the project and to emphasize the impossibility of Chand Builders getting the building plan approved for floors beyond 12. He thought of the possibility of Roopak constructing the building without an approved building plan and the MCA at a later date ordering demolition of the building. If AHFL's name was associated with the project, it would sound their death knell. Ganesh would have preferred waiting for Sanju to get back with more information, but having spoken to her only last night he thought she'd take a few days to do something useful. Even as he kept thinking, he got a call from Stacy confirming the meeting at 10.30 am that morning. He had an hour to go.

He informed Arun about the meeting and said, 'Our last chance perhaps. We'll fight this tooth and nail. I want you to accompany me for this meeting.'

'Sure.'

'Summarize all our points on paper and we'll try our best to talk it out with them. Even if Cedric exerts any pressure on us to sign the release of money to Chand Builders, I'll put my foot down. I may never get along well with Cedric after that, but I'd prefer that rather than sign something that we know for sure is downright fraudulent.'

Arun was unsure of the outcome of the meeting. Would Cedric listen to reason or would he push them to disburse? This was going to be the ultimate test for the CEO. If Cedric listened to reason and took a principled stand, he'd do a lot of good to AHFL and also to himself. But if he pushed for the disbursement to be done immediately, he'd be no different from the foolhardy Karan.

At 10.30, both Arun and Ganesh walked into Cedric's cabin. Karan was already there. The spread of papers on the table indicated that they'd been talking for quite a while. The atmosphere seemed tense and unlike other occasions, this time around Cedric was cold in welcoming them. He merely said, 'Come in guys. Good to see you, Arun. You guys seem to be fully prepared.'

Both took their seats and Ganesh opened his mouth to speak only to be interrupted by Cedric, 'Ganesh, before you begin, I wish to tell you that the Board members have given their approval for a go-ahead on this proposal. Your worry on that count is now addressed.'

'Oh. Thanks for the update. In response to your comment about us being fully prepared, I will begin by saying that whatever we say will be in the best interests of AHFL.'

Cedric somehow took this statement as a personal offence, 'So Ganesh, are you trying to say that what I'm doing is not in the best interests of AHFL? Let me tell you that my responsibility in this organization supercedes yours. Your job is to point out the risks and mine is to decide whether I can take that risk or not. I own the P&L, not you. So please, next time you make a sweeping statement, consider who you are talking to.'

Ganesh and Arun were aghast at the way Cedric had twisted the statement. Still Ganesh, determined not to be swayed from his path, waited for Cedric to make the next move. There was an uncomfortable silence for a few moments. Karan enjoyed the spectacle.

Then Cedric spoke again, 'Ok. Let's absorb what I just said and move forward. On this deal of Chand Builders, which seems to have been fully evaluated by us and found satisfactory, I want to know from you Ganesh, in clear terms, when we'll do the disbursement?' He paused for a reaction and when Ganesh was about to speak, Cedric interrupted him again, 'Ganesh, before you speak, let me tell you and Arun the background so that we are all aligned. Roopak has spoken to me again to request a speedy disbursement. He seems to be a decent guy, especially when it comes to respecting us as a lending organization. He speaks quite convincingly about how he'd benefit by his association with us. This frank admission reflects well on the true businessman in him as far as I'm concerned and I like people who are serious about their business. He has a spectacular track record in loan repayments. He's in a rush and I believe it's time for us to recognize it and reciprocate. So, what's holding us back and why do we need more time?'

Ganesh was thinking where to start, when Cedric continued, 'Ganesh, I've come to realize that we as financiers cannot always hide our inefficiencies. We have to show some aggression. In the earlier situation when you wanted to give a lesser amount of Rs. 250 million, I supported you. You must now appreciate what Karan is going through and also the fact that we cannot continue to ask for time till eternity.'

Ganesh then started to talk, 'Cedric, first of all, we received all the papers for the project only two days ago. We're being asked to complete the entire evaluation in three days when it would normally take eight to ten days.'

It was Karan who spoke, 'What's wrong with that expectation? You've already done the property visit and the valuation reports are positive. Now what's left is the lawyer's report. If you push the lawyer, he can give it to you now. I'm sure he's not going to discover anything new. Plus, we also need to understand that there's a poor customer sitting there waiting to get the money. We cannot keep him in limbo forever.'

'Karan, you'll have to let me complete first. Neither is Roopak a poor customer, nor are we putting him in limbo. When I complete what I want to say, you can decide for yourself who is what. Please bear with me.' Ganesh then turned towards Cedric and spoke, 'As of now the status is that the papers are with our lawyers and we're awaiting the title certification report, on the receipt of which we could say that the basic checks are complete.'

Now Cedric was impatient, 'So when are you getting your lawyer's report?'

Arun answered, 'It will take 3 more days.'

Cedric was stern, 'Why? What does he do with the papers for so long? Why would he need more time? When did you give him the papers?'

Arun answered him patiently, 'We gave him the papers day before yesterday. He usually takes seven days.'

Cedric seemed incensed, 'Does he hatch eggs on them? Why the hell does he need seven days? I'll give you a lawyer who'd do it in a day.'

Ganesh interrupted, 'Cedric, that's not possible. Lawyers do a search in the office of the sub-registrar, going through their records to give us a complete report. It's not possible for them to do it earlier than at least seven days. In this case, we've asked him try his best to do it faster, but I don't expect anything from him at least for the next 3 days.'

Cedric made a gesture of total resignation by throwing

both his hands up, 'You guys do what you want. But tell your lawyer that he just has a day to come back to you with the title certification report. If not, this is the last report we're doing with him. Change the damn lawyer!' It was a completely irrational side of Cedric that Ganesh saw that day.

Despite his growing disquiet, Ganesh kept his temper in check. For a few moments he didn't speak, and then he decided to convey to Cedric the key issues with Megacity. He said, 'Ok Cedric. I'll tell that to the lawyer. Apart from the valuation and the legal checks, considering the size of the deal, we've done some market checks with others and collected some information that does not augur well for us. Arun spoke with some people in Millennium Bank who had declined Roopak's original application for loan on this project. And also, we do not yet have the final approved building plan.'

Karan bristled, 'Ganesh, what's your point? I did tell you that the final plan for floors above the 12th floor was pending approval with MCA. I told you that Chand Builders would give that to us after our disbursement. I did ask you for a special dispensation here. In fact, your valuers should have got this when they visited the site. They didn't. But I gave you this information on my own.'

Ganesh kept his cool, 'Karan, we had known this even before you told us and you didn't tell us on your own, as you claim now.'

'But I did in any case tell you. Recognize that.'

'Ok. Allow me to complete my point. Roopak's people at the site have corrupted our valuers and ensured that they didn't do their job, which was to inspect the property fully and value it properly. The valuers were bribed with gifts and money in exchange for a positive report.'

Cedric found that disgusting, 'This is ridiculous. Why do you have such valuers working for us? Have they done this in other cases as well? And how are you so sure that they were bribed?'

Ganesh felt these were fair questions and answered placatingly, 'I'll surely take it up with them and we'll investigate this. But the fact is that Megacity will have more than 12 floors and in Ayravati that is illegal. Arun also spoke to the valuer of Millennium Bank who confirmed this. MCA will never approve a construction beyond 12 floors in any building. The builder is playing foul trying to dupe us to approve and fund a project that doesn't have the final approval. We can't finance a property that has illegal floors. Let me also add that the same concern has been voiced by another source. Arun checked with Sanjeevani Desai, the journalist, and she also confirmed that any construction beyond the 12th floor would be illegal. So we have heard this from two independent sources and therefore we believe that Megacity is illegal. We must not do this loan.'

Karan was shocked. In all fairness, he had no knowledge of any of these subtleties, except that the approval of the revised building plan by the MCA was going to take more time. He therefore reacted angrily, 'All these allegations about my valued customer are baseless. You're consulting everyone else in the market. I don't know who this Sanjeevani Desai is and what her political agenda is. If I were you, I wouldn't listen to this rubbish. She can say whatever she likes. It's we who need the business. And why do you have to go to another valuer instead of going by what your own valuers say? Why do you have to think that Roopak bribed them? It just goes to prove that you are deliberately looking for ways to sabotage this deal. I've told you clearly that Roopak will submit the approved building plan for the higher floors soon. It's just that he is in a rush for funds now. This is a deal that comes with zero risk. All your allegations are baseless. All of it looks like a figment of someone's wonderful imagination.'

Ganesh exclaimed, 'Zero risk? You're putting the credibility of AHFL at stake, if you go ahead and finance this deal. This Roopak doesn't think straight. He's a mercenary who wants to make money, by hook or crook. He's two-faced. He's trying to defraud the government, defraud the people who buy homes in this project and defraud us by getting us involved in this. He cannot get that MCA approval. I strongly advise you to convey our regrets to Chand Builders ASAP.'

'Ganesh, you're impossible. I'm telling you that the plan will be given to you with all approvals. Don't weigh Roopak on the same scale as any other ordinary customer. He is a shrewd businessman, yes, but he's also a thorough gentleman. He'd never try to commit a fraud of the magnitude you portray. It's dangerous to cast aspersions as serious as these without any proof. Apart from this market information from dubious sources, what proof do you have that MCA will not approve construction above twelve floors? Is it written in the MCA rulebook? If yes, please show that to me. Roopak may have many enemies in the market who are spreading false rumours; let us not fall prey to that. If Roopak comes to know of this, he could sue AHFL. And *that*,' Karan stressed on the last word, 'would be a dent on our credibility whereas taking an exposure on this deal will only enhance it. You're now taking this discussion on a totally different tangent. Cedric, I urge you to intervene now and sort it out; I am tired of fighting this battle.'

Ganesh tried to get Karan to see his view, 'Karan, I agree that I don't have any concrete evidence to prove the illegality of the construction. But from what I've heard, it's clear that there's a problem. You need to think of this as a possibility. What if there's some truth in all these statements? Don't you think as prudent financiers we should at least check and satisfy ourselves on the extent of truth in these statements? The assessment of the proposal has to take all these issues into consideration.'

'Ganesh, you're the one making loose comments without thinking. I repeat, Roopak has admitted that he's constructing higher number of floors there and has applied to MCA for a revision of the building plan. He's promised to me that he'll get it. I'm convinced that he's speaking the truth. For a builder as big as him, this is an ordinary approval. MCA approves all kinds of deviations. So why not this one? Let's not invent stories and kill this wonderful deal.'

Ganesh realized that this conversation was going nowhere. He turned to Cedric, 'Well, I've said whatever I knew about the deal and I now give you my final recommendation. I don't support this disbursement. I very strongly feel that Megacity will have illegal floors which will never be approved by MCA. I don't have concrete proof now. Maybe if you give us some time, I could get it. I don't want to go blind on the risks that have come to light. We're talking of a massive deal and even if you collect the money back, *one* thing goes wrong and the credibility of AHFL would take a beating. This deal carries

a significantly high reputational risk. As your risk advisor, I strongly advise we stay away from this deal. I rest my case here.'

Karan reacted, 'Ganesh is hell-bent on killing the relationship we have with Chand Builders. This is a clean and straightforward deal. We'll not only make a lot of money in it, we'll also gain an association with Roopak that'll help us through the next several years when growth in retail home loans business for us is absolutely critical. He's giving us a project that'll be the pride of the country and we'll get exclusive rights to finance individual flats as well in this project. The only drawback is that we get the approved final plans a bit later. I maintain, as always, that it'll be a monumental mistake, if we turn down this deal.'

Cedric, who had heard both the sides, saw the buck coming around and resting with him. He knew he'd have to take a decision and soon. Karan's arguments were perfect this time, but he couldn't simply ignore what Ganesh said. His quick mind raced through different options. By a process of elimination, he arrived at one final choice that he zeroed in on. He said, 'Ganesh, I face the challenge of finding the middle path which also has to be logical. Very frankly, if I were to accept your allegations on this project; particularly about the illegal construction, I'll need sound evidence to convince myself. And you have none. So it's critical for you to get some form of data or information to back your claim. We can't be found arbitrary in our decisions. We need to inform the customer the reason for rejection of the loan.' He then turned to Karan. 'On your side, you've been presenting your arguments with a great deal of conviction and reasoning. However, you cannot isolate yourself from the issues that Ganesh has raised. If we were caught financing a project with illegal floors, we are doomed. We don't want to shoot ourselves in the foot. There is no choice now than Roopak giving us the final approved building plan from the MCA. If that is done, we go ahead with the disbursement. Not otherwise.'

Ganesh thought over this for a moment and felt that Cedric had been fair in the overall assessment of the situation. So he just said, 'I agree totally. Thanks for your support in insisting on the approved building plan. That'll be one important requirement fulfilled.'

Cedric saw Karan going ballistic. He waved him to calm down and said further, 'Now I want both of you to keep this in mind: we're running against time. We have a customer who has to be attended to urgently. Karan, you'll tell Roopak that he must get the approved building plan. He has to use his entire wherewithal with the MCA and get it out. The minute it is done the loan gets disbursed without any further questions. And Ganesh, you do whatever is required to research and get evidence to prove that the higher floors in Megacity will be illegal. If we get any evidence to that effect the loan gets declined without any further discussions. The game is to see who between the two of you manages to accomplish his tasks *first*. The decision goes in *his* favour. Karan, I agree with Ganesh that as prudent lenders, we should not ignore the requirement of final approved building plan. And there Roopak unfortunately has no choice but to put up with the delay. Sorry.'

Notwithstanding the bumpy manner in which Cedric had started the meeting, Ganesh and Arun felt that he had handled the situation in a fair manner. Now they had some time. Ganesh's hopes were pinned on Sanju. Karan on the other hand looked extremely dejected. He didn't have the courage to go back to Roopak and ask for the final approved building plan, especially when Roopak had clearly told him that he wouldn't be able to give it now. But he had no choice as Cedric had given a final ruling in the matter. But Karan decided to tell Roopak everything that Ganesh said; everything about the allegations on the project; everything about Mishra and Sanju. That was the only way he could convince Roopak of his own helplessness.

The meeting broke up. The race had begun for the collection of their individual deliverables.

Ganesh and Arun returned to their desks. They were very confident that Karan would not be able to get that final approved building plan so easily. Arun called Sanju once again and briefed her on everything that had happened in the meeting with Cedric and impressed upon her the criticality of the information that she needed to gather.

For Arun and Ganesh this day seemed better than the previous day. But neither knew that it would be Karan who would have the last laugh.

Chapter – 19

CONSCIENCE?

27th July 2003

AFTER THE DISAPPOINTING MEETING WITH CEDRIC AND Ganesh, Karan reached his office and called Roopak immediately.

'Yes Karan. When am I getting my money?'

'I need to meet you urgently. I can't discuss everything on the phone.'

'Why? What's happened? Tell me now.'

'My RMQ head Ganesh has made some serious observations about Megacity. He says it's illegal to construct more than 12 floors in any building in Ayravati. He's also saying many other things. I need to meet you urgently. It looks like we'll need the final approved building plan for Megacity after all. The loan may not get disbursed without that document.'

Roopak absorbed each and every word carefully and the devil in him started gnashing his teeth. Roopak asked Karan to come to his office immediately. He then called Dave and Gopal to his office. As soon as they arrived, he started shouting at the top of his voice,

'They have found out everything about Megacity. How? What was to be kept under wraps is now out in the open. Who's responsible for this? I'll kill that bastard. Both of you have been closely associated with this project and know everything. If either of you had goofed up, you better run for your life. You won't be spared.'

Gopal and Dave stood there horrified as they heard Roopak. They had no answers.

Dave mustered some courage and said, 'We are equally shocked, Roopak. We have no idea.'

Roopak yelled back, 'Find out. Find out who that is and kill him on the spot. I don't want him spreading this all over. I want him dead now. Do you understand?'

Dave and Gopal had no response to that and kept staring at Roopak blankly. The next couple of minutes was spent in the most uncomfortable silence ever. Roopak was restless, trying to figure out the course of action. Then they saw his face stiffen. Roopak spoke in a low voice, 'There is no other way.'

He looked at them menacingly and said, 'I am going to ask you for something. This must be done without fail.'

Both nodded, wondering as to what he was going to ask of them.

Roopak said, 'Listen carefully. I need the approved building plan for the entire 20 floors of Megacity on my table by tomorrow morning. If you have it in you, get MCA to approve the plan. Tell the MCA engineer that if he doesn't cooperate, he won't live to see the morning sun. If you can't do that, just forge an approval and give me the forged copy of the approved building plan. But remember, the forged copy has to look exactly like the original. The stamps and seals used should be the real ones used in MCA. The MCA staff has had enough fun all these years with our money and gifts; it's payback time. I want this disbursement from AHFL to go without any hitch and I'll need the approved building plan for it. Gopal, it's your responsibility. You have a liaison guy,' Roopak stopped for a moment, snapping his fingers trying to remember his name, but he couldn't. The impatience went to his head and he screamed, 'What the hell is his name?' Gopal answered in a trembling voice, 'Lokhande, Sir.'

'Yeah, whatever. Tell that guy that he doesn't go home until he gets us that piece of paper with the original stamps and seals from MCA and the signature of the executive engineer. If the engineer refuses to sign, break his fingers and forge his signature. Dave, you block the full page advertisement in all the leading dailies for three days starting day after tomorrow. The caption should prominently say that Megacity has been approved by AHFL and loans are now available, exclusively from AHFL. I want to show that media plan to Karan tomorrow. You guys leave now and I need an update every hour on the progress.'

Dave and Gopal left Roopak's office.

A little later Karan arrived. Roopak welcomed him with a pleasant face, offered him a seat and asked with a sense of urgency, 'Yes Karan. What the hell happened?'

Roopak heard the whole story patiently, only asking some occasional questions now and then. Karan finished by naively saying, 'Roopak, I know all these allegations made by Ganesh are meaningless. You could sue those bastards if you want. But I'd suggest that we first look at some way to get this building plan approved and get the disbursement out. I'll help you with whatever information you need to screw those guys later.'

When Karan finished, Roopak asked a pointed question, 'Karan, you just have to tell me whether you're on my side or not?'

'Of course I am. Your wish is my command. What do you have in mind?'

'First, I want you to know that everything you've heard from Ganesh is true.'

Karan blanched. It was unbelievable. He cried out, 'Whhhaaat?'

'Yes. All of it is true. I hadn't told you before.'

Karan's mouth went dry. He had never in his dreams expected that someone could be so fiendishly devious. He felt sheepish about his assertion all along that Roopak was a gentleman. And he'd been cursing Ganesh for being foolishly stubborn. But now it turned out that he was right all along.

The boot was now on the other foot. He realized that he had been taken for a ride and he felt cheated. As Karan was still absorbing the shock of what he'd just heard, Roopak said,

'I know how you feel. But please don't worry; I'll give you the approved plan by tomorrow for sure. Just tell your guys that Roopak has arranged for the approved building plan from MCA. Keep the disbursement cheque ready tomorrow.'

Karan was unsure of his course of action right now, but impulsively he tried to attend to an immediate doubt that crossed his mind.

'But how would you get the approved building plan so soon? You'd said that it would take longer!'

'Karan, I'll either get you a real approved building plan or one that looks like the real one. You don't have to worry. I assure you that you won't be in any kind of trouble. No one will know the difference. I'll get a perfect job done.'

Karan felt he was hit by a ton of bricks, 'You mean, you'll forge the approved building plan?'

'Yes,' Roopak was unabashed, 'We'll submit the approved plan and get the disbursement. Let me also add that I'll take care of you well. Very well!.'

Karan felt he was falling off a high cliff. He needed to think fast. He got up from the chair with his head lowered. He moved around the table in an effort to settle his mental riot. He went through the arguments in his mind about right and wrong, good and evil, truth and falsehood.

Roopak saw Karan's conundrum and said, 'Karan, if you remain my friend, you'll be unbelievably rich in no time.' He didn't want Karan to think too much.

Karan's heart pounded wildly. He could hear it loud and clear, 'No. No. This is not right. I cannot stoop so low. I have values.' That was what he wanted to say.

But despite himself, Karan felt his strength giving way and his resistance weakening. The temptation was so powerful that finally, after several minutes of thinking, he succumbed to the devil standing by. He felt his clouds of confusion slowly clearing. This timely help to Roopak would go a long way in cementing a professional and personal relationship with him and ensure a permanent flow of future retail business. It would also pave the way in the future for Karan to grab the CEO's seat. This seemed like a golden chance. With surprising clarity, he decided to make the most of it. He could get an assurance from Roopak of an exclusive tie up for all of Chand Builders' projects, present and future, with the promise of an unending flow of business every month. Karan decided to throw his conscience out of the window and get his share of the booty. But he wasn't sure how to convey his state of mind to Roopak. So he asked clumsily, 'Roopak, are you sure that there's no other option left?'

Roopak's cunning and shrewd mind had read the dichotomy in Karan's mind and he decided to reassure the man, 'No Karan. Absolutely none. And I can't let all my efforts go down the drain. Megacity cannot fail. I'll not let your risk guy win and stop the disbursement.' Roopak paused for a moment and then spoke again, 'Karan, I promise you that I won't let you down. You're my friend and I want you to win. If you get the disbursement done, you can be sure of my generosity. I'll sell the project at a premium, with the approval from AHFL. And then the retail business will boom for you. Besides, you'll see your personal bank account soar to new heights. Your lifestyle will catapult to a different league. So don't think further.'

For the first time ever, Karan heard someone make such an open and bold offer to corrupt him. His excitement was palpable. His dying conscience tried to warn him; sound him off that he was digging his own grave. But it was too feeble to achieve much. Roopak's proposal was so damn attractive that Karan was unable to resist it. As his mind struggled thus, Roopak aimed another shot at whatever was left of his conscience, 'As a token, I'm giving you a plot of land on the outskirts of Ayravati right away; it is valued at Rs. 5 million. Keep this as a gift, my friend. The value of this land will grow to Rs. 20 million very soon.'

This last offer pretty much cleared the air for Karan. He had been thinking of buying a plot and now this seemed to him as a fortuitous gift. He took stock of his options: he needed to lie low when Roopak sent the new approved building plan to AHFL. That was it. He further rationalized his decision to accept the gift of the plot of land thus: first, he felt that his own job was just to procure the documents. It was Ganesh's responsibility to check their veracity. So Karan should not be expected to know about the forgery. What if Roopak hadn't informed him and still submitted a forged plan? So it really didn't make a difference. Second, it was just one document that was forged. As long as AHFL made its money, why should it bother them? He was sure Roopak would repay the loan in time. Therefore, in the process, if he himself gained a little something, what was wrong? He thought, 'I should just celebrate for winning the battle with Ganesh *and* for getting the booty.' With his confusion resolved, he spoke with confidence.

'Fine, Roopak. I'm with you. I'll help you pull the wool over Ganesh's eyes. You'll have to ensure that all individual loans from all your projects across the country should come only to me. We should become the largest acquirers in the market. I don't want anything between me and the CEO's seat now. I'm willing to sell my silence only on this condition.'

'Don't worry, my friend. Your personal objective is my goal as well. You and I will go places together. You just wait and see.'

Roopak then fixed drinks for both of them and they toasted their forthcoming victory. Roopak assured him that once the disbursement was done, he'd arrange a larger celebration.

Karan left Roopak with his heart brimming with joy at his new found fortune. He looked forward to seeing Ganesh's expression when he would produce the approved building plan. His own conscience of course lay buried ten feet below the ground.

Chapter – 20

THE CRITICAL DOCUMENT

28ᵗʰ July 2003

IT WAS 10.30 AM AND ROOPAK WAS IN HIS OFFICE WITH DAVE and Gopal. There was a fourth person as well – Lokhande – sitting there with disheveled hair. Every man's eyes were glued to a bundle of fresh ammonia blueprints. These were the building plans of the Megacity project, with the original MCA stamps and seals of approval, thus confirming that MCA had approved construction in Megacity up to 20 floors. The signature of the concerned MCA officer was on all the documents. Only, these signatures were so wonderfully forged that even if the original signatory were to see them, he would not doubt their veracity. These prints had arrived at Roopak's office that morning at 7 am, after being manufactured overnight by Lokhande and some of his close cronies in MCA, who had access to the bona fide stamps and seals of MCA. The date stamped on every ammonia print was 27th July 2003. Roopak had reached the office early enough and was examining the forged copies of the project plans. He'd spent nearly two hours trying to detect the forgery. He examined the prints with microscopic precision. Even with more than two decades of experience in dealing with property papers and building plan documents such as these, he couldn't discover that these ammonia print copies of the 'approved' plan for 20 floors for Megacity were forged. It was a masterful work of forgery. After a thorough study he came to the conclusion that when he himself was fooled, how could people in AHFL, who definitely don't have his depth of experience, see through the forgery. Gopal placed the current set of building plans approved till the 12th floor alongside this new plan that had the approval till the 20th floor. There was absolutely no difference whatsoever in the quality of the papers and shapes of all different MCA seals and the signatures on both the plans. They were all identical except for the difference in the number of floors approved. Roopak was understandably impressed with the quality of work and he praised Lokhande generously.

'Lokhande, this is superb. Splendid work, I must say. You'll be suitably rewarded for this work. But,' he paused and then said, 'Let me bring home to you the truth. You must realize the importance of keeping this knowledge within the four walls of this room. The only option I have for people who try to act smart with me is....,' he got up from his chair, went near Lokhande, took out the revolver from his pocket, held it to his head and said, 'Kill!' He relished the look of terror in Lokhande's eyes and said, 'Keep this in your bloody mind and be very, very careful. Ideally, I'd have killed you, but the only reason I'm letting you go is that I might need your excellent services in the future as well.'

Lokhande, who was now perspiring profusely, said with a trembling voice, 'Yes Sir. I'll hold my tongue.' Roopak then turned to Dave and Gopal and said, 'This applies to you guys as well. Both of you know how ruthless I can be if required. So behave yourself.'

Both men nodded their heads silently.

Roopak then picked up the phone, 'Karan, when can you come to my office?'

'Have you got the approved building plan?'

'Did you have doubts? Come along quickly and pick it up . . . and yes, cut my cheque immediately.'

'Wonderful. I'll be there in a jiffy.'

Karan reached Roopak's office in record time. He scanned the copies of the first set and the second set of approved plans, sanctioning 12 and 20 floors respectively, and his eyes popped out. He couldn't tell the fake from the original until Roopak told him. They looked so damn original that Karan felt foolish for worrying so much. He exclaimed, 'Roopak, *now* nothing can stop your Megacity from getting the seal of approval from AHFL. Plan your advertisement campaign. Just wait till I get back to my office. I'll get the disbursement processed immediately.' Even as he left Roopak's office, the stage was being set in a village near Bangalore, to uncover evidence that had the potential to annihilate these men's dreams.

Chapter – 21

THE CRITICAL EVIDENCE

28th July 2003

AT ABOUT THE SAME TIME THAT KARAN LEFT ROOPAK'S OFFICE with the forged plans, Sanju was nearing Hegde's bungalow for her scheduled meeting with him. Hegde lived in his native village that was located about 200 kilometres from Bangalore. It had taken Sanju more than five hours in her rented car to reach the village. The driver of her car struggled to maneuver the car through the many potholed stretches on the road. But she'd started early from Bangalore and reached well in time for her appointment with Hegde. She located the bungalow and waited in her taxi at some distance from the bungalow. She mentally ran through the questions that she wanted to ask him. She checked her handbag and found both the digital voice-recorders safely placed, which would record her conversation with Hegde and generate that important evidence which Ganesh and Arun had been looking for. She was clear of the purpose for which she'd purchased two voice-recorders instead of just one. After waiting for a good half an hour, Sanju got out of her car and walked confidently into the sprawling bungalow that was spread out over a 1000 square yards plot.

On the porch sat a man in his late fifties, sporting a bald pate, reading the newspaper. As soon as she saw him, she slipped her hand into the handbag and switched on the recording buttons on the extreme right of both the voice-recorders. She then approached him with the respect that befitted his age and said, 'Good morning Mr. Hegde.' He welcomed her politely but colourlessly, 'Good morning, Sanjeevani. Please take your seat. Can I get you some water?'

Sanju was initially conscious that their conversation was getting recorded. But soon she overcame that inhibition and started conversing freely.

'No Sir. Thank you. Since you have other things to attend to, let me come to the point straight away.'

'Ok.'

'Sir, I need some information about the project Megacity.'

'Which project? Megacity? Where's it located? I don't remember the name.'

But Sanju was quick to notice the discomfiture that showed on his face at the mention of the project.

'Sir, please try to recollect. It's a project that's being built by Chand Builders and is located in the heart of Ayravati. The construction started in your period.'

Hegde responded now with a tinge of arrogance, 'Possibly. So what about it?'

'Sir, did you approve the building plans for this project during your tenure as the Municipal Commissioner?'

'During my tenure as the Municipal Commissioner of Ayravati, I approved a lot of things. It's difficult for me to remember all that I approved. But in any case, building plans don't come to the Municipal Commissioner for approval.'

'Sir, this one is not an ordinary approval. Roopak, the owner of Chand Builders, is planning to construct more than 12 floors in this building and you know that twelve is the maximum number of floors that one can build in Ayravati. Roopak must've spoken to you?'

'Sanjeevani, you must be aware that at MCA we always followed our bye-laws.'

'Yes sir. I'm aware. That's the reason I'm asking you if you have any idea of this project. For an issue as serious as this, he couldn't have approached anyone other than the Municipal Commissioner himself. This project has been under construction for more than a year and a half and construction should've commenced during your tenure as the Commissioner. Knowing Roopak, I'm sure he spoke to you.'

With that last line, she hammered home her point.

Hegde was clearly uncomfortable. He wanted to get rid of her fast, but he knew Sanju well and hence he was sure she wouldn't leave without getting what she wanted. He also remembered personally pledging his silence to Roopak. He did a quick rethink and decided to share with her some parts of the story that he felt were harmless and then be done with the conversation. He was completely unaware that Sanju was recording their conversation. He spent some time trying to fake loss of memory and finally said, 'Yes. I think Roopak approached me for a special approval for this project.'

'Thank you, sir. Can you tell me what you told him?'

'I refused the request. Roopak and I had this conversation only once and the issue was killed then and there.' He thought that would stop her in her tracks. But Sanju was not giving up so easily, 'Sir, did you get a formal application from Chand Builders for this special approval or did he just discuss this informally with you?'

'He came to get my in-principle clearance, which I declined.'

'Sir, did they make a formal application?' Sanju repeated her question.

'I don't remember.'

'Sir, please try to remember. He must have made a formal application to MCA.'

'Maybe. But how does that matter? As per the norms of MCA, whenever we get a formal application we have to accept it. We accepted it like any other application. My staff informed me that an application had come. I just told them to reject it and send a rejection notice to Chand Builders.'

'Are you aware if they sent a rejection notice to him?'

Hegde was getting infuriated at the incessant questioning and he tried to trivialize the issue, 'Sanjeevani, I was on the verge of retirement and I had plenty of other, perhaps more important, things on my plate. I think I instructed my staff to issue a rejection notice. I don't know if they actually sent one or not. Anyway, for me this was just one of myriad issues to close before my last day. So there was no way I could keep track. But I do want to know, why are you so interested in knowing about Megacity?'

'A friend of mine works for AHFL. They've received an application from Chand Builders for a builder loan of Rs.500 million against Megacity. Since I've researched buildings and builders, this friend of mine asked for my advice. I only need a confirmation that MCA has already rejected the application of Chand Builders seeking permission to build more than 12 floors in Megacity. With that confirmation he can stop the loan from getting disbursed to Chand Builders and prevent AHFL from funding an illegal building.'

Hegde merely said, 'Whatever; don't involve me in your communications with AHFL. I'm out of the picture now. You shouldn't quote me anywhere.'

'Sir, I won't quote you unless it becomes really necessary. Your statement is very important, because this issue concerns the civic discipline on a subject that *you* stood by during your working years. One last point: did you actually instruct your staff to send a formal rejection letter to Chand Builders for their application to build more than 12 floors in Megacity?'

Hegde was fidgety, 'Yes, I made a remark in the file on the cover page. But let me make myself clear, Sanjeevani: please don't drag me into any controversies. I asked my staff to issue a rejection notice. I don't know what happened after that and it wasn't my job to track that either. Let's bury this discussion here. You aren't authorized to use this discussion anywhere.'

Sanju was like an albatross around his neck. She pursued her goal doggedly. 'Sir, will you hold this view even if you know that your earlier decision is going to be overruled and Chand Builders may go ahead and make a monster of a building which would violate this key rule in the bye-laws of MCA: a rule that came into existence because of the high seismic potential in that region! Don't you think it's your moral duty to speak against it? Please help us make a public statement on this.'

'I don't want to get involved in this. This happened during the course of my career and at that time I acted in the manner that my conscience advised. I rejected the deal. Beyond that I couldn't have done anything. Yes. You can say that I should have checked with my staff whether they actually sent a rejection notice or not. I didn't because I had several other things to attend to before my last working day. And I never looked over the shoulders of my staff unless it was extremely critical. And this was definitely not a critical item.'

Sanju was extremely attentive to every word that Hegde said. She caught on to his words: *Yes. You can say that I should have checked with my staff whether they actually sent a rejection notice or not. I didn't...........not a critical item.'* This statement perturbed her. In the last few minutes Hegde had mentioned twice that he was not aware whether a formal rejection notice was sent to Chand Builder by his staff or not. Why was he emphasizing this point about his lack of awareness of whether the formal rejection was actually sent or not? It struck her as very odd. Besides, was this issue so unimportant? Or did he actually know that the rejection notice was not sent and chose to remain silent about it? Or did he perhaps issue the instruction himself, withholding a formal rejection, thereby keeping the application in a 'pending for approval' status? Several questions crossed her mind. She probed further, 'Sir, do you then believe that there is a possibility of your staff not having actually sent the formal note of rejection to Chand Builders? Is it possible that they kept the file with them or hid it somewhere so that it couldn't be found?'

This directly indicted his erstwhile team and indirectly Hegde himself. Offended, Hegde now raised his voice, 'Sanjeevani, what're you trying to say? If you wish, you may go and ask the staff who're still there. For me it's a closed chapter and…....'

Sanju interrupted him, 'Mr. Hegde, is it that you are actually aware that a formal rejection *wasn't* sent to Chand Builders and also what your staff did with that file?'

This direct attack shocked Hegde. He was taken aback. But he recovered quickly and snarled at her, 'Do you understand the repercussions of what you're saying? I can sue you for making these false allegations. The interview closes now. You can leave this place.'

She was persistent, 'So, you were an accomplice in this deed!'

Hegde screamed, 'I said leave! If you don't, I'll have to get you thrown out of this place.'

She shrugged casually, 'Ok. I'll leave. One last question: may I quote you? That is to say, can I say that you had declined the application of Chand Builders to construct beyond the 12th floor in Megacity, but due to your busy schedule, quite justifiably, you didn't check if a formal rejection notice was issued?'

'No. You do not have the permission to quote anything I've told you. If I'd known this, I would never have agreed to meet you.'

Sanju said softly, but loud enough for him to hear, 'If need be, I'll surely quote you.'

Hegde was enraged. He was frothing at the mouth as he said, 'In that case, if you quote me without my permission, I'll completely deny everything that I've told you. You can't prove anything. Try getting that old file out of MCA. There're thousands of such files that come and go. You'll never be able to find it. I'll maintain that no such project ever came to me. You'll cut a foolishly sorry figure. Go ahead and quote me generously.'

Sanju was appalled at Hegde's audacity and complete apathy towards the issue on hand. She tried to reason with him one last time, 'I'm sorry if I bothered you too much. I just feel that you should take a stand on this issue. I feel that you should come out in the open and state clearly that you warned Roopak not to go ahead with the project. If you don't take that stand, you'll be cheating your own conscience.'

'I can tell right from wrong. I repeat, if you ever try to quote me, I'll deny everything. And let me warn you: Roopak is a fiend and can go to any extent to remove obstacles from his path. If he gets to know of this investigation on his Megacity, he may not hesitate to even kill you. Megacity is his ultimate dream. Leave him alone and let him do what he wants. Why are you so worried? It doesn't impact you. Don't come in his way. I am sure you've better things to do in life.'

This was good enough for Sanju to up the ante and make her point clear to Hegde, 'Sir, you were a civil servant who held an important position in your career. Roopak is blatantly violating something that you had protected in your professional capacity. If you know something and stay silent, you're failing in your moral duty. This could have disastrous consequences. You cannot wash your hands off the past - both yours and Ayravati's. About the possible threat to my life, please don't worry. If there is one good thing I have learnt from my life, it is to stay true to my beliefs. Your threats cannot stop me from calling a spade a spade.'

'Enough. Now get out of here. I'm calling the guards.' He rose from his chair and took a few steps to call someone. Sanju took out one of the two voice-recorders from her handbag, rewound the tape and pressed the 'play' button. The sound from the voice-recorder reached Hegde's ears. In one second flat he realized that he'd been trapped by this woman. Stunned, he turned back.

Sanju now gave him a direct threat.

'Mr. Hegde, I've recorded everything we discussed so far. You cannot ever deny that you didn't know about the illegal floors of the Megacity project. In fact you know everything and if something goes wrong with the project, this recording is good enough to lead the police to your doors. It's therefore beneficial for you that you cooperate with me fully.'

Hegde's face was a study in consternation, stupefaction

and fear. In mellower tones he now asked her, 'What do you want, Sanjeevani?'

'Tell me everything you know about Megacity and about Roopak's plans.'

'Are you going to record everything that I tell you?'

She switched off the voice-recorder and said, 'I'll stop recording now and whatever you say from now on will be off the record. If you tell me the complete truth, I may actually consider *giving* you this singular piece of evidence that I have against you. But that's only on the condition that you tell me the truth and I am fully satisfied that it is so.'

In the next fifteen minutes, Sanju came to know everything, well almost everything that had happened between Hegde and Roopak. Hegde told her about Roopak's audacious attempt to get the building plan approved for 20 floors. He admitted to restraining his staff from sending a formal rejection to Chand Builders. He also narrated as to how he felt totally powerless against Roopak's political clout. He mentioned receiving calls from political higher-ups telling him to cooperate with Roopak and Roopak telling him that he would construct 20 floors regardless of whether he received MCA approval or not. He thus recounted the entire story to Sanju.

And Sanju recorded it all in the second voice-recorder that was still safely in her handbag. This now was good enough evidence to prove to anyone that Roopak was building illegal floors in the Megacity project and that the MCA was hand-in-glove with him.

Sanju believed most of what Hegde had said; although she had a lurking feeling that Hegde had withheld some sensitive details. She thought of a strong possibility that Roopak would also have bribed officials of MCA, including Hegde for their cooperation and silence. Expecting Hegde to admit it on his own was asking for too much. Happy with whatever she got in this visit, she decided to leave.

As promised, she handed over the first voice-recorder to him. Hegde heaved a huge sigh of relief as he took it, not knowing that Sanju carried in her handbag a bomb in the form of a second voice-recorder. With a huge smile Hegde watched Sanju walk out of his bungalow. As soon as she'd stepped out, Hegde went in and dialled a number.

Sanju was satisfied with what she had got out of her meeting with Hegde. She moved to her rented car and after getting in, she tried to call Arun from her mobile phone. Her mobile phone did not catch the signal in that remote village and hence she could not get through to Arun. She checked the time. It was 1 pm. She had to inform Arun of this recorded evidence as early as possible. Sanju realized that she must get closer to an area that could have the required telecom signal to be able to get in touch with Arun. She'd carried with her some packing material. She packed the voice-recorder nicely and secured it with tapes. She addressed the packet to Arun Balachander and wrote his mobile number on it. She also wrote on the packet in bold letters 'STRICTLY CONFIDENTIAL. TO BE OPENED BY THE ADDRESSEE ONLY.' She then asked her driver to start the car and drive back to Bangalore.

Chapter – 22

THE ACCURSED DAY

28th and 29th July 2003

KARAN WENT BACK TO HIS CABIN AND PICKED UP THE PHONE, 'Cedric, I have news for you. Roopak has used his good offices with the MCA and obtained the final approved building plan. It's now signed, sealed and delivered and he's given us a copy of the same.'

Cedric was surprised at the speed with which the plan was obtained. But he didn't suspect any foul play and said, 'Congratulations Karan. You've done what we thought was impossible. I'm happy that we're going to complete this deal with all the paperwork done. I guess there is nothing pending now. Please inform Ganesh and let's meet in my room in 10 minutes.'

Ganesh was shocked to receive the news from a jubilant Karan even as he realized that it was another one of Roopak's dirty tricks. He had a strong suspicion that this was a forged copy of the approval. He squealed, '20 floors? Are you sure, Karan? How can someone construct twenty floors when the approval-limit is only for 12 floors? It's impossible to get this building plan approved so fast. Till about two days back you were saying that Roopak will not be able to get the approval from MCA before our disbursement and that it would take time. How has he managed it so fast from that bloody bureaucratic MCA? It just rouses further suspicions on the deal. I'm certain that this plan that you have, is a forged one and I'll certainly make this clear to Cedric.'

At first Karan was daunted by the fear that Roopak's underhand dealings were now clear to Ganesh. But then he reassured himself that it was just a wild guess on Ganesh's part and nothing more. In any case, Karan felt as long as there was no evidence to the contrary, the ammonia prints and the approval seals on them must be taken as genuine. He shouted back, 'Ganesh, enough is enough. As per the conditions laid down by Cedric, all your terms have been met. You've no goddamn reason now to decline this deal. Apart from silly and baseless allegations, you have not produced any concrete evidence. We have the approved building plans; all the drawings are with me and the disbursement has to happen now.' With that Karan banged the phone down.

He then called Cedric and let loose a torrent of words,

'Cedric, we have a fresh issue now. Without even looking at the approved building plans Ganesh says they're forged and Roopak is cheating us. I am sick and tired of this. I was extremely wary of going back to Roopak once again to ask for the plan. But I did it only for your sake. Cedric, a builder of such credibility will not resort to a silly trick like forging a plan. I've fulfilled every single condition imposed by Ganesh and you. It is only fair that we now disburse the loan without asking for any more questions.'

Cedric asked Karan to come to his cabin. He also sent for Ganesh. Both reached Cedric's office together. Cedric looked at them and said in a stern voice, 'Come on in, gentlemen. Sit down. So how do we go ahead now?'

Ganesh plunged in, 'Cedric, we shouldn't go ahead with the disbursement. Till about 2 days ago we were being told that the approved building plan would take time to come in. How then, I ask, had this been possible in so short a time? As I already said, it is impossible for MCA to have approved this plan. We are being fooled by …'

He was not allowed to complete by Cedric, whose voice had risen, 'Enough Ganesh. Not a single thing you've said has any evidence to back it. How can we take this stance then? I've given you enough chances to prove your point. Now, I cannot go back on my words. Karan has also committed to the customer that on submission of the approved building plan the disbursement would be done. I have to disburse the loan now without any further delay.'

Ganesh spoke softly in pleading tones, 'Cedric. Please try to understand. It's easy to forge a plan.'

Karan now fumed, 'This document isn't forged. It's a genuine document. I'll officially raise this impudence to the Board of Directors and ask for a change of guard at the RMQ helm since no business can ever be done with such a stubborn attitude.'

Cedric added quietly, 'Ganesh. It's over now. We need to disburse. Go and authorize the disbursement without a moment's delay. No more discussions!'

Ganesh walked out of Cedric's office totally disoriented. He reached his office, closed his cabin door and slumped in his chair. He took his phone off the hook and switched off his cell phone. He just wanted to be alone for a few moments. He was deeply affected by both Cedric and Karan bulldozing him into signing a disbursement that he was instinctively opposed to. He moped that he was being treated with utter disregard. That he couldn't prove any of his doubts was extremely unfortunate. He was afflicted by a momentary sense of self-pity and placed his face in his hands in an attempt to stop himself from crying.

Arun walked into Ganesh's cabin and saw Ganesh in a distraught state. He asked worriedly, 'What happened boss?'

'We don't have a choice but to disburse the loan now. They didn't believe me when I told them that the plan is a forged document. As the RMQ head, I feel frustrated that in spite of knowing everything, I'm unable to act on it. If only we could get some damning evidence to prove all this! Where's Sanju, Arun? Can you check if she has something? She's our only hope now.'

'I've been trying for a long time, but can't contact Sanju.

She was going to meet Hegde today. He stays in a remote village and so she must be out in the wilderness somewhere. Honestly, I don't have big hopes from her as she can't give us any evidence. She can perhaps only give us some information and that too if she gets Hegde to speak up.'

Both of them sat silent and crestfallen. After some time, Arun asked Ganesh, 'What do we do now? When do we have to disburse?'

As he asked this question, an officer from the operations unit – where the disbursement cheques are prepared – walked in with a disbursement memo for Rs. 500 million in favour of Chand Builders. The disbursement memo was the voucher that had to be signed by Ganesh to authorize the preparation of a disbursement cheque. Ganesh's signature on this disbursement memo would be the end of everything. A banker's cheque for Rs.500 million would be drawn in favour of Chand Builders the next instant. Once the cheque was cut, the customer would be asked to come to the office of AHFL, complete documentation formalities and collect the cheque. Megacity would then stand formally approved by AHFL.

Ganesh politely told the officer from the operations unit to leave the disbursement memo with him and leave. When the officer left, Ganesh kept looking at the disbursement memo that he'd been ordered to sign by Cedric. He was devastated. He'd faced several other difficult situations in his career, but never one as severe as this where he had been instructed to authorize something that he knew for sure was a fraud. He looked at his watch. It was 2 pm. Four hours to go before the office closed for the day. He decided to somehow spend the next two hours without signing the disbursement memo. He just hoped that some miracle might happen that could influence Cedric to change his mind and stop the disbursement. Then he told Arun to try reaching Sanju again, hoping that she'd have something for them.

But her phone was not reachable. After several attempts, Arun almost gave up. A few moments of deadly silence followed. Suddenly, Arun's phone started vibrating and then let out a shrieking ring. It was Sanju on the line. Arun picked up the phone excitedly and let out a yell, 'Sanjuuuu! Where have you been?'

Sanju interrupted Arun and quickly apprised him of every detail of the conversation that she had had with Hegde. As Arun listened to her, Ganesh could observe from Arun's facial expressions that some positive development had taken place. Arun said to her, 'So that means what we suspected is correct. But Sanju, we're in a tearing hurry here. We've been pushed to a corner and must disburse this loan immediately. Roopak has forged a building plan for Megacity that shows the approval for 20 floors and has submitted it to us. Ganesh tried his best to convince people here that this man is a fraud. But nobody is ready to believe us. In the absence of any immediate evidence, we'd be required to disburse any moment.'

Sanju then told him about the recorded interview and Arun got to know that it contained clear evidence to prove that what Roopak was doing was definitely illegal. Hearing this, Arun's excitement knew no bounds. He was then informed by Sanju that one of her friends was flying by air to Ayravati from Bangalore next day early morning and she would send the evidence – the voice recorder with the recorded cassette in it – through this friend. Arun took down some details about this friend whom he should contact at the Ayravati airport to collect the voice-recorder and closed the phone conversation with Sanju. That voice-recorder was now the only available piece of evidence that could help them establish the fraud being perpetrated by Roopak.

Arun shared this miraculous development with Ganesh. Even though the proof had come in a bit late, they thought they could still present it to Cedric and urge him to reconsider. If the proof was as strong as Sanju mentioned, it'd be easy to prove that advancing a builder loan for Megacity would end up financing illegal floors. Once convinced, Cedric would have no choice but to decline the deal. But somewhere subconsciously both Arun and Ganesh had a lurking fear that Murphy's Law would act, as it always does.

The flight leaving Bangalore at 4.30 am the next day, 29th July, would land at Ayravati at 7 am. Sanju had told Arun that he should expect a call from her at around 3.30 am, when she would confirm to Arun that she had handed over the packet to her friend at the Bangalore airport. Arun could then go, meet Sanju's friend at the Ayravati airport and collect it.

Ganesh and Arun decided that they should leave the office immediately without signing the disbursement memo and somehow remain non-contactable through the remaining hours of the day. They decided not to take any calls from Karan or Cedric. The next morning when they all met in the office, Ganesh would have the evidence with him. He could then play the voice recorder to Cedric and force him to reconsider his decision to disburse the loan.

Sufficiently excited by the prospect of a concrete evidence to prove their point and their just conceived escapade, they prepared to leave the building furtively. They slowly sneaked out of the office and reached the parking lot, got into Arun's car and drove away. Before they left, Karan had tried to reach Ganesh twice in his office, but Ganesh didn't take the call. As they were leaving the office, Cedric had also called once on Ganesh's phone. Ganesh didn't take that call either. He knew that they were calling to check if he'd signed the disbursement memo. He stood firm on his decision not to take Karan's or Cedric's calls and avoided fourteen calls from Karan and three calls from Cedric till 7.30 pm that evening. Arun also had six missed calls from Karan. They were now looking forward to the next stage of news to arrive, which would be very early morning next day, when Sanju would call Arun and confirm that she'd handed over the packet addressed to Arun, to her friend at Bangalore airport. Both of them left the office and reached their favourite coffee joint, Temple Coffee House where they munched some snacks and dunked themselves in coffee to curb their nervousness. They remained there till 9 pm. It was another six hours to go before they would get a call from Sanju. They decided to go home for some rest and meet again at Temple Coffee House in a few hours to receive the message from Sanju. Thereafter they would go to the airport and collect the voice-recorder from Sanju's friend.

* * *

Earlier that day on 28th July, soon after Sanju left his house, Hegde called Roopak and bleated all the details of his meeting with her.

Roopak, after handing over the forged plans to Karan, was just beginning to feel comfortable. He felt that he had arranged for and resolved the most critical obstacle to Megacity:the approved plan. This call from Hegde and the new development about Sanju's involvement in the Megacity affairs, completely unsettled him. What Sanju had done was unbelievable. This Sanjeevani Desai! Why must she interfere in my work? Why try to record a conversation with Hegde stealthily? The questions pummeled him. In Sanju, he could see a huge mountain of a problem brewing. And if someone would get even a whiff of it, his dream of Megacity could crash in no time. He was getting panicky and was uncertain on what he needed to do. Should he inform Karan? No. Karan was on his way to formalise the Megacity approval. So what must he do about Sanjeevani Desai?

As he kept deliberating about this issue over and over through the day, he saw himself coming to the same conclusion again and again. After several hours of such deliberation, he firmed up his decision and looked at the clock. It was 7 in the evening.

Roopak acted quickly. Even though Hegde had told him that Sanju had handed over the voice-recorder, Roopak knew that she was steadfast in her pursuit and personally for him, she represented a major threat given her attempt at getting Hegde to talk. He knew that she was capable of raising this issue in the highest forum and would in all probability initiate a media trial. She was a forceful writer and all her articles had a large readership. He couldn't let her do that. Even though she'd given the voice-recorder to Hegde, the very fact that she attempted to record everything only meant that she was a threat to Roopak's dreams. Roopak again thought over his decision for a while, and then called up one of his nefarious contacts in Bangalore and asked for a favour.

When he connected on phone with his Bangalore contact, he gave the directions, 'Sanjeevani Desai. The investigative journalist. She is somewhere in Bangalore now. Find out where she is. Catch her when she ventures out. Make it look like an accident. Must be done at the first opportunity. No trace should remain. You'll be suitably rewarded.'

The Bangalore assassins absorbed the information and commenced their work immediately. With their widespread network of informers, it took them less than 3 hours to find out where the popular journalist, Sanjeevani Desai, was putting up in Bangalore. It was a 4-star hotel, located near MG Road, a happening place in Bangalore, where people hung out in clubs, restaurants and shops, till late at night.

One of the assassins, accompanied by a well-dressed, good looking, well-spoken woman, landed up near the hotel, where Sanju stayed, at about 10.30 pm. The woman with him gave him a wonderful cover of a friendly couple, happily loitering around. Some discreet enquiries in the hotel confirmed to them that the journalist was indeed staying in the hotel since a few days. All enquiries were done by the woman, who pretended to be a close friend of Sanjeevani Desai. They found out that Sanjeevani Desai had returned to the hotel that evening by 8 pm, had dinner with a few friends and returned to her room at around 10.30 pm. They also learnt that Sanjeevani Desai used a hired car for moving around in the city for her work and that she usually left the hotel in the car by 8 am every morning, and returned by 7 pm. The assassin particularly enquired about the description of her car and learnt that it was a black Honda.

The assassin now knew what he had to do. He made a call to his assistant, got him to arrange for a huge trailer truck and bring it to a point near the hotel. He got the truck parked at a safe distance from the hotel; at a place from where he could see any vehicle leaving the hotel and follow it. He estimated that 8 am in the morning wouldn't be that bad. The traffic would still be light. The truck needed to simply follow the car, smash the car to pieces at a convenient location and disappear. He had done it several times before. He would do it again.

It cost the assassin Rs.4000 to make some helpful arrangements. He paid Rs.2000 to the hotel security guard, for sharing useful information on Sanjeevani Desai's movements. His lady companion's smiling and well-meaning presence, made it easy for him to get the guard to help. Besides sharing useful information about Sanjeevani Desai, the guard also agreed to dial a number immediately, when he would see Sanjeevani Desai leave the hotel in her car. The guard was informed that, friends of Sanjeevani Desai had arranged for a surprise reception for her, and therefore they needed to know the instant when she left the hotel, so that they could be ready. The local drunken cop was paid Rs.2000 to let the assassin park the truck for the night, in a no-parking zone.

THE ACCURSED DAY

By 1 am on 29th July, the assassin had made all the arrangements. His companion's role being over, he sent her off. He then sat at the driver's seat on the truck. The assassin and his assistant, then closed their eyes for a quick nap, expecting to get a call from the guard at around 8 am in the morning.

* * *

A couple of hours earlier, at around 11 pm, Sanju having returned to her room after a busy day, placed a request for a wake-up call at 2 am and went to bed to get some sleep. She had to get up early to reach the airport by 3 am next morning, meet her friend who was flying to Ayravati by the 4.30 am flight and hand over the packet she had for Arun.

At 2 am, the phone in her room rang aloud, the noise amplified by the quiet of the night. Sanju woke up and got ready to leave. She remembered to carry the packet containing the voice-recorder and placed it in her handbag. She had asked her driver to reach the hotel by 2.30 am that morning. She called the hotel reception to enquire if her car had arrived. The car was there. She picked up her handbag, locked her room and stepped out. Venturing out alone, that late at night, was the least of her worries as her own life experiences and her work had toughened her well-enough.

Sanju walked through the reception, out of the main-hotel door, reached her waiting car and got into it. She greeted the driver and apologized for disturbing him at an unearthly hour. The driver acknowledged the greeting, told her that his job often demanded working through the night and hence he was used to it. He turned on the ignition and drove towards the exit gate of the hotel.

The guard who was befriended by the assassin had identified Sanju getting into the car. Although surprised that she was leaving the hotel at that hour, true to his word, he took out his mobile phone and dialed the number he was asked to dial by 'friends of Sanjeevani Desai', who had met him a few hours ago, earlier that night and also paid him Rs.2000 for this help.

The assassin, who was dozing off in his truck, woke up with a start, when the sound of his mobile phone ringing pierced through the silent precincts of the night. Surprised to receive the call at that hour of the night, he recognized the guard's number and took the call. To his astonishment, the guard informed him that Sanjeevani Desai had just left the hotel in her car. It was way too early and he hadn't expected that she would leave so early. But the next moment, the assassin knew that this was the best thing to have happened. An accident in the dead of the night would attract much lesser attention and make it easy for them to get away. He couldn't have asked for anything better. He woke his assistant up, to help him look for Sanjeevani Desai's car.

In a few moments, the two men spotted Sanjeevani Desai's car. The car came out of the hotel, turned right in the opposite direction of the truck and moved on. They waited for the car to go some distance. The assassin, who was on the wheels then started the truck and drove it in the same direction. He maintained a comfortable, controllable distance from the car and followed it, taking care to keep the noise of the truck away from the car.

Even as his eyes kept glued to the car, he saw the car picking up speed and go about a kilometre ahead on the same road, turn left and take the road to the airport. The Bangalore airport was a good twenty kilometres away from the city. The truck followed the car and took the same turn. In the next minutes it became increasingly clear to the assassin that the car was indeed going to the airport. There was many a lonely stretch en-route to the airport. The assassin quickly zeroed in on the location where he would hit the car. The chosen spot was another eight to ten kilometres away. The location fixed was a one kilometre elevated stretch of the road that had a 40 metre deep valley of rocks on the left.

Sanju's car kept moving, followed by the truck. Neither her driver nor Sanju had any suspicion of anyone following them. Given that time of the night, there were very few vehicles on the road.

About a kilometre before the elevated portion of the road, the truck suddenly picked up speed. The distance between the truck and the car, which was around 200 metres all along, reduced quickly. By the time the car had reached the elevated portion of the road, the distance between the truck and the car had narrowed to about 30 metres. The headlights of the truck had become more prominent. The driver of the car noticed the truck covering up the distance fast and saw that the headlights of the truck had started flickering. He continued driving the car at a steady pace. In anticipation of the truck driver wanting to overtake him, he moved the car to the left lane allowing sufficient space for the truck to overtake.

In the next few seconds, the truck was just a few metres behind the car on the right lane. Then in a flash, the truck came dangerously close to the car, took a slight turn to right and in a swift move, turned left and menacingly collided with the car on its side. The driver and the passenger of the car were startled. But all of it happened in a fraction of a second. The hit was so severe that the black Honda car skidded on the road for several metres and then toppled over the railings on the left of the road. It fell into the valley hitting and bumping off rocks before it came to rest at the bottom of the valley, brutally smashed. The digital clock on the car read 3.15 am on the 29th of July.

There were no survivors.

Having completed his work to perfection the assassin quickly scanned the surroundings. There were no other vehicles on the road. Satisfied, he drove the truck away at reckless speed. The assassin confirmed the killing to Roopak at 4 am.

* * *

About an hour before the accident took place in the Bangalore airport road, back at Ayravati, having caught up with a few hours of rest, Ganesh had returned to Temple Coffee House at 2.30 am and waited for Arun. Arun came ten minutes later. They had only been thinking all along about the call that they would get from Sanju any moment now, confirming that she had indeed handed over the voice recorder to her friend in Bangalore. As the time inched closer to 3 am, their heartbeats started to get louder. A reassurance that the packet was on its way, was important for both of them.

Thirty minutes passed. Their anxiety kept growing, but no call came from Sanju. They waited, for they could do nothing else. Another hour passed. No call from Sanju.

They didn't know that the flight had left Bangalore as per schedule; Sanju's friend had also travelled on the flight, but he didn't have the packet with him.

The time kept ticking and it was 5.30 am. Arun tried reaching Sanju on her cell phone, but it was not reachable. Then in extreme desperation, Arun called the Airlines' office to check if the Bangalore - Ayravati flight had taken off and was informed that the flight had taken off as per schedule. He gave the name of Sanju's friend and asked if that passenger had boarded the flight. The answer was in the affirmative.

The possibility of a situation where in Sanju failed to handover the voice-recorder to her friend was frightening. The disbursement to Roopak could not be stopped then. In any case they'd be in a soup explaining to Cedric why they went non-contactable. It would be the funeral of their careers for sure.

* * *

At Bangalore, at the accident site, at around 5.15 am, one of the highway patrol vehicles, with two policemen in it, spotted broken railings on the elevated stretch of the airport road and stopped to examine it. The skid marks on the road and a few broken fragments of a vehicle at the spot made it obvious to them an accident had taken place there. They sighted the car that had fallen off the road. A few minutes of close observation from the elevated road, made it clear that the accident had happened recently. The cops slowly climbed down and reached the fallen vehicle. The large and deep dent on the side of the car indicated that the accident had happened because of collision with another heavier vehicle. They then saw two corpses, severely disfigured by the impact of the hit and the fall. They identified a woman and a man. Quickly both of them made the relevant calls.

The ambulance, the forensic team, more policemen, a crane and a couple of journalists, would arrive at the scene in about 30 minutes. While waiting for the others to arrive, the two cops started to examine the vehicle thoroughly.

The first to reach was their senior inspector, with his team. The name and rank badge on his uniform read, Subir Kuruvilla, Senior Inspector. As he got off his jeep, he quickly climbed down to the car and took an update from the two cops who had discovered the accident.

As a first step, Subir registered a first information report as a roadside accident in which a large sized vehicle that had collided with the black Honda car and caused the car to topple over the railings. At the accident site the police waited for forensic experts to arrive, examine the damaged car and other evidence at the site.

By 6.30 am the accident site had attracted a fair amount of attention. The place was teeming with police, a few local journalists, an ambulance, bystanders and the forensic experts' team. There was a crane waiting there to lift up and tow the car to the police station after the experts completed their work. The forensic experts did their assessment and collected all the details for their report. The corpses were then sent for post-mortem in the waiting ambulance. The owner of the car was to be identified and called for an enquiry. From its commercial number plate, the car was identified as belonging to some taxi operator.

Subir, tried to put things together, as he stood there at the accident site. He called his office and gave the registration number of the black Honda to his officer and asked him to locate the address of the owner from the Regional Transport office and ask him to come to the police station. Subir then examined the things that were obtained at the accident site. He noted that after searching thoroughly they'd just found a water bottle, the car's registration papers and two mobile phones. Subir had known instances where accidents happened at lonely stretches on a highway and if travellers died, groups of people from nearby villages came and pilfered valuables such as gold chains, watches, handbags etc. This was a common occurrence. He was fairly confident that the lady must have carried a handbag. But when the team couldn't find it at the site, he concluded that the handbag must have been stolen. Out of the two mobile phones, one was totally damaged. The second phone seemed to be in working condition. The owner information recorded on the phone revealed to him that the phone belonged to one Sanjeevani Desai. He'd heard of Sanjeevani Desai the journalist, but it was too much of a long shot for him to conclude that so soon. He browsed through the telephone numbers on that cell phone and found frequent calls to one number, to someone named Vinay. Subir dialled that number from the same phone. Vinay came on the line and Subir introduced himself. After a fair amount of questioning, Subir learnt that the deceased was indeed the journalist Sanjeevani Desai, and that Vinay was the fiancé of the deceased. He then revealed the news to Vinay that Sanju had died in the car accident and that Vinay should come down to Bangalore immediately. It was 6.40 am of 29th July.

By 6.50 am, Subir got a call back from Vinay confirming that he would be taking the 9 am flight that morning to Bangalore and that he would reach Bangalore by 11.30 am. Subir asked him to come directly to the police station. After that conversation, Subir switched off Sanju's phone in order to avoid attending to other calls that could come on the phone.

* * *

About an hour before Subir spoke to Vinay, Ganesh and Arun left for the airport at 5.45 am after having waited for a long time. They were overwrought and were hoping against hope that Sanju had indeed handed over the packet to her friend, but had just forgotten to call Arun and inform him. As they thought along these lines, a killer question that hadn't occurred to Arun so far struck him for the first time – was Sanju safe?

He didn't know if his mind was overreacting. He shared this fear with Ganesh as well. Ganesh endorsed the fear. Their only hope now was the friend at the airport. The focus of their thinking shifted from the evidence collected by Sanju to Sanju herself. Even if Sanju had missed passing on the voice-recorder to her friend, the two men were prepared to play hide and seek for one more day and if need be one of them would fly to Bangalore by the next flight and personally collect the voice-recorder from Sanju. But Sanju needed to be safe. It seemed to them that the earth was caving beneath them.

They reached airport at 6.30 am. The flight arrived as scheduled at 7 am. At 7.20 am Sanju's friend walked out. Arun had a placard that had her friend's name written on it for identification. The friend saw them and informed them that Sanju spoke to him in Bangalore and was to see him early morning in the Bangalore airport. He said he had waited for Sanju at the Bangalore airport, but she hadn't turned up. He seemed worried as well. Having conveyed the message, he went away.

Dispirited and blind to the future, the Ganesh and Arun sat in a corner of the airport at 7.30 am in a distraught state. The mental strain of having sparred with Cedric and Karan the earlier day, playing truant from office, revolting against Cedric by refusing to take his calls, insufficient sleep through the night and all the other stresses made the morning in office seem like hell. They wondered what they should do. Should they attend the office today? Should Ganesh simply sign the disbursement memo? That would ease the pressure a bit, but still the insubordination exhibited by leaving the office without informing people and going almost underground would not be pardoned easily. Karan was clearly the winner now. As both men brooded over their next steps, Arun noticed the silhouette of a familiar individual at a distance. As he got up to go near, his phone rang. It was his wife Ananya on the line. He took Ananya's call, but kept walking towards the familiar figure. Ganesh followed him. After a few moments, Ganesh heard Arun yelling on the phone in a troubled tone, 'Oh ......No....No.....No. Ananya, are you sure? When did Vinay call you?' There was a pause, 'Oh my god .... Ok, let me call you back.' Arun's face was panic-stricken as he heard Ananya confirm Sanju's death to him over phone. Arun ran towards the familiar figure, which he recognised as Vinay. Arun ran closer to him and placed a hand on his shoulder.

A flustered Vinay turned around. Vinay then shared with him the call received from Inspector Subir from Bangalore and gave him a description of what he'd learnt about the accident. Arun held him tightly for a few seconds. Vinay was choking and spoke with difficulty.

Arun was in an uncontrollable rage deep within at what had happened. He held himself responsible for this unfortunate death of a soul who he felt had a lot more social, civic and national value than hundreds of Aruns put together. He was also not sure if he should tell Vinay the background of why she'd travelled in that car to that weird location outside Bangalore. Arun put himself in Vinay's position and tried to think. He was convinced that it would deeply upset Vinay to know this later from somewhere else. He had to tell Vinay everything and now. He tried to converse with Vinay.

'When is your flight?'

'In about an hour.'

Arun spoke hesitantly, 'Vinay, I understand your position now, but there's something that I must tell you. This is about Sanju.'

Ganesh stood next to Arun who then took Vinay through the entire trail of events that had prompted her to undertake that fateful journey. And then Arun shared with Vinay his fear that this may not be an accident but murder. He tried to speak objectively, but once he finished, he broke down uncontrollably. Vinay heard all this with a pale face devoid of expression. He felt even more shattered that Sanju should have met such a gory end. Slowly the tears welled up and he hugged Arun, weeping in his shoulder uncontrollably.

Ganesh had by now figured out that Vinay was Sanjeevani's fiancé. After a few moments, when it seemed appropriate, Ganesh took Arun aside and asked him if he'd like to accompany Vinay to Bangalore. That had not occurred to Arun till now. But having been prompted, he felt it was his moral duty to accompany Vinay to Bangalore. Quickly they rushed to the empty ticket-counter to organize the tickets for Arun. Vinay mumbled how grateful he was that he would have a friendly face and a shoulder to cry on at a difficult time.

Arun called home and informed Ananya. Then sparing a thought for Ganesh, he asked, 'Ganesh, you're in a tight spot. What're you going to do today?'

'I don't know. But for you, nothing else is more important than going to Bangalore with Vinay and being with him. And do give me a call as soon as you get more details. I'll handle

Cedric here. I will be in office today surely, though not sure how the day would go.'

With just 30 minutes left for the departure of the flight, the two men entered the airport and Ganesh walked out of the airport. It was 8.30 am of 29th July.

* * *

By that time, the news that the famous journalist Sanjeevani Desai had died in a car accident had spread through the media circles in Bangalore. Hordes of journalists, accompanied by their cameramen had assembled at Central Hospital, where the bodies of Sanju and her driver had been brought for post-mortem. And the reporters had started sending news and stories, which were now being relayed in almost all the local and national news channels. This had by now become the headline news item for the news channels, even as every reporter and presenter expressed severe shock and grief at the death of a deeply respected fellow journalist. The news reports stated that in the road leading to Bangalore airport, a black Honda was reportedly hit by a fully loaded truck that seemed to have smashed the Honda from its side. The telecasts also showed the clip of the accident site. Two bodies drenched in blood were extricated from the damaged vehicle with great difficulty.. While both the corpses were severely disfigured the investigating team had identified one of the corpses as that of Sanjeevani Desai and the other as that of the driver of the black Honda. There was however no trace of the truck that had hit the car. It seemed like a hit and run case.

The news of Sanju's death spread through media circles all across the country like wildfire. While the news took the TV channels by storm, the print media people, although aware of the event, missed getting that item into that day's newspapers, as the accident had happened in the early morning. Therefore the news had still not spread amongst a good majority of the general public who devoured newspapers for their morning dose of news.

Unaware of all the noise that Sanju's death had created in Bangalore and the blaring news channels, Ganesh reached home at 9.15 am. Ignoring the questioning stares of his family members, he went straight to the bathroom, picked up a bucket full of water and poured it over his head in an effort to ease the heaviness in his head, and drenched himself fully. His head was buzzing with too many things. He was physically exhausted as well. His eyes were drooping and dying to sleep, but he resisted sleep. He had to think. In that fully drenched state, he walked into his study and locked himself in there. He plonked himself in a corner on the floor and with a tremendous effort, tried to gather his wits.

He went through each and every stage of his analysis of the builder loan proposal: right from the time when Karan presented it, for the first time in June, till the moment he saw Arun and Vinay leave for Bangalore an hour earlier. He raised several questions to himself. He started with the question whether he and Arun had blown things out of proportion in analyzing the deal. Was it really such a bad deal after all? Should he have just signed the disbursement and closed the chapter? He was playing devil's advocate with himself. He thought of Roopak. The only image of Roopak that came to his mind was of a shrewd, experienced, cunning and a ruthless builder, who could eliminate every obstacle that came his way. But he also forced himself to think that Roopak was known to have dealt with his financiers fairly decently. Then he asked himself why he hadn't approved the disbursement? Was it because Megacity had 20 floors and the top 8 floors were illegal? There was indeed a building plan with those 20 floors approved, which had been submitted to AHFL. So what was the problem then?

The next set of questions pierced his ego. Who knew for sure that it was forged? How could he level such allegations at Roopak? What if MCA had actually made an exception in this deal? Why the hell could he not give the benefit of doubt to the customer in this case, when the customer was financially strong, the property was excellent and the loan amount was a pittance compared to the property value? Everything in the proposal was in perfect order and if he'd simply signed it, things would've turned out easy. Over and above all else, Sanju would've been alive. Then he thought of Sanju, who had laid down her life in the process of collecting evidence for Arun and himself. The question that disturbed him the most was: why had Sanju stretched herself so much? Why did she agree to help Arun and decide to conduct a sting operation on her own in order to obtain the evidence? Arun had just requested her for some help. It was in fact her idea that she should meet Hegde and record the conversation. Was she right in doing that? Why was it necessary to take things so seriously? What would have been lost if this one disbursement *had* happened? Why did she put her life in danger? Perhaps it was her core belief system. It also could have been because Arun requested her personally, and she held him in high regard as a well meaning individual. And who had hell prompted Arun to speak to her? The answer to this question jolted him. It was he himself. Ganesh remembered that he was the one who had, under severe stress and desperation asked Arun if he could ask Sanju for help. And that suggestion had ended in Sanju's death. The more he thought about this, the more he felt mawkish. He felt as if he had killed Sanju himself. A sense of guilt devoured him. If he had simply cleared the loan proposal, this gory end could've been averted.

He didn't know what to do next. He had a tough day ahead of him. Karan and Cedric would be waiting to get the disbursement memo signed and even if he told them about Sanju's death, they wouldn't believe that she'd been killed by Roopak. In fact, it'd be considered impudent to even allege that without any proof. In all fairness, it would be wrong to accuse anyone, even Roopak, of such a heinous crime, without a complete investigation. What if Sanju had actually met with an accident? That was a possibility and couldn't be ruled out. Ganesh felt that he had no choice but to be professional and clear the builder loan the next day. For the first time, his own conviction that the builder loan proposal for Megacity was a fraudulent one, wavered. He wondered if he and Arun had been juvenile and possibly reckless and hence indirectly responsible for Sanju's death. His eyelashes drooped desperately and he dozed off sitting in that corner. But in the next few minutes he woke up with a jerk. The buzzing in his mind due to the overwhelming guilt, topped with the realization that he and Arun could have been more sensible about this loan proposal, kept pricking him uncomfortably. He felt pained from within. The tiredness in his body caused his entire body to ache. He rubbed his eyes in an effort to keep awake. But fell asleep again in that uncomfortable position. When he woke up and looked at the watch it was 10 am. He thought of the office. Karan and Cedric were probably planning on ways to crucify him and Arun. But he was too tired and exhausted and his body and mind desperately needed some rest. He thought he would attend the office in the latter half of the day and face Cedric. He set the alarm for 2 pm and lay down on the cold hard floor to get some sleep. He closed his eyes, leaving his mind in that dangerously undecided state.

* * *

Arun and Vinay, took the 9 am flight from Ayravati and reached Bangalore at 11.30 am. They went straight to the police station. The police station was crowded with a lot of media personnel, who had reached there to gather more information of Sanju's death. When Vinay and Arun reached the police station, at first they were not noticed by anyone. They walked into the police station and met Subir. Vinay produced his identity proofs and explained that Sanju had no other close relatives. The engagement ceremony had been a private affair and Vinay showed some photographs of that as proof that he was indeed her fiancé. He had also called his uncle, who was a retired Major from the Indian army and lived in Bangalore. His uncle signed his statements as witness. Subir then cleared the handing over of Sanju's body to Vinay.

Subir also informed both Vinay and Arun that his team was working to identify the killer truck. He assured them that they would have the truck and the driver arrested very soon. After completing the formalities Subir gave him Sanju's mobile phone. Subir didn't have anything else to give them, but he felt from the expression on Arun and Vinay's faces that they were expecting something else. He asked, 'Vinay, were you expecting anything else in her possession?'

'Yes. She had something for Arun that she wanted to hand over to him badly.' Vinay looked at Arun, who was looking down at the floor, as if in shame.

Subir looked at Arun and felt that there was something here that he should know. He said, 'There is a possibility that some of her things were stolen by the local villagers before the police reached. Was it something valuable that you were expecting?'

Arun was saddened because losing the evidence that Sanju had collected by laying down her life meant that the ultimate objective would go unfulfilled. He was worried that Roopak would go ahead and complete the Megacity project with AHFL's open support. He thought of something and he took Vinay aside and spoke to him softly. Subir was observing them from a distance. He could see Arun explaining something to Vinay seriously and Vinay listening patiently. At the end of their discussion, Subir saw Vinay once again putting arms around Arun's shoulders, hugging him and breaking down. Even as he wondered both of them came back and Vinay spoke to Subir.

'Subir, I don't know if it is feasible. But we want to make a request.'

'What is it?'

Vinay looked at Arun and then again turned to Subir, 'I will let Arun explain that to you.'

Arun organized his thoughts well and took Subir quickly through the sequence of events that were happening in Ayravati, why Sanju had met Hegde and what she was carrying with her when the accident took place. He then made the following request: 'Sanju lived and breathed for the cause she believed in. She died in the process of fulfilling her own belief and to help the cause. Just before her death, she collected valuable evidence against the wrongdoers and was on the verge of nailing them. I suspect that she's been killed. Her sacrifice shouldn't go waste. We must make an earnest effort to find that voice-recorder that she was carrying with her when the accident happened.'

Subir was shocked to hear this new side of the story. Now instead of a road-side accident, it seemed more and more like cold-blooded murder. The investigation had to then take a totally different route. Subir considered it for a while and then advised Arun to give a statement in writing so that he could pick it up for investigation accordingly. Arun did that and Subir then discussed the options with them, 'There is a murder angle to it and that needs to be investigated. The first step is to find the voice-recorder that you're referring to, which can possibly give us some clue to track the culprits. I'll need to release a search team in that area to cast their net. I don't know how long that will take. I'm not even sure if you'll ever get it. But from what you've just said, I promise that we'll make an earnest effort to search for that voice-recorder. I can see that it is important.'

After getting the relevant papers prepared in light of this additional information, Subir asked Vinay to go to the hospital and complete the formalities there.

Outside the police station, the media had got wind of the fact that Vinay, Sanjeevani Desai's fiancé, was there at the police station. They waited for Vinay to step out and were all ready to pounce on him with questions and condolences.

As soon as Arun and Vinay stepped out of the police station, journalists surrounded them. However, Subir efficiently managed the crowd. With gentle pleas and requests to the waiting journalists, he made way for Vinay and Arun to leave for the hospital.

Both men left for the hospital where Sanju's body had been kept after the post mortem was completed.

It was 2 pm on the 29th July 2003.

* * *

Exactly at that moment the alarm went off in Ganesh's study at his Ayravati home. Ganesh opened his bloodshot eyes. It had been a terrible night and a devastating morning. But, surprisingly his mind was now absolutely clear on what he needed to do, having examined all the options. The only thing he would be asked to do and would have to do was to sign the disbursement memo.

Ganesh spent some time with his worried and concerned family, dodging all questions on why he had spent the morning in seclusion and why he had not attended office. He then started for the office to complete what he had decided.

Chapter – **23**

THE DAY OF CLARITY

29th July 2003

THE NEWS OF SANJU'S DEATH HAD GATHERED TREMENDOUS momentum and was spreading fast amongst different circles and sections of media and other forums and industries that Sanju was associated with. However, in the office of AHFL in Ayravati that day in the morning business hours, Cedric and Karan, were sitting wondering what they should do, given Ganesh's disappearance and non- contactability. They had no clue of Sanju's death as the newspapers that they had read in the morning, covered nothing about the incident.

It was 11 am and all their attempts to reach Ganesh

and Arun the earlier day till late evening had been in vain. Cedric was hot under the collar and all geared up to lash-out at Ganesh the moment he appeared before him. But what could he do if the man didn't even show up at the office. The all important thing now was to complete the pending disbursement. Dave's man was already sitting outside Karan's office to collect the cheque. But there was no sign of Ganesh. Karan had conveyed to Cedric that the disbursement could not be delayed beyond 2 pm at any cost, so as to enable Roopak to encash the cheque with his bankers the same day.

As per the rules of AHFL, disbursement memos could be signed only by the RMQ head or anyone else with authority delegated by the same. For a deal of this size however, only the RMQ head could sign and no one else. However, there was a provision in AHFL's corporate policy that in an extraordinary situation, when the RMQ head was not in office the CEO, by virtue of being the head of the organization had the right to exercise all the powers of the RMQ head. Cedric thought that the current situation merited such a status.

Even as he wondered if he should sign the disbursement memo, Cedric realized that it was always easy to bully the risk guys into signing something, but when it came to signing the document himself, the whole thing looked very different. Everything that Ganesh said about the deal suddenly seemed to have a ring of truth. Cedric wanted to avoid signing the memo. But he knew that having got in so deep into the deal, it would be difficult to get out. He knew now for sure that if Ganesh didn't turn up, he'd have no choice but to sign the disbursement memo himself. Karan had already got a disbursement memo prepared in a special format for Cedric to sign. This special format described the extraordinary situation that required the CEO of the company to sign the memo. After playing around with all the doubts in his own mind, Cedric rationalized that everything in the deal seemed to be in order and he could not unnecessarily subject himself to agony pangs at this stage. He decided to wait till 1.30 pm. The sense of anger against Ganesh that he'd felt last evening when Ganesh was non-contactable had turned to frustration by last night. This morning it was a sense of complete helplessness.

He waited till 1.45 pm. No sign of Ganesh. Karan looked at the watch and prompted Cedric.

'Boss, we just have 15 more minutes. Can you please sign it now?'

Karan had got the operations unit to prepare the cheque and keep it ready, so that he could collect it immediately on submission of the disbursement memo. The cheque for Rs.500 million in favour of Chand Builders had been printed at 9 that morning and lay in a locker in the operations department.

When Karan prompted him to sign the disbursement memo, a strange fear gripped Cedric. He had butterflies in his stomach and he felt nauseous. He had never signed a disbursement memo even for a small amount. This one was big. But there was no way out. Frustrated by Ganesh's vanishing act, with a quick stroke of the pen he signed the memo exercising the extraordinary powers vested in his position. Without waiting another second, Karan took the memo from him and walked out of the room.

Karan went straight to the operations department, handed over the signed memo, collected the cheque and passed it on to the person from Chand Builders who was waiting. As per Dave's instructions, the Chand Builders representative took the cheque to the bank where Chand Builders had their account and purchased the cheque. The bank discounted a certain amount from the Rs.500 million towards their commission and credited the rest of it into the account of Chand Builders. Thus in a matter of an hour after disbursement at AHFL, the cheque had been encashed by Chand Builders. The evening daily that day would carry an advertisement that Megacity had been approved by AHFL, bookings in Megacity were open and that loan to flat purchasers in Megacity were available from AHFL; only from AHFL as a matter of fact!

Even after an hour of signing the memo, Cedric wasn't sure if he'd done the right thing. He saw the regular disbursement memo lying on his table. He wondered if Ganesh could come and still sign it. He'd get his own approval replaced by Ganesh's approval on the file. But the next moment he realized that it would be a trashy thing to do. He was the CEO of the company. He had taken the decision to sign under exceptional circumstances. It was fine. But if he could still get Ganesh to sign the regular disbursement memo, Ganesh's approval could also be filed along with his own, thereby strengthening his decision.

Karan returned after completing the disbursement. He told Cedric that the cheque had been handed over and was further updating Cedric about the advertisement campaign that Chand Builders had planned. As Karan sat there briefing

Cedric there was a knock on the door. It was Ganesh. He peeped in slightly and then entered Cedric's office. Cedric was glad to see Ganesh. The first thing that occurred to him was that he should get the disbursement memo signed by Ganesh somehow. Cedric spoke first, trying to keep his cool, 'Good afternoon, Ganesh. The RMQ head is always missed in the organization when on leave, but I never missed my RMQ head as much as I did last evening and this morning.'

Despite the horrific events that had happened earlier in the day, Ganesh maintained a cool exterior. He replied wearily, 'I'm sorry about last evening and today morning.' Looking at his eyes both Cedric and Karan could guess that he hadn't slept well last night. Cedric was unsure if he should probe the reasons for his disappearance the previous day. He decided against it and felt that the priority now was to get Ganesh to sign the disbursement memo. He came straight to the point, 'Ganesh, can you please sign the disbursement memo now?'

Ganesh sat on the chair. He had no knowledge that the disbursement had already happened and that Cedric was only seeking Ganesh's signature to strengthen his own approval. On being told to sign the disbursement memo, Ganesh looked dispassionately at the memo that lay on the table, without putting his hands on it. While he seemed in control of himself, his heart simmered with anger and disappointment at the two people sitting in front of him. His feelings ranged from severe rancour towards the people sitting there facing him to severe anguish at what Vinay and Arun were going through. He wondered if he ought to tell them about Sanju's death and thereby prompt them to reconsider their decision.

He was however mentally and physically tired and couldn't garner the energy to pick up another verbal duel with Cedric and Karan. He was also reasonably sure that nothing would change their minds now. Further, he'd thought through it last night. He was clear that there was nothing else left to be done.

Left with no other option, he signed it. That he was saddened by this act was explicit on his face. He'd never signed any paper under such extraordinary pressure. As he signed it, his eyes moistened with what looked like controlled tears. His thoughts were of his family and he knew his wife would be shocked to know what he'd done. After signing it, he had one good look at it again and passed across the signed paper to Cedric. It was his resignation letter!

The disbursement memo remained on the table untouched, unsigned…

Cedric held the paper that Ganesh had given him in total disbelief. It read:

'Dear Cedric,

After due consideration, I have decided to resign from the services of AHFL. I'll carry with me lot of memories; in particular of having worked and interacted with you.

I'm aware that my stand on the current proposal has irked you but I wish to maintain that whatever I said about the deal right from day one, was what I considered to be professionally correct. My view was based on information and facts that I had collected with the help of Arun. I could not unfortunately prove any of it to you and I do carry a deep regret in that regard.

The reasons for my decision to resign are totally personal. I'd request you to accept my resignation and relieve me from my services at AHFL.

Warm regards.

Ganesh Sukhtankar.'

Ganesh looked blindly at the wall ahead. Karan read Cedric's expression and felt that something was amiss. Cedric was dumbfounded as he didn't expect that Ganesh would take such a drastic step. He was also disappointed that the disbursement to Chand Builders now went solely under his own approval, after his failure to get Ganesh's signature on the disbursement memo. After a few moments of pregnant silence and absorbing the shock, Cedric asked, 'Ganesh, I get it that you're not too happy with our stance on this deal. But is that the only reason for you to resign?'

Ganesh was not in a mood to get into any heavy discussion. He just said, 'Cedric, I have already said whatever I wanted to say. I have nothing more to say. I'm sorry that I didn't take your calls yesterday as I was not in a proper state of mind to talk to you. I felt that we were rushing this deal too quickly, without giving due regard to basic hygiene factors. I tried my best to get you guys look at it from the right perspective. It didn't happen. Please feel free to do whatever you want with this deal. Count me out. I'll continue to attend office to serve my notice period of one month.'

Personally for Cedric, Ganesh's resignation was a huge

setback. He felt sad that Ganesh's glorious career with AHFL should come to such an abrupt end because of a single transaction. Ganesh took Cedric's leave and went to his cabin. His thoughts at that moment were with Arun and Vinay. He resisted the temptation to call Arun and decided to meet him in person when he returned to Ayravati.

* * *

In Bangalore, Arun had been with Vinay all day, running around and helping him with all the formalities related to getting Sanju's body released from the hospital. Hence he didn't find an appropriate time to call Ganesh to check on the events at AHFL. During the day he had sent a text message from his mobile phone to Ganesh to check what happened. Ganesh's response: 'Will update you on return.'

Amidst swarming crowds of journalists, other media men, friends and well-wishers of Sanju in Bangalore, Sanju's last rites were completed in Bangalore that day. Vinay and Arun hadn't anticipated that there would be such a large turn-out of people, who wanted to pay homage to Sanju. After the rites were completed, slowly and gradually the media and other people went away.

Vinay and Arun then returned to the police station to have a good look at the black Honda. The crane that carried the car from the accident site had placed it in a corner of the open ground in front of the police station. The black Honda was in a completely battered shape. The owner of the car had been called to the police station for questioning. Subir had done the questioning, taken all the details and agreed to release the battered car to the owner. The owner of the car was completing his work with the policemen at that time to take possession of his car, for whatever it was worth. All things done, he had the formal custody of the vehicle. He noticed that the car was beyond repair and therefore called a scrap dealer directly to the police station and sold the piece at a throwaway price to the scrap dealer. The scrap dealer came with a crane and took the car with him. Arun and Vinay silently watched the vehicle being taken away. They then left for the airport to take the next available flight to Ayravati that evening.

* * *

As soon as he landed in Ayravati, Arun called Ganesh, despite the late hour. Ganesh picked up the phone and with a genuine concern enquired about the way things had gone in Bangalore. Arun updated him and gave him the bad news that the voice-recorder that carried the evidence collected by Sanju was untraceable. Ganesh felt as if all the evil forces in the universe had come together to plot against him and Arun. Then Arun enquired about the disbursement to Chand Builders. Again, considering the need to urgently bring Arun up the curve, Ganesh told him to come directly to Temple Coffee House and meet him there.

They met at the coffee joint and Ganesh began to talk.

'The loan to Chand Builders has been disbursed.'

Arun remained silent. Ganesh waited a second to see Arun's reaction. His face remained composed. Ganesh continued.

'Cedric signed the disbursement memo.' He stopped talking further. Arun could feel some suspense in the air as he said feebly, 'I was sure you wouldn't have signed it.'

'I didn't sign it. Only Cedric did. He'll be laughing on the other side of his mouth very soon.'

There was silence again. Arun sensed a strange uneasiness in that silence. Then Ganesh told him, 'I'm sorry to disappoint you Arun, but I have put in my papers.'

That statement hit Arun like a punch in the gut. His head reeling, he collected his fragmented mind and asked, 'Boss! What've you done? And why? What will now happen to me? What's your plan for me? That place will now be hell for me, without you around.'

'I understand. But I did that as the last resort. I would have had to sign that blood-stained disbursement memo, if I had continued. I went by my own conscience.'

While Arun was disturbed at the thought of working in AHFL without Ganesh, he realized that Ganesh had, by this act of his, exemplified the ultimate courage of conviction. He could only admire Ganesh for that decision, which reflected enormous clarity despite the noise all around.

He said, 'Boss, I salute you for your decision. You've proved yourself by setting standards that are worth living for and dying for. I'm proud to have been your associate and getting to know you personally so well.'

'The feeling is mutual, Arun. Without a colleague like you, I wouldn't have been able to gather as much information on this Megacity deal as we did. You showed the right path. I just took that path. We complemented each other well.'

'Yup. This stupid deal has dislodged us. We've lost Sanju, Vinay is directionless in life, you've resigned and I don't know what will happen now in AHFL. I don't know how long I'll survive in that environment in AHFL.'

Ganesh tried to bring some practicality into their discussion, 'I feel that you should continue working there. I'll recommend to Cedric that you be given charge of the RMQ unit. I'm confident that you can handle it. Don't screw up your career. You're still young and with your abilities, you have a bright future. And I don't have to tell you that I am always available for any help, support and guidance you would need in your work. Put whatever has happened behind you. I know it's difficult. But you have a life and need to look ahead.'

Arun listened to Ganesh attentively. He decided against doing anything as drastic as Ganesh. But he did resolve that from now on he would only focus on procuring evidence against Roopak and try to get him incriminated. He also decided that he would follow the same no nonsense approach that Ganesh had always practised when dealing with Karan and Cedric.

* * *

Next day, the print media covered the news of Sanju's death. When Cedric read the newspaper in the morning, he couldn't miss the large front-page article that carried the profile of Sanjeevani Desai with a photograph of a smiling and pleasant looking lady. The headline read, 'End of a Warrior'. The article covered in detail the road accident. Besides the front-page headline, in one of the inner pages there was a detailed profile of Sanju. It profiled her as an intrepid journalist, a warm person, a persevering activist and a visionary. It also carried the fact that she'd lost her parents in a building crash during the Gujarat earthquake and that's how she had got involved in fighting for environmental issues and illegal constructions.

Cedric finished reading all the articles covering the accident. For the first time now since the time that Arun and Ganesh spoke to him about Sanju, it occurred to him that in supporting the Chand Builders' deal he had probably made a grave mistake. Everything that Ganesh tried telling him about the deal came back to haunt him. In Ganesh's resignation, Cedric felt he had lost a stalwart. There was a feeling of remorse in his heart. But his mind warned him that he was in too deep to swim back to the surface. And he would be lucky, if he survived till that happened.

Chapter – 24

SETTLING IN

August - December 2003

ON GANESH'S RECOMMENDATION, ARUN WAS PROMOTED AS RMQ head at AHFL and the decision was ratified by the Board of Directors. Karan now felt he had an upper hand as he took Arun to be lesser experienced and not as assertive as Ganesh. Karan nevertheless went to Arun's office personally and congratulated him on his promotion as RMQ head.

However, Arun settled into the new role quickly. He soon came to be recognized for sharpness and maturity in his decisions. Cedric was convinced that he had done the right thing by elevating Arun.

Things gradually returned to normal in AHFL. The

individual loan referrals were now pouring in from the Megacity project. Construction in the Megacity project was progressing at breakneck speed and the possession of the apartments to the respective owners was scheduled for June 2004. Roopak managed the MCA officials well enough to keep them away from this project. The rule of 12 floors did not find specific mention in the bye-laws of MCA and this absence of a clear mention was exploited by Roopak to his full advantage when getting things done from MCA.

There were protests by some environmental protection groups on this construction. They objected to a twenty storied building suddenly springing up in Ayravati. But Roopak managed to silence even such 'trouble-mongers'. With his combined strength of money and muscle power, he nipped every such protest in the bud.

Arun occasionally called Inspector Subir in Bangalore to check if there had been any luck with the search for the lost voice-recorder. But the answer was always in the negative. Arun just kept praying and kept his hopes alive that somehow the evidence that Sanju collected at the cost of her life would be found. He also kept in touch with Ganesh regularly. Ganesh had now joined his family business of automobiles. They dealt in different kinds of automobiles – two-wheelers, cars, buses, trucks and commercial vehicles. They also remodeled different cars in customised designs, thus giving the cars a unique and a fancy look as required by the owner. This business had been started by Ganesh's grandfather several years ago. The business was currently managed by Ganesh's father and Ganesh's older brother. They'd been persuading Ganesh to leave his salaried job and join them. But Ganesh had wanted to chart his own course. Now after his resignation from AHFL, he joined the business, merely as a stop-gap, until he could find another suitable job. But as he got more and more involved, he started to enjoy the business and developed a keen interest. By the end of 2003, he'd been formally inducted as a Partner and was fully settled in the business.

Chapter – 25

THE WAITING

October 2004 – July 2006

THE MEGACITY PROJECT WAS COMPLETED UP TO THE 20TH floor and possession given to all the individual apartment owners in October 2004. The entire project was indeed so breathtakingly beautiful that it left all observers awed. Roopak held a grand opening ceremony where he invited every bureaucrat, every politician, key representatives from every lending organization, known and unknown, in Ayravati and from all the other cities where he had his construction activities. The banners of Chand Builders and its financing partner AHFL were displayed grandly, showcasing their joint effort, Megacity. All key people from AHFL were present.

Arun also attended the function, only to keep the fire of vengeance burning.

Arun had been painstakingly following up with Subir in Bangalore, month after month. These frequent calls from Arun began to irritate Subir at some point and he told Arun that if the voice-recorder was ever found, he'd inform him. But Arun wasn't one to give up. He decided if need be he'd fly down to Bangalore and patch up with Subir. But it was important to keep in touch with Subir, if only to jog his memory from time to time.

Chand Builders repaid their loan installments to AHFL regularly. Roopak had already paid back a sum of Rs.100 million and the loan outstanding had come down to Rs. 400 million. Cedric was in fact quite happy with Chand Builders and even more so with the huge interest revenue that AHFL had earned from this builder loan deal. Karan was having a blast, his own personal coffers swelling with occasional 'gifts' from Roopak and a fantastic salary rise that Cedric had given him for the performance year 2004 as a reward for closing the Chand Builders deal and thereby lifting the top-line revenue numbers for AHFL.

The Megacity project had 180 apartments in all. Nearly 60% of the home owners had availed of loans and all of them had been financed by AHFL. Most flat purchasers were CEOs and other senior management professionals of several multinational companies, bureaucrats and wealthy politicians. AHFL therefore made a killing by giving safe loans to quality customers. Cedric was now convinced that there was nothing wrong with the project. Even the other AHFL staff members in the office who'd seen the sparring between Ganesh and Karan over the Megacity proposal, felt that Ganesh and Arun had overreacted. Unlike Ganesh, who'd left AHFL, Arun had to spend his entire working day in AHFL and very often he received scornful vibes from his colleagues. Whenever he felt low he met Ganesh and spent time with him. And he kept nurturing his strong resolve to nail Roopak sometime, somehow.

Two years – 2004 and 2005 – thus passed. It was mid-2006, when Karan got promoted to the next higher grade in the organization. It was also officially announced that by the end of 2006 Karan would take over as the CEO of AHFL. Cedric was moving to another group company.

Enthused by the success of Megacity where he had successfully built and sold 20 floors, notwithstanding violation of MCA norms, Roopak constructed three more projects in Ayravati, with 15 floors each. The trend caught on and other builders in Ayravati also built a few projects that had more than 12 floors. The MCA became virtually powerless and failed to control this trend. MCA's officers, who were supposed to implement the rule of 12 floors, remained ineffective. Some were easily corrupted while others were just too meek to raise their voice against these violations. Builders wielded enormous clout with the local politicians, who got their share of booty from the sale of the illegal floors in these buildings.

* * *

One morning in July 2006, when Arun reached his office, a messenger from the office of Manohar Mishra, the valuer of Millennimum Bank, was waiting for him. The messenger handed over an envelope to Arun and said, 'Mr.Mishra passed away a few days ago. He wrote this on the last day of his life and asked me to deliver it to you.'

Arun was shocked to hear of Mishra's death and expressed his condolences. The messenger gave him the envelope and left.

Arun opened the envelope. There was a letter to Arun. To the letter was attached another sheet with some handwritten notes.

Arun read the letter,

'Dear Arun,

It's been my privilege to know you. I wish you well. I'm enclosing herewith a note wherein I'd recorded the devastation caused by the tremor of 1951 and the history behind the rule of 12 floors. I'd discussed this with you when you visited my office. I want you to keep these notes, in fact preserve them for the future. I'm aware of the battle that you and your colleague fought against the illegal floors of Megacity. It's unfortunate though that you found no takers for the truth that you tried so hard to establish. I'm now deeply concerned that the situation in Ayravati is deteriorating even as I see MCA losing all control. With Sanju also not around, there's absolutely no one here to protest against the proliferation of these illegal constructions. Please take this up and do what you can. God bless you and for the last time now, I bid you adieu.

   Sd/- (Manohar Mishra).'

Tears welled up in Arun's eyes. He looked at the enclosure to the letter, which was a single sheet of paper with some handwritten notes. He wiped his tears and read the contents of the enclosed paper. Then he carefully placed the cover note and the enclosure back in the envelope and kept the envelope inside his bag.

In these last few years, Arun had waded through myriad poignant experiences, waiting patiently for D-Day – the day he would see Rocpak pay for all his evil deeds.

Chapter – 26

DELIVERANCE

29ᵗʰ July 2006

THREE YEARS AGO IT WAS ON THIS FATEFUL DAY THAT SANJU had been killed. Arun took the day off and headed straight for Vinay's office which was on the top floor of Hotel Airborne. Arun found Vinay standing near a large glass window in his office and looking out into the city. Arun interrupted him softly, 'Hi Vinay.'

Vinay turned around and welcomed him warmly, 'Hi dude, come on in. Good to see you.' Vinay held no grudges against Arun despite his part in Sanju undertaking that fateful adventure. But the trauma of living without Sanju, whom he had loved very deeply, consumed him from within. As opposed to his usual stylish turn-out earlier, he now appeared distraught and dishevelled most of the time. Sanju's absence sometimes threatened to destroy his will to live. In such deeply distressful moments, when Sanju's memory overwhelmed him, he'd often call Arun, meet up with him, spend some time with him and feel better. It was as if an invisible bond united the three of them. Today, Arun had made the call and Vinay had agreed to a meeting eagerly.

Arun and Vinay spent a few hours chatting, remembering Sanju and her work. It felt good. When both of them were a bit relaxed, all of a sudden Vinay enquired about Ganesh.

'How's your friend and colleague Ganesh? Where's he?'

'He has joined his family's automobile business. He's doing well for himself.'

'Arun, I appreciate Ganesh resigning from AHFL following Sanju's death. It needed a strong will to stand by one's own conscience. At times I do feel that I should meet him personally and express my gratitude to him for showing his sincere concern towards Sanju and her cause. Maybe you can help me do that sometime.'

A thought occurred to Arun and he said, 'Why don't we do that today? There would be no better day. Let's drive down to Ganesh's office and meet him. In fact, I've been planning to visit Ganesh's place to look up some new car models there.'

Vinay liked the idea. Soon they were at Ganesh's office. Ganesh was thrilled to see Arun. He jumped from his chair, walked up to Arun and gave him a warm hug. He then noticed Vinay and welcomed him. Ganesh turned to Arun, 'Buddy, I can't describe how happy I am to see you here. You have just blown me by your surprise visit.'

'Well, it is Vinay who should be credited for this visit.'

Vinay smiled and said, 'Ganesh, this is the first time I am meeting you, but from what I've known of you from Arun, I'm at a loss of words to express my admiration for you. Particularly the way you chucked your job and chose the path shown by your conscience – it was awe-inspiring. I only wish we had more people like you in this country with such courage of conviction. And personally, I must thank you for this since what you did represented an endorsement of Sanju's cause.'

'Vinay, I just did what I felt was the right thing to do. If I hadn't, I would never have forgiven myself.'

They kept conversing for a while. A little later Arun asked, 'Ganesh, can you take us on a tour of your automobile workshop where you work on second hand cars? I'm looking to buy one.'

'Of course pal. Come, let's go.'

They all stepped out and Ganesh led them on a tour of his showroom and workshop. The showroom showcased the latest models of cars. There were a few offbeat models which weren't manufactured by any known car manufacturer. When Arun enquired who made those cars, Ganesh explained, 'These car designs are customized and modeled by us. We buy old cars and remodel them in our workshop. We give them a completely new look. These are usually made to order. We make quite a lot of money on these. For e.g, we could buy a damaged car for half a million rupees, remodel it with an additional cost of one million and sell it for three million. It's a lucrative business. The customer doesn't mind paying because he'd never get such customizations on his car anywhere else in the market.'

It was terrific indeed. Ganesh then took them to the workshop where the actual remodeling of the old cars happened. It was a huge workshop. There were a number of technicians in factory uniform working on several different cars, which were in different stages of remodeling. They finished the round of the factory.

Ganesh said, 'Arun, if you want to buy a car, I'd suggest that instead of buying a brand new one, you go for remodeling an old car. I promise to give you a fantastic design at an irresistible price.'

'Yes, Ganesh. But I don't want to remodel my existing car.'

'Who's telling you to do that? I'll show you some old cars that I have. You pick one of those. I'll redesign it the way you want it.'

'Wow, that sounds great. Can we see your old cars?'

'Sure.'

Ganesh took them to the shed that housed all the old and damaged cars.

He said, 'Choose one of these cars and I'll turn it into your dream machine.'

Arun rather liked the idea of having a uniquely designed car. He looked at the old cars stocked there and found that some of them were badly damaged. Arun wondered how Ganesh's workshop could convert such badly condemned cars into swanky ones. He learnt from Ganesh that the stock of cars there had been collected over a period of time by his company.

As Arun continued to scan the stock of cars there, he froze. He saw a familiar looking object there. It was one of the badly damaged cars. It only took him a second to recognize the black Honda in a corner. He shivered; his face turned ashen and his nerves throbbed. It was the same car – the very same car that had been Sanju's grave. How could he ever forget the car? He stood there motionless and dumbfounded for a few moments. Then he raised his right hand, pointing in the direction of the black Honda. Noticing this sudden change of expression in Arun, Vinay and Ganesh looked in the direction of his pointed finger. Vinay saw it as well and he exclaimed, 'Oh my god. This is *that* car.'

Ganesh was amazed. 'Which car?'

Arun was now uncontrollably excited and he cried out, 'That black Honda there. That was the same car Sanju was travelling in when she was killed.'

Ganesh registered it fast enough. 'That Honda?'

'Yes.'

'Are you sure?'

'Absolutely. Where did you get it from?'

Ganesh called up his manager in-charge of purchases and within a few minutes confirmed, 'It was purchased by us from a scrap dealer in Bangalore a couple of years ago. It's been lying there and there've been no takers for it till date.'

Vinay howled, 'I don't know what to call this. Is it a coincidence? Or is it providence?'

At that instant, Arun's mobile phone rang. It was inspector

Subir from Bangalore, who had been investigating Sanju's accident. Amazed at the timing of the call, Arun answered it impatiently,

'Hi, Subir. What a pleasant surprise.'

'Yeah I know. I just called up to apologize.'

'Why?'

'I'm sorry to say that despite months of search, we haven't been able to find your lost packet. I've now lost all hope. We've done all that we could to search for that elusive evidence……..'

Even as Subir spoke, Arun listened to him but his eyes remained glued to the black Honda. The moment Subir made a reference to the evidence something prompted Arun to conduct a search of the car. In an emotionally loaded but confident voice he said, 'Vinay, it's got to be providence. The evidence that Sanju gathered at the cost of her life should be right in there.' He pointed his finger again at the black Honda.

Without wasting a moment, Arun rushed to the black Honda at full pelt. Ganesh, who now understood what Arun was looking for, followed him. Vinay followed Ganesh. Arun excitedly told Subir that he'd speak to him later and disconnected the phone.

Arun reached the Honda, pulled the broken door open, peeped in for a second and then barged inside. The inside of the car was full of dust that had gathered over time. Ganesh opened whatever remained of the boot of the car. He searched the boot of the car. Vinay opened the bonnet and searched there. All the three of them fervently and rigorously searched the battered car, to see if anything lay there; a bag or a packet of some sort. It was a difficult task, because the body of the car was mutilated beyond recognition. The men searched with single minded focus. They got bruised all over in the process since the broken parts of the metal and fibre generously clawed their bodies at every possible opportunity. Arun was the most injured since the inside of the car had been severely contracted due to the impact of the accident. They looked below the seats, in the boot, in the bonnet and everywhere else. Just when they were running out of steam, Ganesh lifted the floor mats in the rear seats, and pulled them out. With the force of the angry pull, a dust-laden ladies-bag fell out of the car with a thud indicating that it contained something heavy. Arun heard the noise and wriggled out of the car. So did the other two men. Arun picked it up, dusted it off and with nerve-wracking apprehension, opened the bag and saw a packet inside with something written on it. The packet was addressed to him and carried a remark written in bold, 'STRICTLY CONFIDENTIAL. TO BE OPENED BY THE ADDRESSEE ONLY'. The sight of the packet made him feverish and his hands started to tremble. He wasn't in control of himself. Ganesh snatched the packet from him and looked at it. He glanced at Arun, who nodded agreement. Ganesh tore open the packet and pulled out a tiny digital voice-recorder.

Following this, the three men hurried to Ganesh's office. Ganesh pulled out a set of new batteries from his drawer and the other two men locked the door of his cabin. A strange nervousness gripped them. Vinay, who was breathing heavily, felt his mind harking back to Sanju, the person he loved; as the memories grew stronger and stronger, he felt overwhelmed by emotions and broke down. Arun was highly agitated, his hands were still shivering and his body shaking. Ganesh was the only one who seemed to be in control. Ganesh replaced the old batteries with new ones and pressed the play button. And then they heard the conversation in full and Sanju's voice therein. For Vinay it was as if Sanju had come alive. He went crazy. After three years of bereavement, today he heard Sanju's voice; the voice that kept him always motivated and moving in life; the voice of his love. He considered himself lucky and thanked god for this unforeseen and unexpected gift whereby he could hear Sanju's voice again. Arun heard the voice of a concerned friend, philosopher and guide, who had gone of her way only for him and in the process lost her life. He tried his best to check his tears. The three of them listened to the entire conversation recorded in the voice-recorder in complete bewilderment. When they finished hearing it, their hearts were pumping abnormally. They were silent for a few minutes.

It was Ganesh who broke the silence.

He looked at Arun and asked, 'What now?'

Arun was too stunned to answer.

Ganesh briefly looked at Vinay. Vinay was looking down at the floor. Ganesh looked at Arun again. Arun looked at Vinay and then at Ganesh.

Ganesh spoke slowly, pacing his words. His voice was a little loud, with a flavor of triumph. 'We're back in business, Arun. Let's get busy.' He couldn't check himself from smiling.

Ganesh's smile caught on and Arun smiled as well, feeling a sense of redemption brewing within.

Within no time, the smiles grew to laughter. Ganesh and Arun were laughing…laughing aloud at the manner in which things had turned around. They were probably celebrating a little too early, but with the fire of revenge still burning within, neither of them had any second thoughts on giving Roopak the fight of his life. They could see that the D-day, the day when Roopak would pay for his sins, was not too far away.

Arun placed his hands on Vinay's shoulders. His voice louder than normal, 'Let's go for it, Vinay. We now have it with us.'

Vinay saw their bouts of laughter with a purposeful smile. Due to his intimacy with Sanju, he had been feeling that the responsibility of taking up and fighting for Sanju's cause was now his alone. But he was now seeing these two men raring to go, ahead of him. He felt overwhelmed. Overwhelmed with gratitude. His mind sub-consciously asking questions as, Who was Sanju to them? A friend? Are there still people in this world, who stake their careers for a friend? In this case, even their lives could be at risk. Is this for real? The noise of the questions in his mind was louder than the sounds of their laughter. He had already acknowledged their feelings for Sanju's cause. But this was the first time he could see the depth and intensity of their belief in Sanju's purpose. And he felt the best way to honour it was to join them in the laughter. And so he did. The little celebration continued for a while.

Then they sat down to plot their strategy. It was obvious

that they would have to take this evidence to the police and courts. But they wanted to act without alerting Roopak in any manner. The element of surprise in this move against Roopak, would be key to nailing Roopak.

Ganesh spoke after some time, 'Ok now. Let me tell you what we should do. A friend of mine is a lawyer specializing in criminal suits. We can speak to him and take his advice. From my limited knowledge of the legal procedures, I think there are provisions whereby, if you have sufficient proof, you can file a criminal complaint against someone, without his knowledge and get an arrest warrant issued. The police will then take him in custody, unless he already has an anticipatory bail with him. At the moment, he doesn't know that we are working against him. Before he gets aware and applies for an anticipatory bail, we must get him arrested. Once he is in custody, the courts will take over. Media will follow. I am definitely banking on a very noisy media trial in this matter. Given that Sanju herself was a popular journalist, the media would only be too happy to give this issue a wide coverage. With media screaming, we can be reasonably sure that the courts will move fast to decide Roopak's fate. Let us take the first step of meeting my friend tomorrow.'

The other two men agreed to the plan.

The next day as planned, they met at the office of Ganesh's lawyer friend.

The lawyer, after fully understanding the background and listening to the voice-recorder, said, 'Ganesh, you guys should first file a complaint with police without much delay and get him arrested. Considering the gravity of the crime, I see no problems with that. This is actually a non-bailable offence. He won't be able to get bail.'

Ganesh asked, 'How do we do that?'

'I will get the complaint prepared in a couple of days.' He looked at the desk calendar and said, 'say by Thursday. We will file the complaint with the police on Friday morning and get Roopak arrested by Friday evening.'

Ganesh wanted to be sure, 'Do you think this could work?'

The lawyer replied, 'No reason it shouldn't.'

As planned the complaint was prepared and filed with the police headquarters by Friday morning.

And, based on this complaint, the police arrested Roopak, the big name of the real estate industry, and placed him behind the bars.

Chapter – 27

THE TRIAL

July 2006 – June 2007

The law took its natural course. The police brought the case before the court for a trial. The court issued directives to police to carry out the investigations thoroughly and present all evidence before the court. The investigating team of the police took control of the full investigation and carried it out meticulously. They identified all the relevant people involved directly and indirectly with this case and questioned them. The interrogations with all of them collectively revealed the entire story, from cradle to the grave. This also paved the way for a series of arrests that included amongst others, the Bangalore assassins who had acted on Roopak's instructions and killed Sanju, the former MCA commissioner Hegde, the concerned MCA officials who had silently abetted illegal constructions, thereby failing in their duties and last but not the least, Karan Agnihotri, soon-to-be-CEO of AHFL.

Following a series of Court debates, the Court ruled different sentences for each of them depending on their involvement in and intensity of their crime. The charges against the arrested people included murder, treason, fraud and breach of trust. Karan's arrest was the most disturbing as no one had known that he was hand-in-glove with Roopak in effecting the disbursement. Though he was released on bail quickly, the damage to his reputation and more so to that of AHFL, had been done. Cedric, who had actually approved the disbursement memo, was let off by the Court on the grounds that he had acted in good faith. The Court however did record a warning to Cedric asking him to be much more diligent in his position. Ganesh felt sorry for this, because he knew Cedric to be a clean individual, sincere about his work.

Ganesh and Arun – the whistleblowers – were applauded by the Court for their indefatigable efforts and single-minded pursuit of the purpose that prodded all concerned to focus on the issue of illegal constructions in Ayravati. The judge also paid homage to Sanju in his judgment, mentioning her invaluable sacrifice – of life, no less – in her efforts to bring these crimes to light.

As the Court trials progressed over several weeks, the case came in for detailed media coverage. The extensive portrayal of Sanju's great work by the media resulted in her becoming the talk of the town. As a natural fallout of the media trial,

AHFL's credibility crashed in the public eye. The share market reacted and brought about an irrecoverable fall in AHFL stock prices. The shareholders and investors lost faith and gave Dr. Sharma, the AHFL Chairman, a tough time seeking an explanation for all that had happened. Dr. Sharma realized that it would take at least another 5 years to get AHFL back on track, with its full credibility restored. He doubted if he'd live to see that day.

Dr. Sharma sat through all the Court hearings. On one of those days, Cedric approached Dr. Sharma outside the Court and submitted his resignation as the CEO of AHFL, assuming moral responsibility for the loss of AHFL's reputation. Dr. Sharma requested Cedric to continue as the interim CEO till he found a new incumbent.

Dr. Sharma also asked Ganesh to join AHFL again. But Ganesh politely refused stating that he was settled in his current work and was happy. However, Arun decided to stay the course with AHFL as the RMQ head, with a resolve to help in the efforts to restore its lost credibility.

Despite the upheaval in Court and the media, Megacity was still standing tall. The Court proceedings had however tarnished the image of the aesthetically superb project. However, the illegal floors were already constructed and were now fully occupied by the residents. The residents who had bought those apartments in good faith, felt cheated. The fact that Ayravati was located in a seismic zone came up for deliberations in many people's forums. There was a growing awareness about the 1951 tremor in the city and the background to the rule limiting the number of floors in a building to twelve. All these events triggered a massive people's rally that carried a message condemning any new construction above the permitted 12 floors in Ayravati. But no one had the courage to either ask or answer the question as to what would happen to the illegal floors that had already been constructed.

Chapter – 28

THE LAST MILE HERO

July 2007- April 2008

THE RAINS ARRIVED AND THREW LIFE OUT OF GEAR IN Ayravati. On one such rainy day, the train from Mumbai chugged majestically into platform number one of Ayravati railway station, piercing the curtain of heavy rainfall. It slowed down and came to a screeching halt. The passengers stepped out one by one. They all seemed enervated and exhausted by the long journey. Everyone left the platform slowly and soon, the platform was empty. There still remained one last passenger in the train who had perhaps overslept in the air-conditioned comfort of the 2nd AC coach. He opened his eyes and sat up on his berth leisurely. He cracked his knuckles, tightened and then released his body muscles in a bid to relax and then let out a loud yawn. He took out his cap and wore it in an unhurried manner, got up, adjusted his cap in the compartment mirror making sure that it rested perkily on his head. Rolling his single Samsonite overnighter, he ambled towards the train's exit door, whistling in style. He came to the door of the train and stood there for a moment with a hand on his hip and looked around the platform. The whole platform was empty but for a few railway porters. The porters looked at him, but none of them made an effort to approach him to ask if he needed any assistance with the luggage. A cool, courageous and don't-mess-with-me look was manifest on his face. He was the new Municipal Commissioner of Ayravati –Surya Mohan, who was also popularly known as *The Bulldozer Man*.

Surya stepped out of the train and onto the soil of Ayravati to take charge as the Municipal Commissioner of Ayravati.

Right from his first day in office, Surya did what he was good at – and what no one else had dared do before. He spent time attempting to understand the history of the city and thereafter identified the illegal floors in some of the buildings on a high-priority basis. With a firm resolve to bring back discipline in real estate constructions he set up a new demolition unit in MCA. The unit released orders to the effect that all the illegal floors in any of the buildings in Ayravati would be demolished.

Surya's team plunged into action. The residents residing in homes above the 12th floor in the buildings were given a few months to vacate the house and relocate. During this period,

Surya's team worked incessantly, convincing the residents to move out.

Surya also submitted a plea at the Court on behalf of the affected residents, requesting the Court to direct the builders who built and sold the illegal floors to compensate the residents, whose apartments would be demolished. With the help of his lawyers, he convinced the Court and got the builders to compensate the affected residents adequately.

By April 2008, all the demolition orders had been carried out - all floors above the approved twelve in all buildings were demolished.

EPILOGUE

29th July 2008

ARUN GLANCED AT HIS WATCH. IT WAS TIME TO MEET GANESH. Arun stepped out of the house, got into his car and drove to Temple Coffee House, where he'd agreed to meet Ganesh. This was the place where they had spent those anxious moments waiting for the call from Sanju on that eventful day, five years ago.

On his way he went past Megacity and a few other buildings that had been demolished by Surya's team. Lost in thought, Arun reached Temple Coffee House. Ganesh was already in. Arun placed an order for his favourite coffee and went to the table where Ganesh was seated. Neither of them spoke for some time.

Both harboured a deep sense of satisfaction at having seen the right from the wrong in the direst of circumstances. The feeling that Sanju's sacrifice finally did achieve its purpose was heartwarming. The events of the last five years had taught them some rock-solid lessons of value and truth. In the time that passed they felt they'd grown a little older, but a lot wiser.

They relished their coffee and spoke of nothing in particular, savouring some light moments. The unstated purpose of their meeting was to silently remember Sanju and to celebrate the victory – of truth and sacrifice over deceit and greed. That they did.

Arun mumbled, 'Ganesh, life always comes a full circle, doesn't it?'

'Of course it does – it either wafts like a pleasant breeze or blazes like a blob of fire, as the case may be. *Jaisi karni, waisi bharni.**'

On that thoughtful note, they left for their respective homes with a committed resolve to lead life the way they'd learnt to live.

E n d

* *as you sow so shall you reap*

www.ingramcontent.com/pod-product-compliance
Lightning Source LLC
Chambersburg PA
CBHW051330020726
47501CB00007B/2014